The Duke Buys a Bride

His breath fell soft and even beside her, and after a while she assumed he had fallen back to sleep until he said, "Give me your hand."

"W-what for?"

"Come now. Just hold out your hand. I'm not going to hurt you. Besides, you still have your knife. Feel free to use it if you feel threatened." She could almost imagine the sarcastic twist to his lips. Warily, she stretched out her hand and he took it, clasping firm fingers around hers.

In the dark, her sense of touch was heightened. His hand felt so much bigger than hers. The fingers long, tapering. His grip strong, the pads slightly rough. Callused. For all his apparent prosperity, he wasn't a dandy then. He used his hands. This should not affect her one way or another, but her chest lifted on a hitched breath.

He flattened out her palm, stopping her fingers from curling inward. Then he began lightly stroking. His fingertips brushed back and forth over her palm, his blunt-tipped nails softly scoring her skin.

Her breath caught. "What are you doing?"

By Sophie Jordan

The Rogue Files Series
THE DUKE BUYS A BRIDE
THE SCANDAL OF IT ALL
WHILE THE DUKE WAS SLEEPING

The Devil's Rock Series
BEAUTIFUL LAWMAN
FURY ON FIRE
HELL BREAKS LOOSE
ALL CHAINED UP

Historical Romances
ALL THE WAYS TO RUIN A ROGUE
A GOOD DEBUTANTE'S GUIDE TO RUIN
HOW TO LOSE A BRIDE IN ONE NIGHT
LESSONS FROM A SCANDALOUS BRIDE
WICKED IN YOUR ARMS
WICKED NIGHTS WITH A LOVER
IN SCANDAL THEY WED
SINS OF A WICKED DUKE
SURRENDER TO ME
ONE NIGHT WITH YOU
TOO WICKED TO TAME
ONCE UPON A WEDDING NIGHT

THE DUKE BUYS A BRIDE

The Rogue Files

Sophie Jordan

AVONBOOKS

An Imprint of HarperCollinsPublishers

First Avon Books mass market printing: August 2018

Print Edition ISBN: 978-0-06-246364-7
Digital Edition ISBN: 978-0-06-246365-4

Cover design by Patricia Barrow
Cover illustration by Jon Paul Ferrara
Cover photograph by Media Photo LLC
Dolphin art © dynamic / Shutterstock, Inc.

FIRST EDITION

18 19 20 21 22   QGM   10 9 8 7 6 5 4 3 2 1

THE DUKE
BUYS A BRIDE

For the Joneses, Michael and Tammy:
It is a truth universally acknowledged, that a writer
must be in want of a good builder . . .
Thank you for helping us build our Pemberley.
May your own happily ever after continue joyfully
into forever.

Chapter 1

In which the hungry wolf wakes . . .

Marcus, the fifth Duke of Autenberry, woke with a startled jolt, face-down in horse shit.

At least he assumed the reeking matter was the product of a horse. Several of the beasts could be heard neighing around him and he had spent a good amount of his life in the stables around horses. He knew the stink of horse excrement.

Pain splintered his skull as he pushed himself up. *Bloody hell.* What happened to him?

Wiping his face with the cuff of his jacket, he sat up fully and looked around, finding himself the subject of scrutiny. Several pairs of eyes stared at him through the slats of the stall. Children, he surmised. The eyes did not appear to be over five feet in height and they talked in high-pitched voices. Of course, that could be his overly sensitive ears.

"When do ye think 'e's going tae wake?"

"Och, 'e's been in that 'orse muck fer 'ours now!"

"No' until the morrow. Whenever my pa drinks 'e sleeps fer days."

"'E's big, isn't 'e?"

"Good morning," he greeted drolly, trying not to breathe too deeply of the surrounding stench.

The eyes blinked at him.

"Och, 'e talks funny!" one small voice exclaimed.

"I don't suppose you could tell me where I am?" he inquired, glancing down at himself and wincing. There was a good amount of dung on his once pristine jacket.

Several giggles and titters met his question.

"Ye dinna know where ye are?" one child demanded rather boorishly. "What kind of dolt are ye?"

"A spectacular one," he grumbled, rising to his feet and ignoring the knifing pain in his skull.

More giggles.

He staggered a step toward the stall door. The children on the other side of the door shrieked and ran. Their footsteps pounded a swift retreat that matched the hammer in his skull. He attempted to lift the latch. No luck. It was barred from the outside.

"Of course," he muttered, leaning against the stall wall and appreciating the support. He burrowed through his inside pocket to locate a handkerchief. He mopped off bits of hay and muck from his face, wondering how he had fallen so low. Had his life really come to this?

He could not recall having ever slept in so undignified a situation. He'd woken in all manner of locations, but always on a bed or a chaise. Once, at school, he'd fallen asleep on his desk when he stayed up late studying.

This was an ignoble first.

Heavy, dragging footsteps approached. No child, he presumed. A jingle of keys preceded a scratching at the door and then the stall door swung wide.

A face peered inside at him, the eyes small, dark beads in a broad, flat face. "Yer awake," the fellow announced inanely.

"I am," he returned mildly, scratching his jaw through an itchy growth of hair as he stared down at his boots. Their high-shine buff had long since faded. His valet back in London would be horrified, but their lack of luster felt appropriate. He felt like his boots. Dull and dusty.

"Thought a night locked up might take the wind out of yer sails."

Ah. So he had been incarcerated. For what infraction, he could not recall.

He glanced around again, seeing the stall for what it was—a gaol. He recalled stopping at an inn (yesterday?) in some remote village.

He could not remember the name of the village. They'd all begun to blur. He'd passed through many of them on his journey north.

He lifted his head and stared at his jailer. "Might I inquire of my crime?"

"Ye 'ave nay memory then?" The man swiped at his red bulbous nose. "Ye practically destroyed ol' Alvin's taproom when John Smithy objected tae yer handling of Rovena."

"Rovena?" The name rang familiar. He fluttered his fingers near his head as if that might help conjure forth the details. "Was she a black-haired lass?"

"Aye." The man nodded.

Rovena was aptly named. The serving wench had roving hands. When she'd served him his dinner, she'd plopped down beside him, her greedy paws making short work of freeing him from inside his breeches and seizing on to his cock right there beneath the table.

A nearby fellow had objected to Rovena's enthusiastic attentions. Perhaps that had been John Smithy.

Marcus remembered little after that.

"If I recall it was more *Rovena's* handling of *me*."

The portly man guffawed. "Call it what you will. The bailiff sent me to free ye. He's already taken the cost for the damages out of yer purse. Lucky ye had enough or ye'd be forced to labor until ye paid it off."

At that, the bailiff's lackey tossed Marcus's pocketbook at him. He grabbed it before it hit the ground and landed in muck. "I'm tae instruct ye tae get on yer horse and leave town. 'Tis market day. A busy time and we don't need the likes of ye loitering about causing any more mischief."

The *likes of him*?

It was almost comical if it wasn't so offensive. He was a bloody duke and they were treating him like some vagabond. True, they did not know his rank, and he might not be dressed in the cleanest garments nor his finest—traveling alone, he knew better than to flaunt his wealth— but they had to realize he was Quality. It was all very unsettling.

"Rest easy. I'm quite happy to leave your little backwater." Straightening, he tugged his jacket into place. "Extend my gratitude to your bailiff for his warm and gracious hospitality."

The man scratched his shiny, bald pate as though confounded.

Marcus didn't bother to assess the status of his pocketbook, although it did feel much lighter.

He'd hidden money both in the heel of his boot as well as the lining of his cloak. He wasn't foolish enough to travel alone into the north country without a healthy dose of respect for the robbers plaguing the countryside.

Marcus passed out of the stall and was quickly directed to his waiting horse. His gelding looked hale and as impatient as he to leave.

A wide-eyed youth handed him the reins. Marcus nodded a curt thanks to the lad and mounted without the aid of a block.

Without a backward glance for the stables that had caged him for the night, he nudged his horse forward into the bustling village, vowing to bypass it on his return journey home. As far as he was concerned, this wretched little place was cursed and he should avoid it and its inhabitants in the future.

ALYSE CIRCLED THE small loft, eyeing her narrow cot pressed against the single gable window. She'd slept in that bed for seven years without fail, staring out the window into the night sky, counting stars and spying on the moon as she waited for the day her life would be her own.

Tonight it would begin. Tonight she would sleep somewhere else.

She'd made the bed today as she did every morning. The gray wool blanket was tucked neatly around the mattress; the thin pillow positioned precisely where her head had rested for seven years. The pillow was worn flat, a permanent indentation at the center of it.

Perhaps where she was going she would have a full, plump, down-stuffed pillow. It didn't matter. She'd accept a blanket on the hard ground as long as it meant she was away from here. As long as she was free of this place.

She approached the window and peered down into the yard. Mr. Beard waited in the carriage for her, bundled in his coat against the cold. His thick, work-roughened hands anxiously worried the reins. He, too, was eager to be on his way and she was fairly certain that it had everything to do with the Widow McPherson. Mr. Beard and the widow had grown close since Mr. McPherson passed away. The only thing stopping them from growing closer was Alyse.

Turning, Alyse studied the small, slope-ceiling room a final time. She had shared this chamber with the Beard children for a long time. When she first came to live here at the tender age of ten and five still raw with the grief from losing Papa, there had been six boisterous children all clamoring for her attention and care. She had been responsible for them whilst Mr. Beard worked his farm.

Only three of the children still lived here and they were scarcely children anymore. The boys worked the farm with their father. They could tend to themselves now. The rest had married and left.

She'd served her purpose. She was no longer needed here. Her purpose would be her own from here on.

Alyse exhaled, feeling much lighter than she had in years. This was it then. She was almost free. Only one more thing left to do.

She lifted her small valise, which held all her belongings in the world. A nightgown. Two spare dresses. A mother-of-pearl comb, brush and mirror set that had once belonged to her mother. Her late father's pocket watch. Her parents' wedding bands. A few hair ribbons. And her family's Bible that held a record of her family history. It was all that was left to mark the Bell family tree—the only thing that proved any of them had even existed. Well, and Alyse.

Turning away from the small gabled window, she left the room and descended the narrow, uneven steps.

Nellie waited below, bouncing a baby on her hip and armed with the same question she'd pelted at Alyse all week. "Are ye certain about this?"

"Yes," she insisted. "This was always the agreement between me and your father."

Nellie scowled. "That doesn't make it right."

Doing this thing today, as awful as it seemed . . . was the only way she was going to make everything right in her life.

She'd worked toward this moment. When life had been its most challenging—and caring for six boisterous children all day definitely qualified—she'd endured. She'd donned a smile. She persisted. Because she knew this day would come. Freedom would be hers.

She covered Nellie's hand with her own and gave it a squeeze. Nellie's young daughter leaned in and swiped at Alyse's hair, mussing her hard-won coiffure.

When she'd first joined the Beard household, Nellie had despised Alyse and resented her presence. The late Mrs. Beard had passed away a few months before and the last thing Nellie had wanted was someone taking her mother's place. Reprisals had been swift. A frog in Alyse's boot. Her hair whacked off while she slept. Her good Sunday dress ruined. She'd quickly hidden her few valuables for fear that Nellie would destroy them.

It warmed Alyse's heart to think how time had changed all of that. Nellie was like a little sister to her now even though she had married and lived on the other side of the village with her growing family.

"Yardley will be there," she told Nellie with assurance.

Nellie snorted and rubbed at her swollen stomach. "Yardley." She rolled her eyes. "Wot do ye know of him truly, Alyse?"

"We were very good friends as children." They grew up together and had been inseparable, running about Collie-Ben and the surrounding countryside. Papa was not yet ill when Yardley left and joined the navy. As children, they had exchanged promises. He would return for her.

They wrote to each other. He told her of his travels. She told him of the marriage Papa arranged for her with Mr. Beard. It did not deter him. He still promised to come for her and he had.

They would be together. Share a life. Live in London. He would apprentice for his father's cousin, a poulter, in Seven Dials. She would find work as a seamstress or even a maid. They'd have a life together and be free. That was the most important thing.

They'd planned for this day and it was finally here. Mr. Beard had agreed.

"Aye." Nellie looked unimpressed. "A lifetime ago. He was a boy then. He's been at sea for a long time. People change."

"We have an agreement," Alyse insisted.

"'E's only been 'ome a few weeks. Ye don't know the man 'e is now and yer willing tae tie yourself tae 'im." She shook her head. "I wouldn't do it were I ye."

Alyse resisted pointing out that her choices were limited. Yardley was her best option. Her only choice.

Choices were everything. Up until now, her life had been without any. Choosing Yardley equaled freedom. She was taking matters into her own hands. She would have a choice in this. Her fate would not be left to others.

Yardley would take her away from here. She'd finally see the world and live outside this little hamlet.

"Don't fret for me. All will be well, Nellie. You will see."

Nellie's scowl only deepened. "I 'ope yer right. Ye deserve good things."

Alyse hugged the girl then. Woman, she amended, as she felt Nellie's stomach between them. The girl she had a hand in raising was about to become a mother for the *second* time.

Alyse was definitely overdue to live her own life. Fortunately, Mr. Beard agreed and wouldn't stand in her way.

As though Nellie could read her thoughts, she spoke near Alyse's ear, "Careful ye are no' exchanging one prison fer another . . ."

She pulled back. "Will you come to the market and see me off?"

Nellie shook her head. "Nay. I cannot watch it." She sniffed and blinked eyes that suddenly gleamed with moisture. "Unless ye want me tae. If ye insist, I'll go fer ye—"

"Nay. Go home."

"Ye'll be sure tae write?" Nellie asked, her wide eyes a little desperate. "I canna bear not knowing—"

"I will. I will regale you with all my adventures away from here."

Nellie smiled uncertainly. "Aye." She nodded. "I 'ope so. Now off wi' ye."

Alyse nodded back. "Yes. I don't want to keep Yardley waiting."

Opening the door, she stepped outside and lifted her face to the cold morning sunshine. Yardley had waited long enough.

They both had.

Chapter 2

In which the dove prepares for freedom . . .

*T*he village bustled at full capacity. Market day always brought people in from surrounding areas. Carriages clogged the lane. Alyse could probably stretch out an arm and touch the carriage seat of a very agitated-looking man driving a cart of potatoes next to them. Vendors hawked their wares. Children ran and screeched as they wove between bodies and between horses. Women gossiped over bolts of fabric. Men discussed the future harvest over barrels of ale and mulled wine.

As they crawled forward, Alyse risked a glance beside her. Mr. Beard stared stoically forward. Nothing too unusual about that. In seven years, they'd had few conversations. Discussions only ever had to do with chores or the children.

She scanned the faces they passed, searching for Yardley.

Of course, she didn't see him. She gave herself a mental shake and wiped her suddenly sweating palms on the knees of her dress. Naturally, he would be waiting in the square. Waiting for her as he promised.

Mr. Beard took them as far as he could—until the lane ended. He pulled to a stop. His knees creaked as he climbed down, tied off the horses and rounded the back of the cart. Reaching her side, he held out a hand for her to descend.

Accepting his work-roughened paw, she climbed down, wincing at the sight of her well-worn boots. The toes were practically worn through. The bite of cold penetrated her wool-covered toes, sinking deep, directly into bone.

At least she and Yardley would be traveling south. It shouldn't be so cold. Perhaps the boots could last her a bit longer. Until she and Yardley were both settled and working and able to buy her new boots.

Mr. Beard lifted her valise and took her by the elbow, leading her through the press of bodies.

The village only seemed more crowded now, her view impeded by so many people. Even though she was not especially short, she could not see over the sea of heads.

She could, however, hear the auctioneer, Mr. Hines, calling out, extolling the assets of a mare up for sale. *Ready for breeding! Sturdy as they come! She can bear the weight of even you, John, and we know how you love your kippers!*

The crowd guffawed at the jest made at the expense of the village's corpulent smithy.

She cringed and refused to consider that he might apply some of that same terminology to her. She was not ignorant to how this was done. She knew how it worked. The auctioneer would talk about her like she was property. Because, in this instance, she was. A difficult notion to bear, but true nonetheless.

She inhaled a sobering breath. The end result would make it all worthwhile.

Roasting meat reached her nose and her stomach grumbled, reminding her that she had scarcely touched her breakfast of toast and cheese this morning. Not surprising. It had been well enough for her to finish her tea. Her nerves were stretched taut, and had been ever since Mr. Beard agreed with her that it was time to dissolve their marriage.

More accurately, they had all three agreed.

Mr. Beard had actually looked relieved when

Yardley and Alyse approached him and suggested the time had arrived to end the arrangement her father had negotiated on her behalf.

She scanned the faces they passed on the way to the center of the square, searching for Yardley. She didn't spot him. No sight of his straw-colored hair anywhere. He hadn't changed much over the years. Same hair. Same soft, boyish features. Even the same fondness for lollies. He always had one in his mouth.

It was some comfort to know that time hadn't changed much about him. Yardley, her dearest childhood friend, who had promised to return and marry her . . . was the same lad.

She reminded herself that he would already be in the square. Naturally he would be waiting close to the dais. His stomach was probably filled with the same amount of butterflies that churned through hers.

As they worked their way through the square, she felt the weight of countless stares on her. She met many of those stares head-on. Familiar and strangers alike. Fixing a smile on her face, she lifted her chin. There was no shame in this day's deed. She'd been forced into this situation by circumstance and she was seeing her way out of it.

She recognized the Widow McPherson standing amid her friends. The pack of them watched avidly as Alyse and Mr. Beard neared the dais.

It was no secret. The villagers knew about this day's business and they were here for the show. Eager as pigs at the trough. *Especially* Mrs. McPherson. Ever since her husband passed away, she had made her interest in Mr. Beard clear, dropping off pies and glaring at Alyse wherever she happened to be standing. Feeding the chickens in the yard. Pinning laundry up to dry. Mrs. McPherson's eyes unerringly landed on Alyse and conveyed her dislike clearly.

Alyse craned her neck, skimming the familiar faces of her neighbors all positioned close to the dais for the best vantage, searching for a glimpse of Yardley. Still no sight of him and her churning stomach took a dive. *Where was he?*

They waited at one side of the dais as Hines closed out the sale of the mare.

While the owner and the buyer moved forward to sign the bill of sale, Hines spotted them and descended the dais. "Ah! Mr. Beard! You've arrived just in time. I was starting to wonder if you'd changed your mind."

At this, Mr. Beard slid a glance to where the Widow McPherson stood. Clearly not. The woman stared back, unblinking, and yet communication passed between them as audible as words.

Mr. Beard had no choice. If he wanted a life with the widow, it had to be done this day. There was no going back. Nor did Alyse want to. She'd slept her last night in that gable room. With an increasing sense of panic, Alyse scanned for Yardley's familiar flaxen-haired head, searching for him.

If he was here, why wasn't he making himself visible? He had to know she would be uneasy until she saw him.

"Mr. Beard." She leaned close to whisper. "I don't see Yardley."

Mr. Beard frowned and glanced around the crowd, his heavily lined face presenting more lines than usual.

"Yardley McRoy?" Hines inquired, overhearing her.

"Aye." Beard nodded, scratching his gray hair.

"Oh, I saw 'im ride out of town early this morn before the crowds arrived." That said, the auctioneer turned away to address the seller and buyer of the mare. As though he had delivered news of no import. As though her entire world had not been shaken and stripped to its core bits.

Her stomach bottomed out, dropping to the soles of her feet. *Yardley rode out of town?*

That made no sense. She shook her head.

"What did ye say?" Mr. Beard reached for Hines's sleeve, tugging his attention back to them.

Hines glanced at them. "Aye, on the south road. Riding hard. Like the devil was after 'im. I had tae get clear tae the side of the lane."

Her face flushed hot then cold as the implication of those words sank deeply.

South. Toward London.

Without her.

He was supposed to take her with him. He had promised they would begin a life together there. They would both find employment and she would see something of the world other than this tiny corner of it. Her life would truly, finally, begin.

He had agreed.

But he had left.

The truth of that descended like an awful poison, spreading its venom through her blood. He'd abandoned her. Left her to be auctioned off, sold to any man struck by the whim to buy her.

Panic swelled inside her. She fought back the tide, taking a deep breath and commanding herself to stay calm. Naturally, this changed everything, but she needn't panic.

She turned to Mr. Beard, seizing his arm. "Mr. Beard. We cannot continue—"

"Alyse." His hand covered hers. His expression was pained. She waited, staring at this man who had been her father's friend. Her husband in name only.

He'd taken her in after her father died, married her so that she might have a roof over her head. In exchange, she had looked after his children. Kept his house. Cooked his meals. Did his laundry. It had been a tolerable arrangement. Fair. A solution to both their problems at the time. *Not* meant to last forever.

She had clung to that knowledge amid the drudgery and loneliness. There would be an end. It wasn't forever.

They'd always understood that the union was temporary. That the day would come when they mutually agreed to end their marriage. The only requisites established were that his children be old enough to fend for themselves and that she find someone else to marry. Someone like Yardley.

A divorce was out of the question. As was an annulment. They did not have the means to achieve such a thing. People from Collie-Ben did not divorce or get annulments. The only way to end a marriage was through death . . . or like this.

Someone would have to buy her from Mr. Beard.

Mr. Beard stared down at her, resolve bright in his rheumy gaze.

The tide of panic swelled over her again. That someone was supposed to be Yardley.

"He's not here," she said. "We can't go through with it today."

She couldn't be sold to some stranger. Her fate could not be tossed to the winds like that. He could not expect it of her. It went against their agreement.

Mr. Beard glanced over his shoulder to where Mrs. McPherson watched them with narrowed eyes.

He looked back to Alyse and gave a helpless shrug. "I'm sorry Yardley isn't 'ere, but I cannot wait, Alyse."

She shook her head. "No, please. You promised my father—"

"I promised yer father I'd give ye a roof over yer head," he said gruffly, nodding as though convinced he had done that. "I promised tae feed and clothe and shelter ye. I did that fer seven years."

She leaned in closely, her voice an anxious rush. She had to make him see reason before it was too late and she was marched up that dais. "So now you will sell me to a stranger? Do you think that is in keeping with the spirit of your deathbed promise to my father?"

Hines's voice boomed between them. "Come. It's time." His heavy gait thudded down the remaining steps toward where they stood. Clearly, he was prepared to escort her.

She stared at her husband, beseeching, hope burning in her heart. She had served his family well for seven years. Certainly he would not betray her in this way.

Beard looked from Hines to where the widow waited.

Mrs. McPherson must have sensed something was afoot. She left her friends and moved closer, her giant bosom cutting through the crowd like the prow of a ship. Her sharp gaze flitted between them. She crossed her arms over her massive chest and lifted both her eyebrows in a gesture that could only be termed threatening.

Sighing, Beard faced her again. "I'm sorry, Alyse. I'm no' a young man anymore. I dinnae have time tae waste. Yer young yet. Ye have yer entire life ahead of ye."

She stared at him in stark wonder and released a shaky breath. A life he was about to sell at auction to some person. Some man.

An entire life bound to a stranger.

Bound to a man in this crowd who could use and abuse her any way he wished.

Was he mad? Did he not see how he could be sentencing her to a life of misery?

She shook her head slowly side to side. No. This was not what she had waited so patiently for all these years. She had not endured for this. The thought—the word—slipped past. "No."

But no one heard her. Her voice was a croak lost amid the loud crowd clamoring for the next item to be auctioned—*her*.

Hines reached her, his thick girth brushing against her side. "Let us tarry no more. Word of the wife sale traveled far and this crowd is most anxious to proceed."

Indeed. The custom was not commonplace. Even in rural parts of the country like this, wife auctions were few. The crowd was hungry for the spectacle. She was the fatted goose and they were famished.

Resignation stole over her as she looked out at the horde.

She hadn't shed a tear when her father died. She'd cried enough before that day, during the months he had been ill. She had loved him more than anyone in her life and nothing had been as terrible as losing him.

Not even this.

She flinched as the rough hemp rope dropped over her head and settled about her throat. That was custom, too. Binding the wife. As though she were nothing more than a field animal. As though she might run.

She released a choked little laugh. She had nowhere to go. Yardley wasn't here. He wasn't coming. She needed to let that dream go and focus on the reality of now. She had to keep a cool head and brace herself for whatever was to come. She lifted her chin and reached down deep, grasping for her composure.

Perhaps it wouldn't be that bad.

Clearly she couldn't go on living as a *non*wife to Mr. Beard. Today would put an end to their union. There was that. That mattered.

The temporary degradation of this auction would be over soon.

And then you will be the wife of someone else.

She fought back a shudder. That terrifying thought threatened to swallow her. *You'll manage. You always do. You'll find a way. Make a plan. Escape if necessary.*

She was sensible. No sense panicking until she knew what she was up against.

As this internal dialogue played out in her head, Hines yanked on the rope, propelling her to move. The frayed hemp bit into her skin. She caught herself, one of her hands flying out and landing on a rough wooden step, breaking her fall.

Mr. Beard reached for her, his hand circling her elbow to lift her up. She pulled her arm clear of him, shooting him a hot glare. "Don't."

She would not give him that satisfaction. He did not get to walk away from this day thinking he had helped her in any way. Not after seven years. Not after promising.

"Come," Hines snapped, looking back down at her as though she were a troublesome child who couldn't keep up.

She regained her feet. Standing on the bottom step, she squared her shoulders and lifted her chin. She'd walk. No one would drag her.

With a satisfied nod, he turned, still gripping the end of the rope. He took the rest of the steps leading up to the platform. The rope tightened around her throat, the length of it stretching taut between them like a long thread of doom.

The hemp tugged around her throat, the rope chafing her tender skin. She ascended the steps and followed Mr. Hines to the center of the platform. The market square looked bigger from up here. People were everywhere. Faces all staring at her with avid eyes. There were more people than she had ever seen in one place before.

She swallowed against the giant lump in her throat and told herself to be strong. *Don't let them see how very scared you are.*

Even if she was.

She'd survive this as she had everything else in her life. She'd make it through this day.

Chapter 3

The hungry wolf spies the dove . . .

*F*ate was conspiring to keep him in this cess-pit of a town.

Marcus guided his mount through the village lane, weaving between carriages, darting children and carts of steaming meat pies, blood-dark kippers and shanks of roasted pork.

He was forced to stop several times. His gelding, Bucephalus, tossed his head in annoyance at the crowd, clearly hating being fenced in and wanting his lead. Marcus could appreciate the feeling. That's why he was on this journey, why he'd departed London. He'd felt fenced in. Choked. Surrounded by people he could not seem to like anymore—himself included.

He patted Bucephalus's neck. "Easy, boy. We'll be free of here soon. I know. I can't wait either."

Straightening, he tugged at the collar of his cloak, grimacing at his own odor. He wondered how far it was to the next village. He was in dire need of a bath, and tonight, he vowed, he would be sleeping in a bed. Preferably a luxurious down-filled mattress with crisp sheets.

Suddenly the traffic in the road thickened and he was forced to stop. He stood in his stirrups and craned his neck, attempting to see what was transpiring ahead to impede his progress.

He could see nothing beyond a throng of bodies, all turned in one direction, their backs to him as they pushed forward in an attempt to gain better view of something happening ahead.

Sighing, he glanced back behind him, wondering if it wouldn't be easier to turn back around and find another way out of town.

A heavyset woman with a face that reminded him of the bulldog his headmaster used to walk around the grounds charged ahead with no mind to anyone in her path—including him and Bucephalus.

She landed a hand on the rump of his horse as she passed.

He called down to her. "What is all the fuss?"

She paused and lifted her jowly face up to him. She motioned ahead, her cheek jowls swinging. "Don't ye ken? There's an auction in the square."

Almost in response to her words, the crowd rumbled and shouts carried forth from the public square.

"It's startin'!" She forgot all about him and pushed her notable girth amid bodies, determined to clear a path for herself.

An auction warranted all this frenzy?

He sent another glance behind him. It wouldn't be easy venturing back that route. He'd be going against the flow of people. Best continue on his path moving forward and make his way around the periphery of the square.

He nudged his mount ahead, curious at what could have incited such excitement in these villagers. Perhaps they were auctioning off a two-headed goat. He snorted at the thought as he nudged inside the entrance to the square.

He pulled up to a stop. People bumped into each other, but were indifferent to the contact, their gazes fixed on the livestock pens ahead.

He followed their gazes, looking to see what these rustics found so diverting.

At the far end of the square, at the forefront of the pens, a dais was erected. His attention fell on the single individual standing on that platform.

It was a female. A rope encircled her neck, the

end held in the grip of a man who cried out to audience.

". . . still in 'er prime. The lass will make a fine bedmate on these cold nights and in the winters tae come!"

He went still, watching.

Even Bucephalus stopped his restless pawing at the ground as though understanding something remarkable was transpiring.

It was unthinkable. Shock rippled through him. They were selling her.

Selling a woman. A human.

The auctioneer continued, "Now I 'ave 'er 'usband's word that she is as pure as the day she came tae 'im. The lass is untouched an' waiting fer a good man tae break 'er in. Now who will it be? Do I 'ear a bid?"

The audience tittered. Necks stretched, heads craning to see if anyone would answer the call to action.

One man broke the crowd's reticence and shouted, "Wot wrong wit' 'er?"

The auctioneer ignored the gibe and continued with his pitch. "A chaste bride, unplowed and ready fer planting if any one of ye fine men is willing tae pay the sum."

A cry went up. "Four pounds!"

The auctioneer groaned and slapped a hand in

the air in rejection of that offer. "Four pounds be an offense fer so fine a maid! We 'ave a virgin 'ere primed and ready . . . trained in the 'ousekeeping arts! Do I 'ear eight? Eight pounds!"

Marcus could never claim to be an exceedingly principled man. His life had hardly been virtuous. He wasn't easily offended, but disgust churned through him as he watched the sordid scene unfold.

These salt of the earth villagers seemed conveniently void of scruples. This—the same village that had seen fit to cast him into the gaol for whatever infraction—had no qualms in selling a woman like she was some bit of horseflesh. Such was the hypocrisy of man. Marcus knew something of that. His own father had presented one face, but lived quite another way. Quite another *dishonorable* way.

As though to hammer home the depravity of the scene, someone called out, "Show us 'er titties! We gotta right tae see wot being offered."

The auctioneer scowled and pointed a damning finger in the direction of the voice. "Mind yer tongue, Liner! This be a proper business. One more foul word from ye and I'll 'ave ye locked up, ye ken?"

The threat must have done its task. There wasn't another word from Liner.

The auctioneer continued to extoll her virtues,

remarking on her youth and cooking skills. "The lass is fit and can labor along any man in the fields! She might be young, but 'ave no fear she be miss-ish 'bout getting 'er 'ands dirty." He grabbed one of her hands and held it up as though the crowd could see. "These little 'ands bear the calluses of 'er labors."

Marcus studied the female. She stood with her hand gripped in the auctioneer's grasp. There was no ducked head or lowered eyes. She stared out at the crowd. Eyes scanning. Searching. For what? Help? An escape? It seemed too late for that.

How was it possible for a man to sell his wife? It was slavery, pure and simple. And how could these villagers support such a thing? He felt as though he had entered another realm where all manner of bizarre things existed. For all he knew, elves might prance past him.

"Can we bid on 'er, Pa?" a boy nearby begged, tugging on his father's coat.

The father looked down at his son before looking back up at the girl on the block. "Nay, lad. We canna pay such a sum."

Marcus looked down at the man, unable to help himself from asking, "Is this normal practice?"

The father looked up at him. His nose wrinkled, confirming Marcus did, indeed, reek of a dung heap. Even so, the cut of his clothing and the fine horse he sat upon had the man doffing his hat. "A wife auction, ye mean?"

"I never heard of such a thing."

"Oh, aye. Not verra commonplace but 'tis a way for a 'usband tae rid 'imself a wife. I seen it a time before many years ago. An older woman then." He nodded at the slight figure on the platform. "No' so young as this. She'll fetch a fine price." The man glanced at the girl wistfully. Marcus turned his attention back to the hapless girl. The bidding had reached nine pounds now. An old man stood beside the auctioneer. Her husband? Why would he wish to rid himself of a young wife?

The auctioneer's voice boomed over the crowd, cajoling the men to dig deeper into their pockets. The onlookers chimed in, hooting and shouting encouragement as well.

"Gentlemen! Wot ye thinking to let this one slip from yer grasp?" He stood behind her and gripped her by the shoulders, forcing her to step forward as though they all needed a better view of her.

Something stirred in Marcus's stomach at the man's thick hands on the girl. Despite all his extolling of her hardiness, she was thin. She could easily break beneath someone bigger and ruthlessly inclined. A description that fit a fair number of men in this crowd.

The auctioneer snapped back her cloak, parting it to reveal her body, still mostly hidden within a sack-like wool gown. She snatched at the edges of her cloak and covered herself again, glaring at the auctioneer.

Marcus felt himself smile. There was fire in her. His smile slipped. How long would it last after this day's unpleasant business? After she was crushed beneath the boot of a man who bought her as though she were a broodmare? How long until the fire was snuffed out completely?

"'Tis a fine body! She'll give ye countless sons tae work in yer trade. At two and twenty, she 'as many a year left tae breed. No green girl 'ere, nay! She can work yer farm, run a 'ouse and care fer bairns." He forced her to turn in a circle. She stumbled slightly as though her shoes were too big.

"But can she work a cock?" an anonymous voice cried out.

The crowd erupted into laughter. The auctioneer stomped his boot on the platform. "Wot scoundrel said that?"

A bent-backed old man in a vicar's collar rebuked the crowd. "Mind yer tongues! I'll not stand fer it!"

Marcus shook his head. But the vicar would stand for such an exhibition as this? As long as there were no obscenities?

The girl's face was fiery red as she faced front again.

Marcus stared at that face, thinking of his sisters, Clara and Enid. Safe back in Town. Pampered and genteel, shopping and taking tea in the parlor and rides in the park. He hoped that would always be so. That this side of life would never touch them as it touched this wretched creature.

The bidding stalled and the auctioneer looked displeased. "Come, men! Ye would let such a fine lass go fer so paltry a sum as thirteen pounds!"

"Why didna ye plow 'er, Beard?" a man heckled. "Ye weren't man enough fer the task or the lass be squeamish?"

The old man turned red-faced.

The auctioneer shouted, "Enough of that!"

"Bite yer tongue, MacDunn, or I'll 'ave a word wi' yer mam!" a heavy matron called out.

MacDunn wasn't to be fazed. He hollered back. "Untried as she is, we've a right tae ken if the lass can perform 'er duties!"

"Aye, thirteen pounds should get us a sampling, Hines!"

Hoots of approval followed this. The girl actually looked alarmed, her gaze flitting over the surging crowd as though Hines might agree to such a thing.

Frustration flashed across the auctioneer's face. He was losing control over the horde and he knew it.

In an impulsive move, he grabbed her by the chin and forced her face higher. "She be fair enough." He peeled back her lips. "And a fine set of teeth. A proper sign of 'ealth!"

Marcus's stomach squeezed anew and he had the urge to vault onto that platform and give the man a good thrashing. He never could stomach the sight of a woman being manhandled. No matter her rank. Farm girl or lady. He supposed his stepmother had something to do with that. She'd raised him to be a gentleman—more than his father ever had. His father always accused him of being weak. Too soft.

He pushed thoughts of Graciela and his father aside. His stepmother was part of the reason he was out here in this godforsaken little backwater. He would not think of her now.

The girl's head sprang forward at Hines. The auctioneer lurched away suddenly, yanking his hands from her as though she were afire. "Ouch! The little 'ellion bit me!"

The crowd laughed in approval.

"Och! There be some spirit in 'er!"

Marcus grinned. Served him right.

The auctioneer glared down at her crossly, nursing his wounded hand.

A man suddenly cried out, "Take off 'er dress!"

The auctioneer flipped her cloak back off her shoulders, revealing her in her ill-fitting brown wool gown.

Despite his disgust at the sordid scene, Marcus couldn't look away. He should turn and leave. One voice commanded that, but another part of himself was rooted in place, taking it all in . . . taking in *her*, this proud girl with fire in her eyes.

The auctioneer gestured at her. "Aye, she be endowed well enough, gents! More than a 'andful there!"

The crowd had fallen eerily silent. Lust gleamed in the eyes of the men and several licked their lips. Every man here was evaluating her, stripping her of her modest attire and imagining her on her back, deciding if she would be worth the coin.

The auctioneer persisted. "Wot say ye? Ye'll 'ave 'er to use fer life. This be no temporary investment, lads!"

At that, the girl's face went even more pale, if possible. She'd suffered all the insults and indignities thus far with admirable mettle, but that declaration made her look as though she might disintegrate into the boards of the platform.

A man called out from one of the stalls at the edge of the square. "Sixteen pounds!"

Marcus examined him. He wore a tanner's apron covered with blood and gore and bits of offal. His skin had a waxy yellow appearance that bespoke of a poor constitution.

When the auctioneer's voice rang out in approval, "John Larkin, my good man!" the girl's pale face turned a shade of green. "Of course ye ken a bargain when ye see one, fine businessman such as ye be!"

The tanner was at least twice her age. Younger than her husband, but still somehow less appealing. He was cadaver-thin, mostly bald with several long greasy strands of hair stretching across his oblong-shaped skull. He smiled at the auctioneer's compliment, revealing brightly yellowed teeth.

"Now do we 'ave any other bids? Anyone else unwilling to let John Larkin beat them and win such a prize?"

Marcus stared at the girl again. Several strands of long brown hair dangled around her face. Her eyes were large beneath a set of eyebrows several shades darker than the brown of her hair. She looked so young.

Those wide eyes scanned the crowd anxiously as though still searching for someone, still hoping for rescue. Escape.

She was nothing to him. Just a peasant girl, but he wished that for her. Wished that she could escape. That someone would rescue her. Anyone.

"Nay? Verra well then! The lass goes to John Larkin fer the sum of—"

"I'll give fifty pounds for the girl!"

Chapter 4

*And the dove finds herself freed from
one cage and placed in another . . .*

*S*old!

The word reverberated in her head.

Sold like livestock. Like goods at market.

Like a slave.

Slave. As awful as that word was . . . the other
words were more awful. All those words shouted
by the jeering crowd that made her feel less than
a person.

A man had bought her. This fact was no small
thing that went unabsorbed in her consciousness.
The knowledge of it bitterly coursed through her.

He was out there somewhere. A face in a crowd
of hundreds. He'd stared at her. Evaluated,

judged her and found her worth the coin. Perhaps his voice was one of the many who yelled horrible, demeaning things at her.

Her heart raced. Her pulse jumped at her throat. He'd bought her for fifty pounds. A significant amount. More than anyone else was willing to spend and that was its own form of embarrassment. So very few had even wanted to bid on her.

These friends and neighbors she had lived beside all her life had stood by as she was haggled over like a piece of property. A few had bid, but most had not. Most had averted their eyes when she looked at them—as though sharing her shame.

No, the men to bid on her had been strangers. Men with leers on their faces and lasciviousness in their eyes. They had come from other villages. Maybe it was easier to buy a woman when you did not know her. When her father had not been a respected member in your community, a teacher to the village children.

All except John Larkin the tanner. She shuddered. Sadly he was no stranger. She had known him all her life, much to her regret.

"Come on, lass." Mr. Hines tugged on her halter. The rope cut into her throat, the rough hemp abrading her skin, forcing her forward. She grabbed the lead and tugged back. He tossed her an annoyed look as though he were the one being mistreated.

She held on to the lead as she followed him down the platform steps, lifting her gaze to scan the crowd, searching . . .

As though she would somehow know *him* when she saw him—this man who had claimed her to wife. As though there would be a sharp moment of recognition when she clapped eyes on him.

She may not have seen who bought her, but his voice still resonated inside her ears. She knew instantly he wasn't from around here. He had been English, his voice deep and impenetrable as a dark wood calling out: *I'll give fifty pounds for the girl.*

She hadn't seen his face but sweet relief had rushed through her to have escaped the clutches of John Larkin. The tanner would not own her. Her fate would not be with him . . . it would not be *that.*

Her nostrils twitched in memory. She could almost smell his stench even now. He always reeked of coppery blood and rotting animal carcass.

Another shudder rolled through her.

Fifty pounds. It was a small fortune. Mr. Beard's eyes had bugged out from his head. She sent him a quick glance. Even now his eyes gleamed with avarice. He shifted anxiously, clearly eager for his money. She knew he had never seen a sum like that in his life. She always budgeted the household accounts and she knew he could never call that amount of money his at any one time.

She was good with numbers. Always had been. Papa had schooled her from a young age. From the time she had learned to walk, she had been taught Latin and French. Her bedtime stories had been Chaucer and Shakespeare. There were only a few books in the Beard household but she had read them countless times. She missed books.

She had been looking forward to moving to London where she could visit libraries. She'd heard they had libraries where anyone could walk in and have access to books. It boggled her mind. When Yardley had abandoned her, he had taken that dream with him.

She swallowed against the lump in her throat. Now she couldn't even imagine what her future might be.

"This way." Mr. Hines led Alyse and Mr. Beard to the rear of the platform near the animal pens where a small table was positioned. Mr. Hines's son sat behind it with ledger books spread before him. He wouldn't meet her gaze. He busied himself scrawling inside one of the ledgers.

She glanced around again, wondering if any

of the curious onlookers watching the proceedings could be him. Her salvation or doom.

"Where's the buyer?" Hines demanded.

"Here he is!" an anonymous voice called.

The tiny hairs on the back of her neck prickled. *Anyone is better than the tanner. Anyone is better.* The mantra whispered through her and she grasped for it, needing it for strength.

For all her curiosity, she could not turn. Could not look. She was too nervous. She felt ill.

He was behind her now. The man whose voice had cracked over the air, saving her moments before she was sold to the likes of the wretched tanner. Nothing could be worse than him. She felt certain of that. Even the unknown had to be better.

John Larkin always made her skin crawl. As far back as when she was a little girl and she accompanied her father to his shop, the tanner had always made her uncomfortable . . . luring her to the side with a sweetmeat as Papa browsed, petting her hair, remarking what pretty braids she had and how far they went down her back.

The few times she had accompanied Mr. Beard to Larkin's shop, he'd always found a way to get close to her . . . a way for his hand to brush or grope some part of her body. Never, in her worst imaginings, could she envision him as her husband. She shuddered again.

She could not seem to stop the reaction. Even though she had escaped that fate, it was enough to make her shake and the bile rise up in her throat. Who knew the untold miseries he would have inflicted on her before she managed to escape?

She sucked in a breath and fought back another shudder. She had vowed to stay strong. Whatever happened today, she'd survive it. Just because she was being cast into the unknown as the wife of a stranger did not mean her life was over.

This stranger would be better than the tanner who smelled of rot and animal carcasses and whose touch made her recoil. Hopefully he was a reasonable man. She could talk him into releasing her. Or she could work off the money he spent to procure her. If that failed . . . well, she would tackle that obstacle when she came to it, but she'd existed as a glorified slave for long enough. She was done living that life.

Suddenly the stench of manure reached her nose. For a moment she wondered if thought of the foul-smelling tanner had conjured the aroma.

Then a deep, decidedly English voice asked, "Where do I pay for the girl?"

Turning, she found herself pinned beneath a deep blue gaze. For a moment, it was all she could see. A dark ring of blue-black surrounding cobalt. Those eyes stared back at her. The air froze in her chest and she had the utterly ridiculous thought that no wrong could be committed by a man with eyes like that.

And yet even as mesmerizing as those eyes were, nothing could distract her from the fact that the man smelled like a barn.

No, worse. She enjoyed the smell of a barn when it was full of fresh cut hay. This man smelled like the back end of a mule. Her gaze swept over him. He was a big man. Tall. Bearded. She could see little more than those impressive eyes and the straight slash of his nose above that heavy growth of hair.

It was difficult to determine his age but his hair was a rich dark brown, very nearly black. Not a strand of gray so he couldn't have been very old.

And this man is your husband.

She was now bound to a man (at least temporarily) that didn't look like he had taken a bath in the entirety of his life.

"Ah! There ye be. Come this way." The auctioneer led them to the table, releasing his grip on the infernal rope, much to her relief. She pulled it over her head, flinging it to the ground as though it were a poisonous serpent. She rubbed at the skin of her throat where it had chafed.

Her skin prickled again and she looked to

the side to find the stranger studying her again. Stranger. Husband. She did not even have a name for him yet.

He looked away then and stepped past her, joining Hines and Beard at the table.

"Jus' need both ye tae sign these documents and then 'ere again in the ledger. My son 'as already detailed the sale. Yer signature is the only requirement." He paused to laugh. "And the money, o'course."

The stranger reached inside his jacket and pulled out a pocketbook. He opened it and removed the money, handing it over as if it were nothing for him to part with such an exorbitant amount. The glimpse she managed told her there had been more inside that pocketbook, too.

Mr. Hines accepted it and handed it to his son. After taking out a small fee for their services, Mr. Hines handed Mr. Beard his cut. "I trust ye are pleased, Beard. She brought a 'efty sum." He turned his attention to the buyer. "And I 'ope yer 'appy in yer purchase." Mr. Hines sent her a stern look. "Be a proper biddable girl and keep 'im satisfied, Alyse."

She seethed, inhaling through her nose.

"You'll not address her by her Christian name."

At this deep-voiced rebuke, Alyse blinked, looking at the dark, bearded man. Ironically, *she* didn't even know her surname. She was Alyse

Bell originally. She still felt like Alyse Bell even after she married Mr. Beard. She always would.

Hines blustered, his face reddening.

Mr. Beard hastily pocketed his money, clearly eager to finish with the lot of them. Especially Alyse. He bent over the table and picked up the quill, quickly making his mark. She knew it well. It was only his initials. JB. Something he had perfected over the course of his life. Those were the only letters of the alphabet he knew.

Her husband-to-be stepped forward and took up the quill next. Unlike Mr. Beard, he took his time reading the document. And there he hesitated. He looked at the words, then to her, then back to the words again. She couldn't read them from her vantage, but she well imagined the substance of the document. They severed her ties to Mr. Beard and made her the stranger's wife now.

"Well, on wi' ye then," Mr. Hines snapped, all goodwill he had felt toward the stranger gone. "I've things tae do yet. Many more animals tae be auctioned."

The man leaned over the table, quill braced tightly between long fingers. Filthy or not, she could not help noticing he held himself differently from other men. At least differently from all the men she had known. The men of the village.

His bearing was almost dignified. Too dignified. As though he held himself above everyone else. This place, these people. Yes. That would even include her.

At last he signed. First the document and then the ledger as directed. The scratch of quill on parchment seemed loud. And then it was done. Documented for posterity.

Like chattel, she was conveyed from one owner to another.

She thought of Papa then and it almost hurt. He couldn't have imagined it being like this. He couldn't have known the indignity of it all . . . the potential peril.

She tried to step forward and peer at his name so she would know who she had bound herself to, know what name she now bore that would never fit. But he stepped back, blocking her view.

Mr. Hines's son quickly sanded the parchments and then folded them, slipping each inside an envelope with neat movements.

Mr. Hines took up both envelopes. "A bill of sale fer each of ye," he pronounced. "Ye'll want tae keep those. Although 'tis a matter of public record now." He winked at Mr. Beard and clapped him on the back. "Yer a free man once again, Beard. Enjoy yer bachelorhood."

Mrs. McPherson was suddenly there. Or perhaps she always had been lurking close. She squealed and clapped her hands, pushing her way into their circle. Clearly he wouldn't be a bachelor for long.

"Fifty quid! Mr. Beard! Och, wot a feat! Never tae believe! Wot a sum fer a bag of skin and bones such as our Alyse!" Her gaze flicked over Alyse dismissively.

Alyse bit back a burning retort for the old hag and shifted awkwardly on her feet, aware of the stranger's scrutiny and uncomfortable beneath it.

"Come." The stranger—her husband—directed.

She *still* did not know his name. She had no idea what to call him.

Before she turned to follow, Mr. Beard reached for her arm. "Alyse."

She stopped and looked at him, bracing herself for his farewell, hoping that she maintained her composure and didn't lash out at him as every ounce her being willed her to do.

Her blood was pumping hard in her veins and her head was spinning already from everything that had transpired. She didn't know how to react if he dared to apologize . . . although she was most certainly owed that small gesture after years of loyal service to his family. He may have given her a roof over her head, but she had earned twofold every courtesy he had ever extended her. She doubted she could accept such an apology graciously.

"'Ere ye go. Dinna forget this."

She looked down. Mr. Beard extended her battered valise for her to take. There was no fare-well. No forthcoming apology—and as much as she didn't want to hear such a thing from him, she was also, irrationally, angered that he did not care about saying good-bye. He didn't want to apologize.

"Oh," she said, the word strange on her numb lips.

She accepted the bag, nodding mutely as her clammy fingers gripped the handle. Turning back around, she saw that her new husband waited. Her eyes briefly met his before looking away.

He pressed on and she followed, adjusting her grip on her bag and walking stalwartly, shoulders squared, chin high.

Mrs. McPherson wrinkled her nose as they passed. "Phew. 'Opefully 'e 'as enough blunt left fer a bath."

Alyse followed behind her new husband, eyeing him carefully, noting the hard set of his shoulders. He did not turn around, however. Nor did she. There would be no looking back. There was only forward. Only the future and she needed to focus on that. On getting that right. She'd endured enough. Even though Yardley had failed her and would not be in her life, she could still carve out a future that was worth something. She wouldn't give up until she had that for herself.

The crowd parted a path for his tall figure. She didn't know if it was his intimidating size or the foul smell of him, but everyone gave him a wide berth.

They departed the square, walking a short distance until he reached a young boy holding the reins of an impressive gelding with a gleaming black coat that her fingers itched to caress.

"Here, lad." Her husband tossed him a coin. *Husband.* She blinked at the strangeness of that. At the *wrongness.*

"Thank ye, sir," the boy exclaimed before darting away to buy a treat with his sudden earnings.

The man pulled himself upon his mount with ease and then peered down at her from his great perch, his deep blue eyes inscrutable.

She looked up at him, hoping he did not intend for her to ride astride with him. She was loath to press her person against his rank body. She would rather walk.

"I'll take your valise." He extended a hand. She lifted her bag up to him. He secured it to his saddle. "Follow me," he commanded in those cultivated tones before turning his mount around.

She hesitated only a moment before moving after him. For now, she would obey. She would be the perfect image of submission. Temporarily. Until she devised a plan.

As difficult as it was for her, she would bide her time. Assess. Strategize.

He was not difficult to keep pace with. The lane was crowded and more narrow than usual with stalls and vendors erected along the edges. Her stomach grumbled at the aroma of roasting meats and fresh baked breads. She really should have eaten more this morning . . . but then she might have retched during the awfulness of that auction. Nellie had been right. Never in her life had she felt so degraded. Damn Yardley for abandoning her. She would never forgive him.

The horse ambled along, unable to move very quickly, but it was still no small embarrassment to walk down the street of her village, meekly plodding behind the man who had just purchased her.

Eyes and indiscreet whispers followed her. It all added to her humiliation.

Perhaps it was a good thing he was from out of town and they would be going somewhere else. Some place where people would not know the demeaning details of their beginning. Bitter bile welled in her throat as she grappled with that fact that she was bound to this man. At least until she figured out how to break free.

Soon the busy street thinned out and they

were at the edge of the village on the road north. He pulled to the side and dismounted. They stood face-to-face. She had to crane her neck a bit to look up at him and she wasn't a particularly short female. She and Mr. Beard had been of like height and Yardley was only a little taller. She swallowed and attempted to look composed, fighting the urge to take a step back.

Outside of the village, away from the clamor and the press of bodies, she realized how very cold it was. Without the shield of buildings, the wind buffeted her, whipping her skirts around her ankles. Shivering, she burrowed into her cloak.

It wasn't only cold. It was . . . lonely. It felt like they were the only two people on earth even though the village bustled just beyond, its din a distant murmur.

Here, in this moment, it was just them and the wind and the crack of branches beneath the weight of snow.

Flurries fell lightly, dusting his shoulders and clumping on the dark fabric of his coat. Big shoulders. She swallowed against the sudden lump in her throat. All of him was big. His body filled out his garments.

She looked him up and down, eyeing every filthy inch of him warily. Staring up at this large bearded man, the realization that she belonged to him now sank in slowly, deeply . . . terrifyingly.

She fought to hold her ground and not back away. Not run screaming into the village as the weaker side of herself urged. How had she ended up here? In this place? This scenario? She had such different expectations for how this day would end.

His blue eyes sparked, sharp and intent above the dark growth of hair covering the lower half of his face, and she suspected he knew the panicked edge of her thoughts.

Silence throbbed between them, matching the pulse racing at her throat. She was bound to this man. She struggled to wrap her mind around that . . . struggled to deny it.

His breath fanned like fog from his bewhiskered lips. He looked practically biblical. Like Moses emerging from the desert. He was fairly . . . *feral*. A man capable of trapping and killing his dinner with his bare hands. His fine diction notwithstanding, there was a roughness to him that locked her jaw and shrank every pore in her skin.

Even after Yardley returned from the navy he had not looked this virile. Indeed not. Her childhood friend was not as broad. Not as tall. In truth, five years in the navy did not overly change him. He did not look very different from the boy of her youth who lived next door to her. She doubted he could even grow a beard. And perhaps that was some of his appeal. His very familiarity, his lack of change, brought her back to far more pleasant and less grueling days.

This man—this very un-Yardley type of man— could crush her.

She swallowed against her tightening throat. He could drag her into the woods and she would be helpless to fight him. Her blows would rain uselessly.

He was strapping. Young. At least young*er* than Mr. Beard who had celebrated his sixtieth year just this past Christmas. But not as young as her Yardley. Yardley was a boy compared to him.

A fresh flash of anger shot through her. No. Not *hers*. He was not *her* anything anymore. Perhaps he never had been. If he'd been hers he would have been here for her and she wouldn't be standing across from this man—this stranger— contemplating the ways he might destroy her.

She groped for that elusive composure of hers and inhaled, catching a fresh whiff of the man who'd just bought her for fifty pounds. She winced and covered her nose.

Say what you will but at least Yardley did not reek.

They continued to assess each other. It reminded her of when the Beard family introduced Moody, their calico cat, into the household. The family hound and the cat had a stare-off that lasted weeks. Whenever Alyse entered the kitchen, they were always in their respective spots, glaring at each other with wild eyes, growling and hissing low in their throats, waiting for the other to make a move or sound. She did not know who she was in this situation—the cat or the dog. She'd always felt them equally matched. Currently, she did not feel equally matched. No, she felt quite pale in comparison to the man towering over her.

"Your name is Alyse Beard—"

"Not Beard. Not anymore," she replied hastily. Not ever really. "My name is Alyse. Alyse Bell."

She had never felt like Alyse *Beard*. She was Alyse Bell. Always had been. Even if legally she was not.

Now, she supposed, she bore yet another name . . .

A name she didn't even know. How strange was that? She didn't even know the name by which the world identified her.

He made a noncommittal sound. "Very well. Alyse Bell." Apparently he was in agreement that they didn't share a name either. There was that at least.

He continued, "Don't think this means anything. We are not truly bound to one another."

She opened her mouth several times but then closed it, bewildered, unsure how to respond. He was in possession of a bill of sale that said differently.

A beat of silence passed before he added, as though sensing her confusion, "I am *not* your husband." His gaze was almost cruel in that moment, eyes blazing a dark blue in the obscurity of his unshaven face, like a dark loch, promising untold secrets. "Let us be clear. You are not my wife."

Chapter 5

*And the dove blinked, rotating and testing her
cramped wings within her new cage.*

There was no misunderstanding his words,
but that did not lessen her confusion.

He'd bought her like a sack of grain, and he
had a deed of sale to prove it.

What kind of man bought a woman at auction,
but did not want her?

She was no longer Mrs. Beard. Like it or not,
she belonged to this stranger. She was his even if
he didn't want her.

"Doesn't it, though? Mean something?" She
moistened her lips. "There is . . . documentation.
A bill of sale?" She glanced in the direction of

the village. She could still hear Mr. Hines's voice in her head, his words ringing in her ears. *Sold!*

If that didn't mean anything to him, then where did that leave her? Free? Dare she hope that he meant to let her go?

Her hand moved to her throat, brushing the skin there. She could imagine she still felt the fraying rope, thick and choking, sawing into her skin. Staring at this man, she did not *feel* free. She felt trapped as ever.

"Perhaps this rural little backwater may consider a wife auction a legitimate method to marry two people." She could hear the sneer in his voice. "But I assure you, the civilized world will *not* recognize what a bunch of provincials deem a wedding."

She bristled. Pride stiffened her spine. He uttered the word *provincials* like it was something dirty on his tongue. She was certain he considered herself one of said *provincials*. He might as well have called them all idiots. She didn't know whether to be insulted or relieved. Relieved, she supposed, if he did not consider this arrangement binding and it gained her freedom.

She resisted pointing out that her father had been a schoolmaster and that she had been reading and writing and speaking French quite well by the age of five. She might not have traveled outside this little hamlet and she might be as poor as a church mouse but she was no idiot. She kept that to herself, though. Let him think her a provincial. Someone of no value. She didn't want to persuade him into keeping her.

"By all means, if you think you have no obligation to me, don't let me keep you." She motioned in the direction of the snow-draped road even as her mind feverishly started working through what she would do once he left her here. Specifically, how could she acquire the funds to reach London? And assuming she did, how would she subsist there while she looked for employment?

Mr. Beard didn't want her anymore. He'd made that abundantly clear. Even though he'd made a pretty penny selling her she knew he would not part with any of it to help her. Mrs. McPherson flashed across her mind. The widow would likely take a broom to her if she even spotted her approaching the house. She'd clearly staked her claim on Mr. Beard and she did not want Alyse lingering.

Nellie would want to help but it was doubtful her young husband would permit it. As apprentice to the blacksmith, they could barely fend for themselves. Also, they had another baby on the way. Alyse couldn't burden them.

Her Not Husband narrowed his eyes. He considered her for a long moment, his expression dark and brooding, impossible to read.

Alyse waited for him to mount his horse and leave her, certain he was on the verge of doing that very thing.

"I did not say I have *no* obligation to you. I accept my responsibility," he finally said, his blue eyes as grim and solemn as an undertaker.

And she, presumably, was a responsibility?

"What does that mean precisely?" she asked distrustfully. He'd dismissed the legitimacy of their union, after all. What did he consider them to be if not man and wife?

"We can work out some manner of arrangement. Is there somewhere you would like to go? Do you have any family . . ."

"To foist me upon?" she finished bitingly.

He hesitated before nodding. "In a manner . . . yes."

She resisted pointing out that if she had any family to rely upon she would never have found herself at the center of a wife auction. He did not know anything about her, though. For all he knew, her family was the kind that gladly let one of their own be sold in a sordid public display.

He didn't know she was an orphan. He would not know she'd had loving parents once upon a time who were rolling over in their graves because she was in a predicament such as this. The thought of her parents was almost enough to undo her.

She took a shuddering breath and tried not to think of them. "No. I have nothing. No one." She pointed at her valise on his horse and wondered why it stung her pride so much to admit that to him. Her pride had already suffered such a thorough stomping today. She did not think it could still feel anything.

She had been wrong.

"That is everything," she added. "My life is in that bag."

He stared to where she pointed, his forehead furrowing. "No friends or—"

"No one," she snapped.

He digested that and asked, "Then is there somewhere I could escort you?" Even as he asked, his eyes glittered with frustration. Perhaps anger. He didn't want to be here with her. Her chin went up a notch higher. Well, that made two of them. "Some place you would like to go?"

Where she would *like* to go? As though it was that simple. As though her life was full of so very many choices?

"I should like to go to London." Since he was asking, she might as well be honest.

He winced. "I've come from there and I'm not going back. At least not any time soon."

She laughed once roughly, the sound pulling at the back of her throat. That would be her luck.

He came from the place she most wished to go. "Any place then. Preferably a larger city."

Somewhere she could lose herself. So that she might find herself.

He gave his head the slightest shake. "So am I to understand you have nothing? No distant relations? No funds?"

She fidgeted. "Yes."

"So I could take you somewhere but there would be nothing waiting for you once you arrived there."

Was he saying this so that she could feel . . . *better*?

She held his stare, knowing she was soliciting his pity and hating him right then. She suspected she had already done that once today when she stood on a block wearing a halter. Her dignity begged for a reprieve and she didn't want him feeling obligated toward her. "Yes," she answered slowly. "That would be true, but I can fend for myself."

"Can you?" Skepticism laced his voice. He crossed his arms as though he really were seeing her. Seeing how very pathetic and alone she was and she despised that.

She squared her shoulders, trying to look more. Bigger. Stronger.

He scanned her, unmoving. "Have you any

skills that would make you desirable for employment?"

She angled her head sharply and suppressed a snort of derision. "You were at the auction, were you not? I think you heard the extolling of my attributes."

He nodded slowly. "You worked a farm, did you not? You can cook, clean, sew." He clipped each of those words as though counting off a list.

"Aye." She had essentially been the family servant. No task too menial or grand. She did them all, including managing the household ledger. She mentioned that then. "I managed the household."

"Ah." He snapped his fingers. "A housekeeper then. You sound aptly qualified to that task."

Housekeeper. That would be an improvement over unwanted wife, she supposed. She eyed him suspiciously. Was he implying he would help her find a situation? It was almost too much to hope.

"I have a position for you. I'm on my way to my property in the north. On the Black Isle."

The Black Isle was far north indeed. It was quite the opposite of where she wished to go. Inverness was the closest city and it was hardly London.

And yet he was offering her work.

She looked him up and down again. "You've property there?"

"I do. Kilmarkie House. It's at the top of the peninsula, near the point."

Her mind immediately tracked back to her geography lessons with her father. "Is it true you can see dolphins there? In the sea?" Scotland might be surrounded by sea at every side but she had never seen the ocean, much less dolphins.

"That's what I hear."

She blinked. "You've never been there yourself? And this is your property?"

"No, I haven't visited, but I've heard dolphins are visible from the shore. Whales, too."

What manner of man owns a property he has never before seen? Was he very rich then and simply averse to bathing?

"I've heard it's very beautiful," she admitted, mulling over his offer. The Black Isle. It wasn't London, but she would be seeing more of the world. And she would like to see dolphins. That was one incentive. "Would I earn a wage?" She could work until she saved enough money and then move to London. Or anywhere at all . . . hopefully with a glowing reference in her pocket.

"Of course," he replied with no inflection to his voice.

Of course?

He acted as though she should expect fairness when life had taught her to expect very little. If life were fair then she wouldn't be here with him and rope burns on her neck.

"I didn't bid on you in that auction for free labor," he added with a touch of indignation.

She resisted asking why he did bid on her. Sometimes it was best not to ask questions.

She nodded decisively. "I accept your offer."

She would not be getting any better offers at this time and well he knew it.

The dark whiskers surrounding his lips twitched. "Very well." He looked her over quickly. Turning, he swung up onto his mount again. "Wait here." With no further explanation, he turned about and headed back into the village.

She watched him ride away, wondering what precisely was happening. Why was he going *back* to the village? Certainly he was returning for her? He'd taken her valise with him. She shivered a little and hugged herself, hating how reliant she was on this man—her Non Husband. A man whose name she still did not know. She bristled. Apparently he had not deemed her significant enough to properly introduce himself.

She stood at the edge of the road for some time before she stepped to the side and leaned against a tree. As much as she wouldn't mind sitting, the ground was covered in snow. Her dress and cloak would be soaked and then she would really be cold. She looked down, considering her too-tight boots and tattered garments. She was not attired for traveling north into the Highlands. It would only get colder.

Minutes ticked by and she glanced up at the cloudy sky. The afternoon was well on its way. Her stomach grumbled and she wondered if they would eat any time soon. Whatever the case, she knew she would not ask him.

"Alyse!"

At the sound of her name, her gaze popped up. She scanned the road.

Nellie approached on foot, holding her very swollen belly with one hand.

Alyse sprang away from the tree and hurried to meet her friend, her heart immediately clenching in concern for the girl she had looked after for so many years.

"Nellie! What are you doing walking all the way out here? It's far too cold for you. You should be off your feet."

Nellie breathed heavily. "I 'eard wot 'appened. Oh, that damn Yardley! I wish 'e'd never come back! And m'father! I'll never speak tae 'im!"

"Shhh, now." Alyse rubbed a comforting hand over Nellie's back. "Don't distress yourself."

"Ye canna go wi' 'im." Her gaze darted around. "Where is 'e? Did 'e abandon ye 'ere?"

"Nay, he'll return. I'm just waiting here for him." At least she thought he was returning.

Nellie's face crunched up with tears. "I 'eard 'e was a giant and reeked like a barn."

Alyse winced. "Aye, but he can bathe." One would hope.

Nellie shook her head, her face crumpling. Fat tears spiked from her eyes and tracked down her cheeks. "Nay. Ye canna go wi' 'im!"

"Shhh, don't distress yourself."

"Ye deserve better, Alyse. Better than m'father, may a blight fall on 'im." Her lip curled in a sneer as she continued her tirade. "Better than Yardley . . . and better than some monster of a man!"

Right then the monster returned.

They turned in unison at the sound of clomping hooves. Her Non Husband trotted along the road, kicking up a small spray of snow. Another much smaller horse trotted behind him with an unwilling air . . . as though the beast resented being pulled out of whatever warm stall he'd occupied. No. She peered around her Non Husband atop his great beast. It was not a small horse. It was a mule. He led a mean-eyed mule.

He stopped before them and before she could inquire about the mule, Nellie charged ahead, ready to resume her tirade.

"Listen 'ere! Dinna think ye can abuse 'er!" She

shook a fist, her other hand holding her swollen stomach, looking rather absurd in her intense ire. Certainly not a visage of intimidation. "I'll find ye if ye do! I'll spend all m'days 'unting ye down! I'll make ye pay, God 'elp me!"

It was impossible to read if his expression cracked beneath the dark pelt of his beard, but he only gave a mild blink. He inclined his head once and she couldn't help thinking that nod rather regal. Arrogant, but regal. "I give you my word no harm will come to your friend."

Nellie held his gaze for a long moment as though measuring the value of that promise. The silence was uncomfortable and Alyse cleared her throat.

Sniffing and looking partially satisfied, Nellie turned and embraced Alyse with a clucking sound. "Ye take care of yerself. Where will I direct m'letters?" She cast another suspicious glance over her shoulder. "I 'spect to 'ear from ye and assure myself of yer well-being."

"I'll be at Kilmarkie House in the Black Isle." She gave Nellie's gloved hands a reassuring squeeze. "Don't fret yourself."

"Outside Inverness," he contributed.

Nellie cast him a glare, clearly unwilling to warm to him. It would take more than his promise not to harm her to accomplish that. "I will write ye and if I dinna 'ear back . . ."

"I know . . . you'll send an army." She squeezed Nellie's hands again.

"Nay, I willna need an army," she said loudly, looking at him and speaking to him rather than Alyse. "I'm a good shot by my own right."

Alyse nodded, her lips twitching. "Thank you," she whispered to her friend.

"For wot?"

"For making me feel loved in this world." This morning she would have said she had more than Nellie to call friend. She'd thought she had Yardley, too.

Nellie released a strangled little cry and hugged her again. Alyse laughed and patted her on the back. "I look forward to your letters. I want to know all about the baby. Now go on with you. Get somewhere warm."

Nellie stepped back with a sniff, swiping at her red-tipped nose. She nodded. "Aye."

Alyse faced her Non Husband, looking up at him perched in his saddle. "Am I to assume the mule is for me, sirrah?"

He nodded once.

She peered around the gelding to consider the smaller creature. The mule's large dark eyes seemed to stare back at her in equal consideration.

"It . . ." She paused and ducked her head to peek under the animal. "*He* seems small. You expect me to ride him? Are you certain he can hold my weight?"

"Mules are sturdier than you think."

Still, she hesitated, staring at the animal as though it might suddenly transform into something else before them. Something resembling a full-sized horse.

With a resolute nod, she told herself this mule might not be as ornery as every other mule on the face of the earth. "Very well. Let's be on our way then."

He dismounted and approached her. She took several steps back before she could stop herself. Nellie hissed from where she stood, looking ready to pounce on the bigger man regardless of her condition.

Shaking her head, Alyse told herself not to be so jumpy.

After all, he didn't want her as a wife. He pitied her and had offered her a position as his housekeeper. If he was to be believed, she should be overjoyed. She had employment. She would earn a wage and soon she could go anywhere she wanted.

If he was to be believed, she would eventually be free.

Chapter 6

The wolf had no notion what to do with a dove.
The creature was so clean and fragile.
He came from a world of wolves where doves did not exist.

Marcus helped her mount although she could probably have done so without assistance. As she pointed out, the beast was not very large.

"Perhaps I'll call him Tiny. Or Little Bit," she muttered as she arranged her skirts.

Even though he didn't want to be amused, his lips twitched as she settled herself atop the mule he'd purchased for far more coin than the nag was worth. Bloody extortion.

The animal was all to be offered in the stables and only through much coaxing had the stable master parted with the mule. All other horses available for sale were being auctioned in the square and nothing would have prompted his return there. His taste for auctions had been efficiently dispatched. He doubted he would ever attend one again.

He stared at her for a long moment as she finished arranging her bedraggled skirts and cloak to cover her legs. Even so, the barest amount of thick wool socks peeked out above her worn boots. No woman of his acquaintance would wear such meager garments. Nor would they bear the indignity of riding such a creature. It would be absurd. The soles of her boots might actually graze the ground. His father had owned greyhounds that were taller than this mule.

And yet she didn't utter a protest. Of course not. She was of lowly roots, was she not? He'd bought her for fifty pounds. She wasn't going to complain about her manner of conveyance. She was accustomed to far worse.

Even as he told himself this, his stomach knotted. The entire mess made him uncomfortable. He did not like to think of himself as a procurer of humans. Even if pity and altruism had motivated him.

He looked away from those unusual eyes of hers, feeling nearly as uncomfortable as he had watching her on that block with a harness around her neck. He didn't *own* her. Nor was she his wife.

No court of law would decree their marriage valid. He could imagine, however, a court would pronounce him responsible for her. He winced. He did possess a bill of sale, incredible as that seemed. Tucked inside his vest pocket, the paper felt like an unrelenting weight pushing against his chest.

Not that he needed that bill of sale to tell him he was responsible for her. He'd opened his mouth and purse for her. He accepted his duty to her. She was penniless and without a roof over her head. He couldn't abandon her.

Your father would . . .

His father, were he in Marcus's shoes, would take full advantage of her. Use her up and then toss her aside once he'd slaked himself.

Not me. I'll not do it. I'll not touch her.

And that reminder bolstered him. The last person he ever wanted to be like was his father. Not since he'd learned the truth about him. Not since he discovered the precise nature of the man who had sired him.

He exhaled. As of now she was his employee. That's all she was. All she would ever be.

There were only minimal servants at Kilmarkie House. A caretaker and his family managed the property. He'd gotten a sense from his last correspondence with Mr. Shepard that they would appreciate the help. His wife was in poor health.

Alyse could slide into the role of housekeeper easily enough.

Resolved, he gathered up the reins and handed them to her.

She bent, reaching for them. As she did so, her nose wrinkled.

He glanced down at himself and was reminded of the fact that he spent the night in a stable. It was rather humbling. Women desired his company. It was the simple state of his life.

Not that it should matter to him. His ego wasn't so fragile as that. She was not even to his tastes even if she were available.

"Here you go," he snapped. "Take them."

She accepted the reins. He moved ahead and mounted, ignoring her friend who still stood in the road, gawking as though he were some two-headed spectacle intent on devouring Alyse.

He heard the muffled sound of their voices behind him as she exchanged hushed words with her friend. Then the mule followed, its hooves clomping over the snow.

"C'mon, Little Bit." She clicked her tongue. The mule issued a braying whinny of protest. "Ow!" she exclaimed. "He bit me!"

An apropos name then.

He slowed his pace slightly with a grimace. "You must show him you're in control," he called back.

"I don't think he agrees. Ouch! Stop that, Little Bit!"

At this rate, it would take them months to reach Kilmarkie House. "Perhaps he takes exception with his name?"

"Oh, should I just address him as 'mule'? What makes you think that impersonal designation would not offend him?"

Sighing, he dug in his heels and circled around to check on her.

Just this once he'd help her. She was his employee. He should not dote on her and give her unreasonable expectations that their relationship was anything beyond that of employer and servant. He needed to keep them both carefully in their respective roles. A challenge perhaps considering they would be traveling together in such close proximity, but not unmanageable. He hadn't bought her off that auction block for any nefarious reasons. Pity drove him. She had looked so hapless and tragic and unnervingly courageous standing before that unsavory mob.

His father would call him weak for giving a damn what happened to some peasant girl. Especially a scrawny thing like her. She was hardly the type of female Marcus preferred. It should prove no struggle to resist her, proximity or not.

He moved Bucephalus alongside her.

The mule danced skittishly to the side.

"Oh, I don't think he likes you so close," she sang nervously.

He reached between them and loosened the slack in the reins. "Shorten your lead. His mouth is sensitive. A light touch will satisfy." He bent and dropped his hand just below her knee, squeezing her calf once through the fabric of her garments to indicate where to nudge the mule.

She flinched at his touch and yanked her leg away.

"Use your legs to direct," he snapped, not even bothering to defend his actions. She was understandably uneasy.

When he looked up he caught her leaning away and averting her face, reminding him that his odor still offended. He pulled away, offended in turn, which was perhaps unreasonable. He did stink. He knew that.

He didn't *want* to feel offended. But he didn't want to repel her either . . . this girl he had saved. It very well might be the one good selfless thing he had ever done. So yes. It mattered to him, he supposed. It mattered what she thought of him. Or at least that she realized he wasn't some groping letch.

"Keep close," he snapped. "He should follow Bucephalus."

He trotted ahead as she called behind him. "Your horse's name is Bucephalus?"

"It is."

"He's a lovely animal."

It took him a moment to reply. He was still seeing her flinch in his mind.

She continued, "The name suits him even if it is a mouthful."

After a few moments, he heard himself explain, "Bucephalus was—"

"The horse of Alexander the Great. Yes. I know."

He had to resist sneaking another look behind him. The peasant girl he had bought from that little backwater knew Ancient Greek history? He never would have thought such a thing. It made him wonder what other surprises she hid.

He saw a flash of her on that block again, her wide topaz eyes set deeply beneath darkly arched brows, snow falling lightly around her. Initially he'd been taken aback by the spectacle, marveling at the surreal quality of it all. The absolute absurdity of it.

But now it struck him. She'd been the unearthly one. Some untouchable wisp of a fairy. A dove with pale clean wings pinned to her sides, unable to fly away as humanity raged and frothed around her in all its stark ugliness.

He knew something about the ugliness of man. Even as untouchable as she had seemed up on that block . . . ugliness would have seized her if he hadn't done something. He'd known that.

So he'd done something.

He urged his mount a fraction faster as if needing more space between them.

He just had to get her to Kilmarkie House and then he could secure her as his housekeeper and have all the space he needed.

Chapter 7

*The dove paced the confines of her
new cage, learning its parameters . . .
learning all she could about her new prison.*

*A*lyse reached down and rubbed her calf
where Little Bit had nipped her. She knew there
would be a bruise later. Thankfully the beast had
ceased trying to eat her for a snack. She didn't
know if it was because of her Non Husband's
instructions or if the animal simply decided to
increase its pace to something beyond a crawl.

Little Bit still didn't move fast enough. It was
a nuisance. The man ahead of her was forced
to slow his pace and she knew it annoyed him
from the hard-eyed glances he cast over his
shoulder. She resisted pointing out that *he* was

the one who had purchased a mule for her to ride. Except he was her employer now, so she held her tongue.

She stared at his broad back moving ahead of her—at the filthy fabric of his dark coat. He appeared to have spent some time rolling on the ground. It baffled her. Clearly he was a gentleman. He spoke with cultured accents. He possessed property and funds enough to buy her and a mule. And yet he looked a mess.

Deciding it would behoove her to better know the man she was stuck with, she cleared her throat. "Where are you from?"

A beat of silence passed before he answered, "I live in England."

She rolled her eyes and stopped herself from retorting, "Obviously." She did not want to provoke him. As much as she was loath to admit, her life was in his hands now. He could still abandon her. Toss her in these very woods where her body would be picked apart by wolves. She shivered before she could help herself.

It would well serve her not to be too difficult of a traveling companion. Just as it would serve her not to lower her guard with this man. She knew firsthand that a person could say one thing and then behave in a contrary manner. Just because he promised her future employment did not mean he would keep his word. Wisdom bade she be on her guard no matter what words he spoke.

His shoulders lifted on a sigh. His voice rumbled back at her, his reluctance to speak evident, and yet he did. "I spend most of my time in London."

Another five minutes passed as they plodded along.

Nothing else from him.

She moistened her lips and glanced around at the surrounding snow-draped trees. "I've never been this far north of Collie-Ben before." In truth, she'd never been anywhere outside of her village before.

Hooves clopped on the path, one after the other. A steady, hypnotic cadence. She sank deeper in her saddle, telling herself to embrace the silence as it appeared it would be the background to their journey. That would be fine. A refreshing change from the boisterous Beard household.

Except the humming silence fed her doubts as they rode along. Her gaze fixed on his back. She was placing a great deal of trust in this man. What if he was lying? He could be lying about any number of things. His intentions. His destination. His promise of employment. She knew nothing of this man.

She took a deep breath and tried to suppress her unease. She needed a calm and level head.

She was alone now. Truly alone. No husband willing to claim her. No friends. No children to look after. It was just Alyse. She had only herself to rely on and she required her composure and wits.

She exhaled, wondering if she should simply slip away. Escape into the woods on her dawdling mule. The image was almost laughable.

"I don't believe you ever told me your name," she said, compelled to fill the silence and squash her wild thoughts.

He stopped and wheeled his horse around. "Did I not?"

"No, you did not."

"How remiss of me."

"Well, it was quite an eventful day," she allowed.

"Indeed. My name is Marcus." He hesitated and then added, "Weatherton."

She nodded a single time, testing the sound of that name in her head. Marcus. Weatherton. Marcus Weatherton. She rolled that over inside her mind, and then she was bold enough to take it a step further. Alyse Weatherton. Mrs. Alyse Weatherton.

No. She gave her head a hard shake. That was not her name. He had made that much clear. It would never be her name. She stared at his hard-eyed visage and shivered. A relief to be certain.

She had no wish to be trapped in marriage to him.

She swallowed against her dry mouth. "A pleasure to meet you, Mr. Weatherton." It was the polite and proper thing to do. Even if a couple hours late.

He made a grunting sound, and she was quite sure he was not pleased to meet her. Still, she would make an effort at manners. Her father had always taught her the importance of grace and civility.

Still, it would better serve her if she grew to know Marcus Weatherton and learn for herself what manner of man he was, so she asked, "If you have never before visited Kilmarkie House, what inspired this visit now?" In the midst of winter, no less.

He considered her a moment longer before turning his horse back around and continuing forward. She urged her mule to follow. He protested with a braying neigh, but reluctantly obliged. She could relate.

"This is not the most hospitable time of year in the Highlands," she added, hoping it would invoke more response from him.

Her suspicious mind worked busily. *What if there was no Kilmarkie House? What if he lied?* Her pulse throbbed at her neck and her gaze darted to the trees again.

Moments slipped past, but he still did not respond.

The trees felt thicker, pressing in, blotting out the light. Hard to imagine her best chance of refuge might be in those dark depths.

With a shaky breath, she continued, "Although I hear the Highlands are lovely any time of the year. I imagine covered in snow they are quite majestic."

At last, he asked in a wearied voice, "Do you plan to talk the entire journey?"

"Have you an aversion to conversation, sir? We will be in each other's company for a long time and I thought it might help."

"Help? With what? I don't require pointless banter."

Pointless banter? She huffed out a foggy breath. The man did not win points for charm. She reminded herself that he was not a friend, not a companion . . . not even anyone she could trust. She wanted only to know him so that she might better arm herself. Not because she cared to personally know him.

She supposed she needed to expect less from him. He was simply her employer.

"I confess there is one matter that has been weighing on my mind," he said.

"And what is that?"

"How did you come to be on that auction

block?" He didn't look back as he asked the question, but she could still almost imagine those dark blue eyes on her, measuring her, judging her . . .

It was so easy for him, a man of means, to ask something like that in a voice rife with judgment. For him it was unthinkable. He could never fathom himself in such a situation. Because he would never be in such a situation. The truth of that angered her unaccountably. Why should it be her lot in life? Or any woman's?

"I married Mr. Beard when my father died. That was the arrangement they made when Papa took ill and it became clear he would not live long."

"Your father did this to you? Auctioning you for any stranger to buy?"

She stiffened in her saddle, her hands suddenly damp where they clenched her reins. He didn't understand. Again, he was full of scorn, passing judgment without all the facts.

"He did it to protect me," she said tightly.

He made a sound. Part laugh. Part grunt. "Well, that worked out, didn't it?"

She shook her head slowly. Her father loved her. He'd tried his best. "We should all have a crystal ball to see into the future. He thought he was doing the best thing for me. I would help Mr. Beard raise his children and work around the farm and when I was old enough, I would choose a new husband for myself and he would buy me from Mr. Beard at market." It had seemed the perfect solution. She nor her father imagined it would end like this—with her bound to a stranger.

"Incredible," he muttered, loud enough for her to hear.

"It should have worked!"

"But it didn't."

She sank back in her saddle, stung at that truth and feeling deflated. "He was supposed to be there . . ." she whispered, the betrayal of Yardley's abandonment cutting deep, the wound still much too fresh.

He stopped abruptly and turned his horse about in one well-guided circle. "What did you say?"

Her mule pranced and hedged away, not comfortable in such close proximity with the much larger gelding. She could understand that. She didn't particularly care for close proximity with his master either.

Marcus Weatherton stared down at her with hard eyes from atop the much higher perch of his mount. He repeated himself, canting his head. "What did you just say?"

She cleared her throat and flexed her damp hands around the reins. "I didn't say anything . . . to you." But she had spoken aloud and she heartily and intensely regretted that right now as he pinned her beneath his unblinking stare.

"You said: *he* was supposed to be there."

"Well, if you heard what I said why are you asking me?" She knew she sounded cross, but she could not help it. He did this to her. He put her on edge.

She shivered, knowing it had nothing to do with the cold. No, it had everything to do with him and his arctic stare. She cast another look around them, at the thick press of snow-dappled trees. She knew nothing about this man and yet here she was in the middle of nowhere exchanging tense words with him.

He ignored her inquiry, stubbornly pushing, "*Who* was supposed to be there?"

She fidgeted, ashamed to confess her abandonment, to reveal how very unworthy she was. Her own friend, the man who had promised to marry her, changed his mind and left her with no explanation. That was the worst thing of all in this. Theirs had not been a passionate love, but she thought their friendship deep and true. She thought he would make a fine husband. She would have been a good wife to him.

"A lover?" he pressed, his cunning eyes sweeping over her and making her tremble anew. He laughed once, the sound harsh, his teeth a straight flash of white amid the dark pelt of his beard. "Of course." He tilted back his dark head as though examining the sky, lips snapping shut over his teeth.

She watched him, feeling an odd stirring in her gut at the sight of him.

His broad hands loosely gripped his leather reins, but there was a restrained air about him. As though he might jump to action at any moment with those powerful hands of his. The wind had temporarily stilled and she was spared the scent of him. He was quite the virile specimen with that lush dark head of hair and his large frame. Those blue eyes far too calculating, too . . . observant. She shifted upon her saddle. They saw too much.

"What did he do? Make all sorts of promises and then fail to appear?"

She sniffed and moistened her wind-chilled lips. "How did you know that?" How could he guess so accurately?

He snorted. "I know something about the manner of men." He looked angry then, his eyes fierce. "Your lover promised you the world between kisses and then would have let you be sold to someone like that tanner. That should teach you. Trust no man."

She shuddered, remembering the repulsive tanner and how very close she had come to becoming his wife. He would have wasted no time claiming his husbandly rights. And perhaps more. He would have claimed her soul, too. Then she would have been as dead inside as all the animals whose hides he tanned.

She didn't bother to correct that Yardley had been more friend than lover. He'd been her longest friend. Her truest, she'd thought. His letters to her during the years of her marriage had been her one light in the darkness. She'd read them again and again, until the parchment cracked. She'd absorbed his every word, memorizing his descriptions of the far-off places he visited and drinking in his promises of their future away from Collie-Ben.

Yes, there had been a few kisses between them. Her first kiss when she was fourteen, before he left. Then one just a few days ago, sealing, she thought, their commitment to each other. Both chaste. Obviously neither tempting enough for him to commit to being her husband at the final hour.

Trust no man. She mulled that for a moment. "So I should not trust *you* then?"

She studied him for his reaction, waiting and expecting his assurances that he was a good man. That he was a gentleman. That he would never harm or deceive her in anyway. That seemed the natural response.

But it never came.

Chapter 8

The wolf wasn't like the other wolves. He craved solitude.
He had nothing in common with a dove.
He feared he might crush her.

The village was similar to the one they'd just left. Similar thatched-roof buildings. A smithy shop where loud clanging could be heard. A stone church with a neighboring graveyard. Hopefully this time he would make it through the night and not end up in a gaol.

At least it wasn't as crowded. They maneuvered through a few streets easily enough until they located a large inn. As they arrived before the building, the delicious aroma of roasting meat reached his nose. His stomach grumbled, reminding him that he hadn't eaten since the hunk of bread and cheese he'd bought off one of the vendors in Collie-Ben.

He glanced over where she sat atop her mule, swaying slightly. She looked exhausted. Likely she was hungry, too. She could definitely use a little more meat on her bones. He felt a stab of guilt for not seeing better to her comfort. He should have acquired food for the both of them before he left Collie-Ben. He would order them a hearty meal. Hopefully that would help fortify her. He didn't need her to sicken.

The instant the thought passed through his head, he cringed. There he went again. Overly concerning himself with her welfare. It was hardly typical protocol between employee and employer. He needed to keep perspective on who she was, who he was and most important who they were *not* to each other.

So I should not trust you then?

He hadn't answered her question. He'd told her to trust no man. He wasn't about to contradict himself and tell her he was the exception. It was better if she knew to stay on her guard. Better for her. Better for him.

They turned their mounts over to a stable lad, who made no effort to hide what he thought of Marcus's aroma, taking several steps back. Damn it all. Finally, he'd have that bath and everyone could stop treating him like a leper.

"We're verra full. 'Aven't got two rooms. We've only one room available," the innkeeper said to his request for two rooms.

One room. That silenced him for a moment. He glanced at her face as he digested that. She turned to stare at him, her eyes wide and un-blinking, questioning and fear-tinged. He hated that fear. Hated that he was the one who put it there.

Clearly she hadn't thought this far ahead. Neither had he. He hadn't considered sleeping arrangements. He had assumed separate rooms would be available.

"Take it or leave it." The man glanced between the two of them with a curious light in his eyes, clearly marking the tension.

Glancing back at the innkeeper, Marcus slapped down his coin on the counter. "We'll take it."

It couldn't be helped. There was only one room. She might be nervous about the situation, but he wouldn't so much as brush a finger against her. He did not intend to endure another night in a barn, however. Or even outdoors. It was far too cold for that. "Can you send up a bath, too?"

As the innkeeper led them upstairs, he casually remarked how the market day in Collie-Ben brought forth more business than typical. "Nae complaint 'ere, though. Always 'appy fer business." He unlocked the room and led them inside. It was comfortable enough. Airy. Fading sunlight streamed through the curtained window. The bed wasn't nearly as large as the mammoth contraption he slept in back in Town, but he wasn't one to thrash and kick about. At least none of his bed partners had complained of that before. He'd keep a wide berth.

The innkeeper took his leave, promising to have a bath sent up forthwith. The door shut behind the man and they were alone. Again. Only this felt different. This was different. They were alone in a bedchamber. He deliberately avoided glancing to the bed again. He could taste the tension in the air. She was nervous, her fear as tangible as copper on his tongue.

She moved to the center of the room, and rotated in a small circle, her worn valise at her feet. Her gaze flitted about, assessing . . . marking, it seemed, for potential escape routes. She always had that way about her. The way of a cornered animal looking to take flight.

Exhaling, he turned to the fireplace that burned at a low dwindle. How in bloody hell had he ended up in this situation? It was a sad sorry state. He'd left London and all his family and friends behind in a fit of temper.

Most of his temper had worn off, but now he just felt tired. Jaded. In no mood to see any of his family. He knew he couldn't hide forever. They were his family. He couldn't turn his back on his sisters.

For weeks now, he had claimed his solitude. Time for himself to get away from Society. Except he had cast that aside today when he bought this girl. He could be alone right now, kicking off his boots and stripping off his clothes in a room to himself, reveling in his isolation. Instead he had to worry about being a well-behaved gentleman and conducting himself as a proper employer would.

He stoked the nearly banked flames to life. It gave him something to do and gave her time to compose herself. He suspected she needed that. He stabbed at the logs until they crackled, flames licking over their gnarled skin. Rising, he turned to face her. She hugged herself, her arms tight around her torso.

"You needn't look so frightened."

She nodded jerkily. "I know. I'm not." Her words said one thing but those gold-brown eyes another.

"You're not convinced of that," he countered. "But then that's a good thing."

Her chin went up. "Never trust? Correct?"

He nodded. "That's correct."

He sank down onto a wingback chair that was surprisingly more comfortable than it looked. The cushions were worn but plump, and he released a gratified sigh.

He waved at the other chair across from him, flanking the other side of the fire. "Have a seat."

She shook her head. "You said we were not to be . . ." Her voice faded, but he knew what she was thinking, what she could not bring herself to say. She worried he was going to demand intimacies.

"Not what? People who sit in chairs?"

She flushed.

He continued, "I meant what I said. We're not married. I have no designs on you—"

She gestured around her. "But we're sharing a room—"

"You heard the innkeeper. There were no other rooms to be had."

"And you've requested a bath be brought up," she challenged.

"Would you prefer I not bathe?" He arched an eyebrow at her, knowing full well everyone in the world preferred he did.

At that, her lips pursed and he knew she could smell him even from where she stood. "Of c-course . . . only where am I to go during your—"

At the moment, a knock rattled the door. He rose and passed her to open it.

Several lads carried in buckets of steaming water. They pulled back the screen in the corner and poured water into the copper tub. Nodding deferentially, they took their leave.

He rubbed his hands together in anticipation as he eyed the water.

An older woman arrived with soap and towels. "Can I get ye anything else, sirrah?"

Alyse looked rather desperately around her, her mouth opening and closing as though she wanted to ask for something. Something like a weapon. Or a ladder to escape out the window.

"Yes," he said. "Do you have a parlor where one might take tea?" He nodded to Alyse. "I would like some privacy for my bath."

"Oh." The woman nodded, tucking her plump hands inside her pinafore. "Yes, we do." She nodded to the door, eyeing Alyse expectantly. "Shall I escort ye there, ma'am?"

Alyse nodded rapidly, her eyes alive with relief. "That would be wonderful."

"Come now." The woman walked out the door, waving her to follow.

Alyse quickly trailed after her. And that was a bit of irony. He knew a good amount of females who would have been grateful to ogle him at his bath. This one wanted no part of that.

"Go on with you," he tossed after her. "Perhaps they'll serve biscuits with that tea."

She paused, bestowing him a tentative smile and then she was gone, shutting the door behind her.

Turning, he started stripping off his clothes.

He cast them aside with relish, determined to never wear them again.

Sinking down into the bath, he moaned in pleasure and leaned back in the copper tub. After a moment, he dunked below the water's surface. Coming up, he reached for the soap. Lathering his hair, his hands drifted to the thick bristle covering his cheeks. He hadn't shaved since he left London. He hadn't cared to bother. It felt rather defiant, eschewing his customary shave each morning. And that felt good. Casting aside the trappings of his life felt damn good.

His father would have hated the beard. As would his stepmother. They wouldn't approve of anything he was doing. Shunning his title. Journeying to some forgotten piece of property. *Buying a woman off an auction block . . .*

They wouldn't know him at all. He wasn't certain he could claim to even know himself anymore.

He dragged his fingers through the beard. It was damnable itchy.

THEY DIDN'T SERVE biscuits with the tea, but the room was cozy and the chair thick and comfortable and her cup warm in her hands. As crowded as the inn happened to be, the small parlor was unoccupied. Voices and the clang of dishes carried from the neighboring taproom full of patrons. That seemed the popular place to be, and she was glad for the privacy of this room. Glad that she was not forced to be above stairs with him as he took his bath.

As she sank deeper in the plush chair, she contemplated leaving this place, this village. Bolting. Fetching the mule from the stables and going back to Collie-Ben where she could prevail upon Nellie or Mr. Beard. Except the idea made her flinch. It was problematic. Nellie was in no position to offer assistance and Mr. Beard was unwilling.

She sighed. The more viable recourse was to stay. Keep on with Weatherton and hope that she remained unmolested in his company. Hope the offer of employment was legitimate. Hope that this was the only night they would be forced to share a room.

It was all a risk, of course. One she would take while staying ever alert and ready to protect herself.

Her gaze narrowed on the tea service beside her chair. Even though the maid had not bothered to supply her with any biscuits or sandwiches there was a small butter spreader. Hardly the sharpest of knives, but it was . . . something. She reached out and picked it up, tucking it inside her bodice.

She actually dozed off in front of the fireplace, waking abruptly when a garrulous pair of women entered the parlor.

"Och!" one of the women exclaimed, looking Alyse over critically. "Didn't know the room was already occupied." She tugged off her fine-looking gloves with a sniff and glanced at the innkeeper as though he needed to rectify this.

Alyse glanced at the clock above the mantel. She'd been gone nearly an hour. She rose, brushing a hand against her bodice. The butter spreader was still there. "I was just leaving."

The innkeeper looked relieved that he did not have to ask her to leave. She exited the parlor and made her way up the stairs and down the corridor to their room. *Their* room. She cringed.

Weatherton should have had enough time to finish his bath by now. She knocked on the door tentatively. Muffled footsteps sounded and then the door swung open.

She looked up, expecting to see the familiar sight of Weatherton.

Only it wasn't him. A younger man stared back at her, the tall lean lines of his body filling the threshold to capacity. He was so handsome she actually blinked as though needing to clear her vision. Smooth-shaven. Square-jawed. Aquiline nose. Lips well-shaped, the bottom full. Like he'd just finished kissing someone. She stopped breathing altogether at that unsolicited thought. She held it in for several punishing moments.

It had been a long messy day. She exhaled. He was quite certainly the prettiest man she had ever seen and the sight of him addled her head.

"I-I'm sorry," she stammered. "I must have the wrong room."

He angled his head and looked at her curiously. Then his voice came—cultured and deep, a rub of gravel on her skin. Gooseflesh broke out over her skin and she rubbed at her arm. "Alyse."

The instant he spoke, she knew. His deep tones washed over her and her gaze darted to his eyes. Those familiar blue eyes. There was no mistaking them.

Dear God. This was the man who bought her. Her employer. He'd bathed and shaved and was positively transformed.

He was . . . beautiful.

No no no no. He could not be this. He could not look like this. She could not be stuck with . . . *this.*

She wanted to disappear into the floorboards.

He wore fresh clothing. Dark trousers and a white lawn shirt without a cravat. It gaped open at the neck, hinting at a well-formed upper chest. In fact, all of him was well-formed.

If she had any doubts as to the validity of their union, this confirmed it. She could *not* be married to this man. She wasn't. He was as far removed from her as the moon itself.

It was as he said. They were *not* man and wife and she would do well never to forget that—to never let herself be so seduced by his looks that she dared to dream for more from him.

"Forgive me. I did not recognize you."

His lips twitched and she knew he was enjoying this . . . enjoying discomfiting her. Men who looked as he did could not be unaware of their impact on the female gender. He was aware that he had unnerved her—she who had made no attempt to hide her distaste for his aroma—and he was amused at the reaction.

He stepped aside so that she could enter the room. Grasping for the fraying ribbons of her composure, she crossed the threshold into his room. *Their* room for the night.

"Did you enjoy your tea?" He shut the door after her.

She nodded mutely, struggling to find her tongue as she drifted forward and stopped before the fireplace. She held her hands out to its warmth.

"I trust my person does not offend your nose anymore." Oh, he was really enjoying this.

She nodded jerkily, not allowing herself to

look at him again. Not yet. That first look had
been bad enough. His beauty was imprinted on
the backs of her eyelids. Of course the man had
no wish to be her husband. With a face like his
and pockets that ran deep, why would he want
someone like her?

He continued, "I've asked that dinner be
served in our room. I confess I did not sleep well
last night. My accommodations weren't idyllic."
Even with her back to him she could hear an edge
of derision in his voice. "I would not mind retir-
ing early tonight so that we might get an early
start in the morning."

Her gaze swerved to the bed at his mention of
sleep. She nodded in agreement. What else could
she do? Did she think he would molest her? He
had established that he had no interest in her for
base purposes. Clearly he could find any number
of willing bedmates far more attractive than she
if that was his inclination.

Except she knew that cruelty defied logic. He
could hurt her simply because he could. His pretty
face changed nothing. She needed to remain on
guard.

Sucking in a deep breath, she rubbed her
slightly warmed hands together. At her inha-
lation, she felt the press of the butter spreader
inside her bodice. Silly as it seemed, it was a com-

fort. Somehow just having the cutlery in close proximity made her feel stronger.

Turning, she faced him again, telling herself that he didn't need to know just how little she trusted him. Blast. The sight of him was no less astonishing than it had been when he first opened the door.

"You're looking at me as though you fear I might gobble you up."

Apparently she was more transparent than she thought.

She relaxed her features. "Not at all. I . . . thank you," she managed, aware that she should probably at least appear to be appreciative. She hadn't gotten the words out before. It was probably overdue.

He arched an eyebrow as though mildly surprised. "You're thanking me . . . why?"

She swallowed thickly. "You saved me from a wretched fate." She motioned around them. "You're caring for my needs. You've offered me employment." It was all true, she supposed. If he delivered all he claimed and didn't perpetrate any dastardly deeds against her person, she owed him her gratitude.

His expression turned inscrutable again. She could not fathom his thoughts . . . specifically whether he believed in her show of appreciation.

"If you execute your duties well at Kilmarkie House then it shall all be repaid."

She nodded. "I will serve you well as a housekeeper and pay you back for your kindness."

"Kindness," he mused. "I've been guilty of many things. Never that."

Not exactly a bolstering personal recommendation. She eyed him warily. He stared back. Tension throbbed on the air between them, and it derived from her. He looked calm and unaffected. A man in control . . . who held all the power in this scenario.

A knock at the door spared her from replying. Weatherton bade them enter. The innkeeper stepped inside, holding the door open for two servant girls carrying in trays.

The girls gawked at her Non Husband, one practically walking right into the table in her distraction.

"Sheila!" the innkeeper snapped. "Where are yer wits?"

Sheila snapped into focus and set the tray upon the table before the fire. They quickly unloaded a bounty of food. Smoked salmon. Bannock. Tatties. Creamed turnips. Plump slices of shortbread.

Before departing the two girls dipped deep curtsies to her Non Husband, allowing him to look down the front of their dresses. They did not once glance in Alyse's direction, instead feasting their eyes on the attractive man before them.

"Please let us ken if we can be of any other service tae ye, sir."

"Any at all," the other girl seconded, her eyes looking him up and down as though he were a tasty morsel she might like to bite.

"Out wi' ye now!" the innkeeper barked.

The girls scurried from the room, darting longing looks over their shoulders.

Alyse couldn't feel too much annoyance. He was exceptionally handsome. She could understand the need to gawk.

In the wake of the serving girls, the innkeeper nodded at them. "Ring the bell if ye need anything more, sirrah. Madam." He ducked out and shut the door behind him.

Weatherton motioned to the table. "Shall we eat?"

She nodded.

He moved to pull out her chair. She stared at him for a startled moment. She knew men extended such courtesies to ladies, but it was a strange world indeed when she would be on the receiving end of such courtesy. Where one might perceive and treat her as a lady. Earlier today she wore a halter and stood upon an auction block. Now a gentleman held out a chair for her before a table laden with fine food and drink.

She took a seat, feeling dowdy in Nellie's old dress. She smoothed a hand over her lap, wincing as her roughened palms snagged on the fabric. Further evidence that she was no lady. The fabric was not even delicate. Simply coarse wool.

He sat across from her and poured wine into her glass.

She copied his movements and lifted her glass, sipping the dark red liquid tentatively. "That's good," she murmured.

"Have you ever had claret before?"

She shook her head and took a deeper sip.

"Not too fast. It can go to your head."

Her eyes widened and she set her glass down. She didn't need to become addle-headed around him.

He leaned forward, peering at her.

She pressed a hand to her chin. "Is there something amiss? On my face?"

He shook his head and tapped at the side of his throat. "What is right there?"

Her hand moved to her throat, mimicking his move. "I-I don't know."

"Are those marks?" he asked intently.

"Oh." She dropped her hand, instantly knowing. She'd spied the marks herself in the chamber's dressing table mirror. "I'm sure they're just from the rope."

His expression clouded. Apparently he had

forgotten she wore a halter like an animal. It would not be so easy for her to forget. Even after the bruises disappeared, she would remember. She would always remember.

She searched to change the subject. "How long should it take to reach your property?"

He slid his fork into his salmon as he replied, "A little over a week. Perhaps two. Weather permitting."

That long? She would be stuck with him— *alone*—for so long?

She went straight for her shortbread. She couldn't help herself. She had a sweet tooth and shortbread was a rare indulgence. Mr. Beard thought sugar an extravagance.

She bit into her first bite and moaned at the taste. She couldn't help herself. It had been a good while since she ate and she could not recall the last time she ever consumed shortbread so sweet and moist as this. She stuffed more into her mouth while cutting another bite, cramming that in as well, forgetting all decorum as her stomach cheered in joy.

With her cheeks stuffed, her gaze collided with his.

He leaned back in his chair, his glass held idly in long tapering fingers. He watched her with hooded eyes. Unreadable eyes.

She set down her fork and worked to chew

and swallow the copious amount of food in her mouth.

"Hungry?" he murmured.

She pressed her napkin to her lips, wondering if the bite would ever go down. He must think her a glutton.

Nodding, she reached for her claret and took a tiny sip to help. "I have not eaten since this morning." *And I have not eaten this* well *since Papa passed.* Oh, she'd never starved in the Beard household. They had chickens and pigs on the farm. Vegetables from the garden. But a meal like this was the type she only read about in books.

"Eat," he encouraged with a wave of his hand. "Go on. You need some meat on your bones."

After a moment, she picked up her fork again and resumed, stealing glances at him. Despite how hungry she was, practically falling upon her food, he finished before she did and was left studying her as she finished. It was unnerving, but she did not let it deter her. She ate every bit of the food before her.

"You speak well for a . . . country girl."

He hesitated before arriving at the word *country* and she wondered what word he really wanted to use. Provincial? *Peasant?*

He meant she didn't sound like a rustic.

She'd been told that before. Others in the village claimed she put on airs.

"My father was a learned man. A teacher. Originally from Newcastle."

"Ah." He settled his hands on the arms of his chair.

"I can keep household accounts for you," she volunteered, happy to point out her usefulness.

"You read and write then. As the auctioneer said."

She stiffened at his reference to her time on that platform. "Yes. I can read and write as Mr. Hines had advertised." She squared her shoulders. "And I'm quite good with numbers."

"That should be useful."

"And I could be useful in London, should you decide to take me with you when you return there." Hope stirred in her chest. She couldn't resist. He was from London and that's where she ultimately wished to go.

A shutter fell over his eyes. "I think not."

She sagged a bit in her chair. "Well . . . something to keep in mind." She could not relinquish that dream. Someday she would get there. She'd serve her time as his housekeeper, earn enough money and then go. Be free.

"No," he announced, his tone emphatic.

The single word jarred her. As though he

could read her thoughts and was pronouncing *no* to her private longings. She bristled . . . until she realized he was simply being curt.

"I don't know my plans," he continued, "but should I ever return to London I see no need to bring you with me. I've offered you a respectable position at Kilmarkie House. That should suit you."

That should suit you.

She stared at him in mute frustration. The skin near her eye twitched. Here was another man deciding her fate, telling her what should *suit* her. Papa, as much as she loved him, had done the same for her at the age of ten and five. Then Mr. Beard made all the decisions and now this Marcus Weatherton was deciding things.

She lifted her chin and fixed her gaze on the crackling fireplace. "The position shall suit me . . . for the time being."

He snorted and her gaze shot to his. "As though you have so many options, Miss Bell."

She inhaled sharply. Flinging her helplessness back at her did not endear him to her in the least. He might look like some knight from her girl-hood dreams, but he was quite the boor if he had to remind her of her helplessness.

Well, she wouldn't be helpless forever. Once she put enough money aside, she would have choices. The freedom to go wherever she chose.

Independence. This was the modern age. A woman led the realm, for heaven's sake. She could go wherever she wanted. Be whomever she wanted.

He stood and rang the bell.

Soon the simpering maids returned to clear away the dishes, still casting him beckoning looks as they worked.

Alyse remained in her chair before the fire, unsure what to do with herself as they gathered the dishes. Again, it was quite an unfamiliar experience to be the one waited upon. She would never grow accustomed to such treatment.

He asked, "Would you like me to ring a bath for you?"

Her head snapped around at the offer.

She scrutinized him, resenting the instant urge to say yes. She would adore the luxury of a hot bath but she hated relying on him for anything more. She had taken so much already from this man who wasn't her husband.

Her feelings were all ajumble. Distrust. Resentment. She didn't want him to be *nice* to her. But, of course, she didn't want him to be cruel and harm her. It was confusing. She *needed* him to be a good man.

He nodded once as though she had answered. "I'll assume that's a yes. I'll take my leave, so you can have your privacy."

Before she could find her voice again and decline, he was gone, the door clicking behind him.

She sighed. Just as well. She really did crave that bath . . . as though the sordid events of the day could be washed away and she could be reborn clean and new. Wishful thinking.

Soon the simpering girls returned with kettles of hot water for her bath. They quickly searched the room with hungry gazes. Finding Weatherton absent, they simpered decidedly less and moved about with much more efficiency.

They prepared her bath and helped her out of her clothes as though she were a child. Or someone important.

As though she were not like them. This morning she had woken like them. Perhaps even beneath their station.

As she was freed from her garments, the butter spreader clattered to the wood floorboards. They all stopped and stared.

She cleared her throat and found her voice. "Ah, there it went. I thought I misplaced it at dinner." She bent and picked it up as though her actions were the most natural thing in the world.

They watched her as though she was a half-wit, but they didn't do anything as she placed it on the nightstand.

Soon they were pushing her into the fragrant water. They'd sprinkled some kind of floral-smelling concoction into the water and it was heady and wonderful.

"Nae need tae fuss now. We'll 'ave ye smelling sweet and yer body warm and pink fer that fine man of yers."

Her face caught fire. Clearly they thought she and Weatherton were in fact married. She opened her mouth to explain and then closed it. She was sharing a room—a bed—with the man. It was easier to let them make their assumptions.

"Och, a man like that must wear ye to the bone," one of the maids lathering Alyse's hair mused with a chuckle. "First I couldn'a imagine what 'e saw in a skinny thing like ye, but now I can see."

"You do?" Alyse looked up at the maid.

"Aye," the other one replied. "Ye've a woman's body tae be sure. Plump lovely bosom on ye."

"Aye, men love tae suckle."

Her face burned even hotter at such bold language. Instantly, she was assailed with the image of her Non Husband's dark head nestled at her breasts, his mouth at her flesh.

It was scandalous and wrong. She didn't know him . . . she didn't trust him, but a deep throb started between her legs. She pressed her thighs together in an attempt to assuage the ache, but that only seemed to make it worse. Oh, she was wicked to have such thoughts.

"And men love tae be suckled in turn," the other girl reminded with a giggle.

Blast. Would they cease talking?

"Wot man dinna love that?" the other maid agreed as she dunked water over Alyse's hair, rinsing it free of soap.

Alyse frowned, struggling to imagine such an act. How could a man be—

She gasped. Now it wasn't only her face burning. Understanding dawned and she felt as though her entire body might combust. She didn't utter another word, simply listened in stunned silence at the maids' ribald exchange.

They dried her off and slipped her simple cotton nightgown over her head. She felt like a child as they seated her before the fire, toweling her hair and then setting to work brushing the long, tangled strands.

"Lovely 'air," one of them remarked.

Alyse blinked drowsy eyes, feeling quite content as they pampered her.

"Ah, ye look ready tae fall over. Let's tae bed wi' ye."

She let them put her to bed, feeling like a child. No one had coddled her this way in years. She knew her mother must have but memories of her were only vague. Papa was more pragmatic. They would read by the fire and she would tuck herself into her own bed at night.

She settled into the comfortable bed, permitting them to pull the down-filled bedding up to her chin. She was more tired than she realized. Yawning deeply, she folded her arms over the coverlet. Her lids drooped.

"Ah, get some sleep, ma'am."

She heard their footsteps move toward the door and the hinges creak open as they prepared to leave the chamber.

"Ye'll be needing it wi' a man as virile as yers."

Her eyes flew open at that parting remark and the full reminder of her situation asserted into her. Apprehension seized her.

The door clicked shut. She lay there for some moments, curled on her side, tense and queasy as she considered her Non Husband returning soon. His big body climbing into bed with her. Lying so close. Radiating heat. All night. And he no longer smelled foul enough to make her retch. Indeed not. He smelled of soap and virile male.

Seized with sudden impulse, she sat up and reached for the butter spreader where she'd dropped it on the nightstand. She immediately felt better as her fingers wrapped around it. She didn't have anywhere to hide it on her body, so she slid it beneath her pillow, still clasping it in her grip. Sighing, she willed the tension to leave her body.

The day had very nearly melted away. The curtains were drawn on their second-floor room, but murky light crept in around the lacy edges. She lay there, rigid, ears straining for any little sound signaling his possible return.

Even as tired as she was, there was no way she could relax enough to fall asleep. It was impossible.

That was her last thought before her eyes drifted shut.

Chapter 9

*The wolf's father taught him how to hunt.
Because, as he had explained, that's what wolves do.
Hunt prey.*

*H*e stayed downstairs longer than he intended.
The innkeeper invited him to use the private parlor and he sat in front of the fireplace, drinking a damn fine glass of whisky as he contemplated his situation.

Life was strange, to be certain. Not long ago he had very nearly died from an injury to the head. He had succumbed to a false sleep for days. The physician had warned his family that he may never wake. His temper had gotten the best of him the day of his mishap. He'd come face to face with his father's by-blow and harsh words had been exchanged. Then blows.

It was strange to consider that had he not survived, had he never woken from a false sleep, he would not have been passing through Collie-Ben in the exact moment Alyse Bell stood on that auction block before that hungry mob.

One might say it was destiny. If one believed in such things. Marcus did not.

Life was made of choices. His choices had led to this moment and his choices would lead him out of this situation.

She was his now . . . his responsibility. An uncomfortable fact. He'd never had such a burden before. True, he had two sisters, but after his father died his stepmother had stepped to the helm in all matters concerning them.

He felt as though he'd arrived at a reasonable solution—one he could live with. He'd offered her the role of housekeeper. By all standards, it was a boon for someone of her background. She could be fairly independent in such a role, collect a decent wage and live in a fine residence with her own bedchamber. It was far better than her previous prospect as wife to the tanner. She'd be safe and that was something she couldn't have said before.

So why did he still feel uneasy? The bill of sale burned a hole inside his jacket pocket. He felt it there like a brand against his chest. It was simply parchment and ink. Except it claimed the woman upstairs was his wife.

Downing the rest of his drink, he set it down with a clack on the side table. Enough. It was done. He'd freed her and given her employment. He'd let it trouble him no further.

He wanted a bed and to see the backs of his eyelids so badly he could taste it. She'd had ample time to finish her bath.

He made his way upstairs, knocking lightly and waiting several moments before entering the chamber. Just as he suspected, she was already in bed—a lump beneath the covers. The fire crackled, casting the room in a red-gold haze.

He closed the door behind him, locking it. After a night spent sleeping in a barn stall, the bed beckoned.

He settled into a wingback chair and removed his boots. Standing, he followed with his shirt. His hands hesitated at his trousers. Naturally he didn't sleep in his breeches. He usually didn't sleep in anything at all.

He eyed the enticing bed, craving the sensation of clean sheets on his skin.

The girl was asleep with her back to him, facing the window, hugging the far side of the bed. He wasn't a wild sleeper. He didn't thrash about. At least he had never been accused of that. They need never come into contact.

Bloody hell. He shook his head. He never slept in his trousers. He wasn't going to start now. He yanked his trousers down.

She was safe from him. He would not touch her. He didn't want this woman for a wife. Hell, he didn't want a wife at all. Not yet. Perhaps not ever. He wouldn't dare consummate their union and he refused to take advantage of her. Alyse Bell was safe from him.

He slid beneath the cool sheets and groaned as the bed sank beneath his weight. His tired muscles cheered at the comfort cocooning him.

He studied the back of her beneath heavy lids. She hadn't even stirred. He doubted she would. The day had been long and exhausting for both of them. She could be naked, too, and launch herself at him and he doubted he would even react. He just wanted sleep.

ALYSE'S EYES FLUTTERED open to sunlight streaming on the air, tiny motes of dust and particles suspended in its beams.

It was an alien sensation. Waking to sunlight. She was always awake before the sun came up. Before anyone else in the house had roused, she was up, starting the fire and fetching the milk and getting breakfast underway.

She'd never slept so late before. The realization froze her to the bed. She clutched the pillow against her head, her senses on high alert, prodding the air around her.

A sigh stirred somewhere behind her, confirming that she wasn't alone. He'd come to bed. While she slumbered this man, this *stranger*, had slipped into bed beside her and she had slept on, blissfully, totally unaware, totally vulnerable. She shuddered at this horrible realization. It shouldn't come as such a surprise, but it was no less shocking.

She held herself motionless, waiting to see if that sigh meant he was awake. Her hand brushed something beneath the pillow and she was reminded of the butter spreader she had tucked away the night before. It was still there. She gripped it tightly, at once feeling somewhat more secure. It might not be the most ideal weapon but it was better than nothing.

After a moment of continued quiet, she pushed back the covers and eased away from the body at her back that was radiating heat in a strangely welcoming manner. Welcoming, she would guess, because it was so cold outside of the bed and for no other reason. The fire had burned itself out sometime during the night and when she expelled a great breath she could see it like fog on the air.

"Awake, are you?"

Her feet hit the floor and she whirled around at the deep voice, her long plait of hair flying like a rope and landing with a soft thud over her shoulder.

He was all casualness, lying flat on his back with one hand tucked behind his head. Her gaze crawled over him. All over his naked chest. He was unclothed. Her breath caught. At least what she could see of him was unclothed. The bedding was bunched and gathered around his narrow waist.

She gawked again at that chest. She couldn't help herself. It was nicely formed with ridges of muscle along his stomach. Not an ounce of fat detectable. Unusual for a privileged gentleman. He had the means for indulgence. Food. Wine. Ale. She'd seen enough of the gentry in her life to know that a good many of them were on the portly side. Not him, though. Her gaze skittered along the shape of him hidden beneath the counterpane. Surely he was wearing *something* beneath.

"What have you there?" he asked.

She followed his eyes to the butter spreader clenched in her hand. In her scrutiny of him she had forgotten she had it.

It was rather ridiculous. Warmth flushed her face and yet she did not lower her arm. It felt the thing to do—brandish a weapon with this man so near and in such an obvious state of undress. She wasn't exactly attired modestly either. The entire scenario felt . . . precarious and ripe for tragedy. *Her* tragedy, if she were not careful.

A corner of his mouth curled and he added, "Is that for protection?"

She gave a stiff nod.

"From me?"

She nodded again. "It seems . . . advisable. One can never be too safe."

His smile faded and for a moment she thought she had offended him. Until he replied, "Indeed not."

Of course, he would agree. Trust no one. Was that not his sound advice?

Abruptly, he moved, launching himself from the bed, flinging back the counterpane and revealing that he was, indeed, naked.

He marched across the chamber. Her mouth dropped open with a croak as she gazed at his bare buttocks.

"You slept beside me without a stitch on!"

He stopped beside the chair where he had draped his clothing. Turning, he sent her a quick glance, arching a dark eyebrow as he reached for a garment. "I always sleep naked."

She jabbed her butter spreader in the air toward him, careful to keep her gaze trained above his waist. A tricky task. "Not with *me* you don't!"

"As this was the first time we slept together, I did not realize we had established protocol."

He was maddening! "It is common sense . . . common decency! I may have agreed to be your employee but I did not agree to such—" She waved her butter spreader madly, sputtering, "To such intimacy!"

"You agreed to share a bed with me," he replied with utter equanimity. "That amounts to intimacy."

"I might have agreed to that on this one occasion, but I did not expect you to disrobe. This is wholly unacceptable!" Even as the words spit from her lips like arrows, her gaze swept over him. Over all of him. Including south of his waist.

Good heavens. Her face erupted in fire.

He wasn't the first nude male she had ever seen. Stepping in to play mother to young boys, she had, of course, observed the male body. And yet none had looked as he did. So large and very virile. Her gaze locked on his manhood. So very . . . *very*.

He shrugged as he riffled through his garments, searching for something. "Sorry," he announced without the slightest apology to his voice. "It's my custom. Should the occasion ever occur again you shall just have to close your eyes."

He moved toward her then, his strides easy,

but all of him was still very much naked and very much distracting.

"Would you please dress yourself?" she snapped with a small stomp of her foot.

His arm stretched out to her, offering something for her to take. She frowned, flashing a quick glance down, too wary to take her gaze off his face for long—as though his expression determined everything, specifically whether or not his intent toward her was ill-disposed or not.

"Here. Take this. As long as you are going to arm yourself you might as well do so with something that could actually draw blood."

She inched closer to peer at what he was holding in his hand. It was a sheathed dagger. The hilt looked interesting. Gem-studded? No. Leather with colorful threading.

"You're giving me a . . . weapon?"

"Yes, I am. An effective one."

A long beat of silence passed between them before she reached out to accept the dagger.

He released it to her and then turned away. "Now if the *occasion* should arise again where we share a bed, you will be properly armed. Just be certain not to stab me in your sleep."

She watched mutely as he dressed himself, trying not to appreciate the way his muscles and sinew flexed with his movements. It was rather hypnotic. She told herself she could admire him rather clinically. It didn't mean anything.

Dressed, he faced her fully again. "I'll go downstairs and see about getting us some food for the journey. We're getting a later start than I intended. Ready yourself while I'm gone."

She nodded wordlessly.

Then he was gone.

She stood unmoving for a moment, staring at the door and then down to the dagger in her hand. She'd never seen such fine craftsmanship. It was a costly piece. She pulled it free of the sheath, assessing the blade. It looked sharp enough, glinting in the light. He was correct. It would serve as a much better weapon.

With a grunt of satisfaction, she secured the dagger and dressed for the day.

Chapter 10

*Above all, wolves are survivors.
They are even known to gnaw off their
own limbs when caught in a trap.*

*H*e regretted their late start. They should
have gotten on the road much earlier. Marcus
knew that within an hour. It was colder than yesterday. The snow was coming down harder and
the mule did not favor the conditions, braying
loudly as though that might result in a change of
circumstances. Their progress was agonizingly
slow.

Alyse Bell, however, didn't complain.

He couldn't see much of her face. She'd burrowed inside her cloak and only her eyes peered
out in thin slits at the world.

He checked on her several times, circling around in an attempt to prod her mount forward. He liked to think it helped propel them onward, but even so, it became increasingly evident that they would not be reaching the next town before nightfall. A definite dilemma. Stuck out in these conditions after dark was certain cause for alarm.

He scanned the road and surrounding country-side through the flurry of snowflakes. The quiet landscape stared back at him, snow-blanketed and sleepy, indifferent to the wet cold seeping into its bones. Mother Nature was unfeeling in that way.

As evening approached, his desperate need to find them shelter only increased. They couldn't bed down out in the open, unprotected from the elements. He was on the verge of circling back around again and lighting a fire to that mule's stubborn arse when he spotted the smoke above the treetops, a gray plume against the darkening sky. The sight of it lifted his spirits.

He called to her over the howling wind and gestured ahead. She gave a nod of understanding. He led them off the road and through the trees, hoping it was a dwelling ahead that they might prevail upon for shelter. He broke through the foliage and paused on a rise that overlooked a small crofter's cottage.

He released a grateful breath, not fully realizing until that moment how worried he had been.

"There." He nodded to the small house sitting at the base of the hill. Smoke chugged from its chimney. A slapdash structure beside the cottage hardly qualified as a stable, but it could be nothing else.

The mule rolled up beside him and stopped. "Do you know the people who live here?" she asked doubtfully.

"No, but they will board us for the night." He said the words matter-of-factly, without looking at her.

"How can you be so certain?"

"They're crofters. I'll offer the proper incentive."

She made a sound that was part snort part grunt.

He slid her a look. "Something amuses you?"

"You are so confident your money can buy anything, are you?"

"Take a look about, Miss Bell." He gestured to the house. "They appear to be in need. Why would they not leap upon the opportunity to earn a few coins?"

Her eyes sparked with something that resembled resentment. "Money can't get you everything," she grumbled.

The words were scornful, but there was a stubborn refusal to them, too. As though she wanted them to be true, and yet she had her doubts.

"It got me you," he snapped.

Her hissed breath was the only reaction she gave but it was enough. Enough to tell him that he had hit a nerve.

Feeling rather foolish, he looked away from her, his chest tight with discomfort at this sudden flash of introspection. The girl made him think about things he would rather not.

Money had given him a life of leisure, power and position others could only dream to live. He knew that, but he had never really contemplated it at length. His life was simply one of privilege. It's all he had ever known.

And yet he was running from it. Leaving that life behind.

The place was even smaller up close. He couldn't imagine a great many people lived under its roof. A dog barked somewhere inside the house.

The front door opened as he dismounted. A young man stepped out, clearly alerted of their arrival by the beast that charged out with him.

The mule let out a long bray of disapproval at the sight of the sheepdog.

The canine must have taken the sound as an invitation to rush forward because he lunged at the mule with several wild yips.

"Fergus! Come."

With a whimper of longing, the dog obediently trotted back to its master, tail tucked.

With a quick pat on the dog's head, the man reached behind him to close the door to his house. He hadn't bothered to don a coat. Even so, he didn't shiver as he stood in his wool shirt and suspenders, snow falling down on him. His boots scuffed over the ground as he advanced a few steps, eyeing them cautiously. The dog inched forward as well, surveying them in mutual yet restrained suspicion.

"Good eve'," the crofter greeted, squinting through flurries.

"Good evening," Marcus returned. "Frightful weather."

"Aye." The man nodded slowly and looked to the sky. "Storm coming."

"Indeed."

The girl muttered behind him, "You mean it's only going to get colder?"

Ignoring her, he fixed his attention on the crofter. The man was younger than Marcus but his face was weathered and lined, testament to a hard living.

"Might we impose on your hospitality and take shelter here for the night?" Marcus reached inside his coat for his pocketbook. "I will compensate you, of course."

"We're a mite crowded." The crofter paused, his gaze skipping over them, considering, taking in everything. "'Ow much?" he asked, clearly tempted despite his reserve.

Marcus glanced at the small house again. It was badly in need of repair. A new roof. Even the door needed replacing. Drafts doubtlessly slipped in through the cracks in the wood. "Enough for you to make all the repairs necessary on your home."

The man said nothing, but his nostrils flared slightly as he continued assessing them.

Alyse muttered something more under her breath, but this time Marcus could not make out the words. He was beginning to suspect the lass had a great many things to say on all manner of subjects whether anyone wanted to hear from her or not. Even when her mouth wasn't speaking, her eyes were. Not an ideal characteristic for a housekeeper. The role usually required deference. Nothing of this girl smacked of that particular character trait.

"Verra well," the Scotsman replied at last. "Settle your mounts for the night."

Marcus nodded. "Thank you."

Before moving to the barn, he caught a flash of movement in one of the windows. A young woman peered out, a babe in her arms and two more barely out of nappies crowded beside her. Now Marcus understood what the man meant. Crowded indeed. Where did they all sleep? Where would he and Alyse sleep?

With a mental shrug, he told himself as long as they had a roof over their head it would suffice.

It surpassed freezing to death on some desolate road.

"Did you have to say that?"

He faced Alyse. She glared at him, looking most aggrieved. "Say what?"

"That remark about his house needing repairs?"

He motioned to the cottage. "It's no secret. Anyone with eyes can see that."

"Aye, he is undoubtedly aware and didn't require the reminder. You needn't have humiliated him. Some people have no control over their situations." High color crept into her cheeks and he suspected she was not merely talking about the Scotsman.

"Indeed. Situations can be out of one's control. Which is why he needs my money." He snatched the reins and started guiding Bucephalus to the stables. "And for the record, I don't think I embarrassed him. He didn't so much as blink an eye."

"Of course he wouldn't want to *appear* embarrassed. He has his pride."

"You act like you know the man."

"I know . . . his kind." Again, her eyes told a greater story . . . that she was not purely talking about the man back in that cottage.

She entered the stables behind him, huffing a little. The walls of the building did little to shield them from the cold and he was heartily glad they didn't have to sleep in the stables overnight. "He's like every person I grew up with in Collie-Ben. I *am* his kind. Poor but proud. We don't like our shortcomings flung in our faces, especially by the likes of you."

"The likes of me?"

"Aye." She nodded her head, looking him up and down as though he were some manner of vermin.

"And pray enlighten me. What am I that is so very unsavory to a poor crofter?"

"A gentleman. Someone born with a silver spoon in his mouth that has never known a day of deprivation in his life." Her chest lifted on labored breath and there was a slight rush of pink to her cheeks that had nothing to do with the cold.

"That's what he sees, is it?" he asked, pausing before adding, "Or is that what *you* see?"

Staring into those strange topaz eyes, he read the truth there. This was what *she* thought of him. She didn't even know how true her words were. He was as blue-blooded as they came.

"Perhaps it's what we both see."

"Perhaps," he allowed, feeling unaccountably angry. He wasn't certain why. She spoke the truth. He didn't know what it was like to go without, and since when was that a shortcoming?

Besides. Why should her opinion of him matter?

He stroked Bucephalus on his velvety nose. "And yet I offer something you both need."

For her, it was freedom. For the crofter, an improved home.

"See here," he began, "I don't regret saying what I needed to in order for us to achieve shelter for the night." He shrugged as he closed his gelding up in a stall and then guided her mule into the neighboring one. "We needed lodging. He did not look ready to agree. Forgive me if my candor hurt his feelings, but in case you didn't notice, this isn't the kind of weather you want to get stuck in overnight."

That said, he turned his back on her and fetched some hay, reminding himself yet again that he shouldn't care what his soon-to-be-housekeeper thought of him.

Without being directed, she copied him and fed her mule. She was no delicate miss. She knew work. He watched as she hefted a pitchfork that he knew was substantial in weight. She didn't so much as grunt from the effort.

Satisfied that their animals were tended, they walked back out into the evening. The temperature had dropped in just those few minutes they were in the stables.

They crossed the yard. Just as he was about

to knock on the door, the young woman he had spotted in the window pulled it open for them.

"Come in and warm yer bones," she commanded.

They stepped inside the single-room cottage. She closed the rickety-thin door behind them.

The cottage, however ramshackle it appeared, was far warmer than outside and his body instantly sighed with relief.

The husband sat at the table, eating from a bowl. He looked up at them as they set their bags on the floor and removed their cloaks. The crofter's wife took them and hung them on pegs.

"I've a stew. Can I get ye both a bowl?"

"Aye, thank you," Alyse responded before he had a chance to say anything—almost as though she doubted his ability to be polite. He, a man raised in polite Society and schooled in the prettiest of manners.

They sank down on a bench at the rough-hewn table.

Marcus glanced around the tight space, wondering where they would sleep. The two toddlers whispered in the bed where they were tucked beneath the covers. One of them waved a rag doll above her face.

His gaze landed on a fur rug spread out before the fire. He supposed that would be better than the stables or exposed to the elements.

"Where are ye traveling?" the husband inquired.

"The Black Isle."

"This time of year?" He tsked and shook his head. "Ye wouldna see me 'eading that far north."

Alyse slowed the stirring of her spoon in the bowl. She looked at Marcus, an eyebrow lifted in inquiry.

He arched a brow, staring back at her. It wasn't difficult to read her thoughts. He knew she would prefer London. She'd voiced her desire to go there already.

But he wasn't going to change his plans for her. He was going to the Black Isle and she could bloody well like it or go her separate way.

He sipped a spoonful of broth. London was the last place he wanted to go.

Foolish or not for this time of year, he was going north.

Kilmarkie House was as close to the ends of the earth as he could get and right now that sounded just about right.

Chapter 11

The dove was sensible.
She knew other doves were free of cages.
She'd heard their weeping and knew freedom
did not always guarantee happiness.
That was another battle that must be won.

They ate quickly and then Alyse helped the lady of the house with the dishes. It was the least she could do. Weatherton might be paying them for their hospitality, but it wasn't like Alyse to sit idle—especially when the young woman looked so very weary. Several strands of hair fell loose and dangled around her pale face. Her hair looked like it needed a good washing, but she imagined it was a lot of work to heat water for a bath.

"Thank you," Alyse murmured as they dried the last bowl and put it in the cupboard.

"Of course, and ye may call me Mara. We dinna get much company 'ere. It's nice tae see another woman's face." She smiled tentatively.

"Yes. It is nice," Alyse agreed, smiling back, recognizing Mara's loneliness.

She knew about loneliness. She'd felt it for several years under the Beard roof. Even surrounded by people, the ache had been there, gnawing deep. Sometimes it was worse when others crowded about. Worse than when she was lying alone in her narrow bed at night, imagining a future elsewhere. Strange, she supposed, that one should feel alone when surrounded by others. It shouldn't be possible then.

"I grew up in Abderdeen." Mara's voice snapped her from her musings. "Have you ever been there?"

Clearly the woman was keen on conversation. "No. I have not."

"Oh." She looked a little disappointed. "It's lovely. Our 'ouse was a stone's throw from the sea. My family is still there, the whole lot of them. I'm the only one tae move away." At this, a cloud fell over her eyes. "I've seven brothers and sisters and between all of us there are thirty-three nieces and nephews."

"Goodness, you have your own army. It must

be nice to have such a large family." If Alyse had family, she wouldn't be in this situation now. She wouldn't have been forced to sell herself.

Mara nodded proudly. "Aye, we were always a boisterous clan. I 'aven't seen them since Sally was born." She nodded forlornly in the direction of where her two children slept. Alyse could only guess which child was Sally, but whatever the case, Mara had not seen her family in a number of years. "I miss them," she whispered, her voice thick with emotion.

Alyse nodded back in sympathy. It could not be pleasant being heavy with child and no female around for company or support. She would not be the first woman to endure the labors of childbirth on her own. Especially not out in remote areas like this. Hopefully her husband would support her through it. It was hard to say what manner of man he was. He still looked sullen across the room—doubtlessly from his interaction with Weatherton.

At the thought of him, her gaze skipped to her employer. He was already looking in her direction, blue eyes deep and unreadable.

She was only a day gone from Collie-Ben but she understood the desire for a feminine voice and soft gaze. Her employer was all hardness. No softness or kind words from him. With any luck, she would find that at Kilmarkie House.

Perhaps in another servant. It would be nice to have a friend. At least until she managed to get away to somewhere of her choosing. That's what mattered the most to her. Her ability to choose. To decide where and how she would live. Right now she would do what was necessary, but someday she would have a choice.

She would endure as always and not be so foolish as to expect softness from this man. In truth, any man. Not anymore. She was on her own. Even if she was fortunate enough to make a few friends, she would never again fully trust.

"Come. I'll see ye both settled in fer the night. The wee ones can sleep wi' us." Mara crossed the small space of the main room, her gait waddling, and motioned them up the narrow ladder to the loft.

Of course they assumed she and Weatherton were husband and wife. She sighed, dread running through her. Which meant another night sharing a bed with him.

Everything inside her rebelled at this lie they were perpetrating. Even for only one night. Even if they would never see these people again. Of course, it was for the best to let Mara and her husband live under that delusion. Better that than explaining their complicated situation.

Except was it really a lie?

Alyse shoved that grating voice aside. There

would be none of that. She would not entertain such thinking. They had both agreed that buying her off that auction block did not constitute a marriage in reality. The act might have served to dissolve her marriage to Mr. Beard but it did not bind her in matrimony to Weatherton. She didn't care what some deed of sale claimed.

Mara's husband had already moved to the bed and was scooting the children to the center to make room for the four of them. He hardly acknowledged them. After Weatherton embarrassed him he'd avoided their gazes. Understandably.

"I'm sorry we can no' offer ye better accommodations," Mara said.

"This is quite generous. Thank you," Alyse quickly assured.

"Yes. Thank you," Weatherton echoed as he motioned for Alyse to ascend the ladder.

"You first," she insisted and she wasn't certain why. Perhaps she wanted to be closest to the ladder, her means of escape, the one way out of the loft in case she needed to make a hasty retreat.

Weatherton nodded and climbed the ladder. Alyse stared up at the shadowy ledge he ducked inside. The long length of him disappeared. She inhaled a shuddery breath. She was expected to follow him. To disappear in that dark little den with him.

Her throat thickened and her hand moved to the pocket of her skirts where she kept her dagger. She felt the same panic pressing on her as she had when facing the auction block. The uncertainty. The sense of being penned in. Trapped.

Here she was again. Alone all night with him.

She'd done it before and yet this time felt different.

She *should* feel a little more at ease, more reassured after last night and this morning. He hadn't harmed her. In fact, he'd given her a dagger should she ever feel the need to defend herself.

And yet . . .

The dark little cave looming above her was so very different than the spacious room they had shared last night. Odd as it seemed, last night already felt a lifetime ago.

Her fingers closed around the rough wood ladder. She peered above her with another shaky breath. There was only darkness up there. And him.

"I know it's not the most inviting . . ." Evidently Mara did not miss her hesitation and she misread it.

"Oh, no. Not at all. It's perfectly suitable. We're so grateful." Alyse fixed a smile on her face and hardened her resolve to climb. "Thank you."

Mara nodded amiably. "Well. Good night then."

Alyse watched as she ambled toward her bed, her hand braced against the small of her back and felt a fresh stab of guilt for adding to the woman's discomfort by forcing her children into the bed she shared with her husband.

With a shake of her head, she reminded herself that they would be well compensated for the single night of discomfort. That gave her some consolation. Readjusting her grip on the ladder, she lifted her skirts with her other hand and began to climb, mindful not to miss a rung.

Arriving at the top, she peered into the dark loft. She couldn't even make out the shape of him in the unremitting blackness. There wasn't much to the loft other than the mattress. She patted with her hands and crawled forward a few inches before bumping into the bed.

She eased down a knee, testing, making certain she wasn't going to collide with a man's body. Fortunately, she didn't come into contact with him. Evidently he had bedded down on the opposite side of the loft and she wasn't climbing atop him. She winced. That would have been awkward.

The space was tight. The shared air passed back and forth between them.

She stretched a hand above her, fingertips meeting the ceiling that was only a scant inch above her head. Cramped, indeed. He was much taller than she was. If he sat up too suddenly, he would bang his head.

She lowered her arm and settled down onto her back, arranging her dress around her. She lay stiffly, unaware how close he was to her. It was disconcerting. She was, in effect, blind. He was near, but she had no idea where he was.

She only knew that they were not touching. Relief coursed through her. She could almost convince herself she was alone. That he wasn't up here with her.

Except she could sense him, feel him, his bigger body radiating heat beside her.

Expelling a breath, she laced her fingers together over her stomach and willed herself to relax. It was futile. A slat of wood couldn't be any more rigid. Minutes slid past. She unlaced her fingers and her hand drifted to her skirt, patting where the dagger was tucked away, feeling its comforting shape. Ironic indeed that the item gave her such comfort as he had been the one to give it to her.

She turned her face to the side on her pillow, staring where she knew him to be, where she heard the steady fall of his breath.

Everything is fine. Everything is fine.

The refrain ricocheted through her mind. He'd had plenty of opportunities to harm her and had not.

It could be far worse. She knew that. She could have been sold to someone else.

Her mind drifted to the image of the tanner and she had to fight back a surge of bile. All those uncomfortable encounters from her girlhood flooded over her. His disturbing stare. The occasional brush of his hand on her person. She could be married to him right now. Enduring *that*.

Instead she was here with this man who had not made one threatening move against her . . . who even tolerated her wayward tongue.

The reminder made her feel better.

Better enough for her body to finally relax and drift to sleep.

Chapter 12

The dove told herself it was well
and good to be without family.
There was not room enough in her cage for others.

*S*he woke with a scream hot in her throat. She lurched upright. Tears scalded her cheeks as she stared into blackness, bewildered, confused. Terrified.

The darkness was so thick it sat on her skin like a heavy blanket. She was blind to the world, but visions flashed across her mind.

The tanner's leering face. Rough, dirt-crusted hands, grabbing her, hurting her. The smell of him, foul and bitter as copper in her mouth.

"Alyse," a voice rasped. Hard hands shook her.

"No!" She surged, fighting like a wild animal, striking out with fists, desperate to get him to go away. To leave her alone.

"Alyse! Stop! Stop! It's me."

His words meant nothing to her. They buzzed meaninglessly in her ears. She only saw the tanner. Felt his touch on her. Battled the suffocating fear.

Those hard hands slid down and gripped her wrists, lifting them and pressing them into the mattress. She surged, trying to break free, but her arms were pinned, immobilized.

"Miss Bell! Alyse!" She felt his warm breath on her face. Her own breath escaped in crashing pants.

"Oy! Anything amiss?" a voice called out, startling her. Another voice. A second voice? That didn't make sense.

A dog joined the din, releasing several growling barks.

"Fergus, quiet!"

Gasping, she went still as stone and assessed, taking note of the mattress under her, the pop of crumbling wood in a fireplace somewhere in the distance, a big body against her own trembling form. Then other voices. Small voices. Children's voices.

Instantly, she knew where she was. It struck her all at once. She remembered the events of the day.

Alyse swallowed back an epithet.

Blast it. She'd acted a fool, waking the entire house. She blamed it on thinking of the wretched tanner before she fell asleep. Thoughts of him had filled her head and followed her into her dreams.

"I . . . I had a nightmare," she whispered, her tone tormented even to her own ears. Mortified . . . apologetic.

"Evidently," Weatherton whispered back. "Can you assure him I'm not killing you up here?"

"I'm f-fine. Just a nightmare. I'm s-sorry for disturbing your rest," she called down, wincing at the sound of Mara earnestly humming the children back to sleep.

Mara's husband grumbled beneath his breath and stomped back toward the bed. His dog whined, nails scraping the wood floor as he scurried below. "Enough, Fergus," he snapped. "Go back tae sleep."

After a moment, Weatherton whispered near her ear, reminding her of his presence. Not that she forgot. How could she forget? He was . . . everywhere. His breath fluttered her hair. "Well, that was fun. Not a dull moment with you, Miss Bell."

She cringed and laughed weakly, the sound hoarse.

The hands on her wrists loosened, but he didn't

move and she was achingly aware of the big body covering her own.

"You can get off me now."

"Can I? I suppose I should count myself fortunate you did not go for that knife I gave you and skewer me."

"It won't happen again." She doubted she would be able to fall back to sleep at any rate. Her mortification ran deep and would keep her tossing and turning.

He didn't move but he released her wrists and balanced his weight on his arms on either side of her head.

"What was your nightmare about?" His deep voice came out softly, curious and almost . . . kind.

She fidgeted. His kindness made her uncomfortable. Not that she wanted cruelty from him, but she did not want to like this man. She wanted indifference. She wanted to feel toward him what any employee might feel toward her employer. Cool indifference. Aloofness.

"Nothing."

She didn't want to share her nightmare with him, her fears. She didn't want to expose herself and be vulnerable. Contrary to how they met, she was no fragile flower.

He'd already seen her at her most vulnerable

on that auction block. She needed to show him that she was strong.

"I'm not weak, you know," she heard herself blurting. Great. Denying it so emphatically probably made her appear that very thing.

"Weak. You? No, I didn't imagine you were."

"You needn't mock me."

"I'm not mocking you."

"You bought me. I was like a . . . a slave up there." She hated admitting it. The truth sounded so much worse uttered aloud.

"I thought you were very brave. You didn't flinch. Didn't cry or beg. I don't know a single woman who would have stood as proudly as you did up there."

She couldn't breathe. Did he mean that? She blinked furiously, feeling the burn of tears. Now she would weep? Over his flattering words? She really was daft.

Silence stretched between them and he finally moved, sliding off her.

She exhaled, the tension in her chest easing. There was a slight rustling as he settled down beside her.

Only he wasn't finished with her.

He continued talking. "You needn't be embarrassed, you know. It happens to all of us."

Was he actually trying to make her feel better?

He'd already done that, surprising her with his flattering words. Couldn't he just hold his tongue? She didn't want to share and swap stories with him.

She didn't want him to be so *nice*.

Still. He'd piqued her curiosity. "What happens to all of us?" she grudgingly asked.

"Nightmares."

"You have nightmares?" It shouldn't amaze her. Just because he was a big, arrogant man with expendable funds didn't mean he wasn't human.

He paused a beat. "I talk in my sleep. At least that's what I've been told."

And who told him that? Immediately, she told herself she didn't care. He could have had a thousand bed partners—he was certainly physically appealing enough—and it was none of her business. It had nothing to do with her. She didn't care.

"I didn't talk in my sleep. I screamed," she began, "like I was being murdered and woke up these nice people. It *is* embarrassing," she replied in hushed tones. "First we take their children's bed and now I ruin their sleep."

"It's only a single night. We'll be gone tomorrow and leave them with a pocketful of coins for their trouble."

His reasonable tone and reasonable words did serve to comfort her.

"Don't worry," he added. "Go back to sleep, Alyse."

She sighed. "I don't think I can."

He didn't respond. She stared blindly into the dark, wishing she could see his face and then she remembered his face was far too good-looking and definitely weak-knee inducing. Given their proximity and the intimacy of their circumstances, it was probably better she couldn't see his features.

His breath fell soft and even beside her, and after a while she assumed he had fallen back to sleep until he said, "Give me your hand."

Her pulse jumped at her throat. He wanted to touch her? "My hand?"

"Yes."

"W-what for?"

"Come now. Just hold out your hand. I'm not going to hurt you. Besides, you still have your knife. Feel free to use it if you feel threatened." She could almost imagine the sarcastic twist to his lips. There was definitely humor to his voice.

Warily, she stretched out her hand and he took it, clasping firm fingers around hers.

In the dark, her sense of touch was heightened. His hand felt so much bigger than hers. The fingers long, tapering. His grip strong, the pads slightly rough. Callused. For all his apparent prosperity, he wasn't a dandy then. He used his hands. This should not affect her one way or another, but her chest lifted on a hitched breath.

He flattened out her palm, stopping her fingers from curling inward. Then he began lightly stroking. His fingertips brushed back and forth over her palm, his blunt-tipped nails softly scoring her skin.

It was a delicious sensation. Gooseflesh broke out over her skin.

Her breath caught. "What are you doing?"

The physical contact was more intimate than she had experienced in years. Her kiss with Yardley had been brief. Chaste. Weatherton's fingers running over her quivering palms felt . . . personal.

"I used to do this to my little sister. It always put her to sleep. She was a headstrong child. Never wanted to sleep and miss out on anything."

She didn't know what was more shocking. That this hard man petted his little sister to sleep or that he was petting *her*.

Her stomach felt funny. Bubbly like she drank too much of Mr. Beard's ale and then went sledding down a hill. Not that she had gone sledding since she was a carefree child but she remembered the plummeting sensation in her stomach.

"That feels . . . nice," she admitted, wondering why her body was starting to hum, like all her nerve ends were tingling.

"Clara never lasted very long. Usually this put her right to sleep. Course I haven't tried this on her since she was a child of eight."

"How old is she now?" She yawned.

"Fourteen. Almost fifteen."

"Might be trickier with me. I'm not an eight-year-old little girl." She opened her mouth wide on yet another yawn that belied her words.

"Yes," he agreed. "You're not a little girl."

In her suddenly drowsy fog, she thought his voice sounded gruffer, thicker. She didn't know what that signified, if anything, but she shivered. Even though she wasn't cold anymore, she shivered.

She supposed his tickle-soft touch on her palms had something to do with that. Her hand felt like a lead weight. She let it droop. He caught it and lowered it onto his chest.

She felt his shirt against the back of her hand.

A lethargic smile curved her lips. "Breaking custom tonight, are you?"

"I beg your pardon?"

"You're wearing clothes."

"Ah. Yes. Well, this entire journey has been one for breaking tradition, I suppose."

"I suppose it has." Not that journeying *anywhere* was a custom of hers. This entire trip, in fact, was a break in tradition for her.

His fingers continued their sensual assault on

her hand, creeping up her wrist and forearm in slow, measured strokes and then back down again. *Sensual?* When had his touch become sensual?

She gave a slight shake of her head and told herself it was relaxing. *Not* sensual.

"Is your sister in London?"

"Yes," he answered.

She thought about that for a bit. He clearly liked her. Clara. So he would return eventually.

As though he could read her thoughts, he asked, "Why do you want to go to London so much?"

Her lips worked before she arrived at her answer. "I've never been."

"So? I've never been to Warsaw, but I've no overriding desire to go there."

She laughed once, lightly, and then sobered. "My father visited London. He told me about it. The buildings and people. The museums and galleries. The theaters. The bookshops."

"It's crowded. You can't breathe there."

"What do you mean? There's air there like anywhere else."

"Not like anywhere. Not like here."

She turned that over in her mind. Perhaps she had built London up in her mind. Perhaps the most important thing was to simply get away from Collie-Ben, where she was known as the girl married at the age of ten and five to old man

Beard . . . and now where she would be known as the girl sold at auction.

Anywhere else was preferable. As long as it was someplace else. As long as it was away.

"I suppose the air can be different," she agreed as his fingers traveled over her skin, "in certain places." Life at the Beards' had smelled of sweat, the air cold and ripe as an onion field, but next to him the air felt . . . warm. Electric. Not easy to breathe necessarily, but still different from Collie-Ben. Better.

And that was a rattling thought. She shouldn't enjoy being near him quite so much. At that thought, she pulled her hand away. "Thank you. I'm much relaxed now. I should sleep quite well."

Rolling onto her side, she pulled deep inside herself and feigned sleep.

Chapter 13

The dove never felt frail. Never weak.
Her heart always beat strong beneath her feathered chest . . .
ready for the day the cage door flung open.

The good news was they left early the following morning and reached the next village well before nightfall.

Alyse only offered the sparsest of words as they traveled. She was too preoccupied with her thoughts. She almost didn't feel the cold at all as she recalled how she fell asleep last night with his fingers tracing her palm and his deep velvet voice talking to her about dreams and his little sister and places where the air flowed clean. It was unnerving. Nothing about it felt like something that should have happened between them, and she thought of little else as they traveled deeper north.

She thought about it *too* much.

When they arrived at the village the only lodging to be found was more of a boardinghouse than an inn, and it didn't boast a bounty of bedchambers. Once again, they were forced to share a room. At this point, it felt par for the course and she experienced only a momentarily flash of unease.

They had shared a bed twice now. She'd endured it both times with no mishap—well, if one did not count a great sense of awkwardness.

The boardinghouse was operated by Mrs. Collins, a widow who currently looked them over critically, clearly trying to decide whether or not they were married.

Alyse knew she looked bedraggled and hardly a proper match for the better dressed Mr. Weatherton. After a night spent sleeping in his clothes and road-weary from two days of travel, he still looked annoyingly fresh. His manner and bearing declared him a gentleman whilst all of her shouted *awkward* and *peasant stock*.

The widow slid a registry toward Weatherton for him to sign. "I will put ye and yer wife in the yellow room. In the spring it 'as a lovely view of my garden." Fingers laced stiffly before her, Mrs. Collins studied them carefully, likely to see if they would correct her assumption that they were man and wife. "I operate a good and moral establishment," she added.

"We would stay at nothing less," Weatherton replied with ease, clearly not rattled by her judgment. "And we shall have to stop here for the night when we next journey south," he added amiably, flashing her a devastating grin.

"Och, that would be lovely, sir." Mrs. Collins tittered, her double chin jiggling, the sharp condemnation fading from her eyes as she preened beneath Weatherton's charm. "And might I inquire yer final destination?"

"The Black Isle."

"Ah. I've a cousin who lives near in Inverness."

As they bantered back and forth, Alyse glanced down at the book, noting that he had signed them in as Mr. and Mrs. Weatherton. It was a necessary subterfuge. Just like the night before when they had let Mara believe they were married. They could not risk offending the proprietess and being turned away.

Alyse did not spot many servants about the house as Mrs. Collins led them from the foyer. Just a young lass lugging two buckets down the stairs. The widow addressed the maid as they passed her on the stairs. "Gregoria, back tae the kitchen wi' those buckets for more water." She clapped her hands briskly. "Make 'aste now. Our guests want to wash before dinner."

"Yes, mum."

Once on the second floor, Mrs. Collins opened the door to their chamber and then glanced down at the watch pendant pinned to her bodice. "Dinner is in 'alf an 'our. Dinna be late. It be yer only chance tae eat. I dinna keep the kitchen open all 'ours." She followed this stern warning with a softening smile for Weatherton. "I vow it will be worth it, sir. My scones 'ave been known tae keep a boarder 'ere an additional night."

"I can hardly wait," Weatherton replied.

It soon became clear that Mrs. Collins had a hand in everything that occurred under her roof. Not only did she herself admit guests into her home and escort them to their rooms, she served dinner downstairs in the dining room, carrying in the food with the help of Gregoria and presiding over the feast with a judgmental eye.

When Alyse declined the leek soup, the old dragon poured some into a bowl for her anyway, tsking her tongue. "Ye'll love it."

"Er, thank . . . you," she murmured, picking up her spoon.

They dined with three other guests. Mrs. Collins directed each of them where to sit with the authority of a queen. Alyse didn't feel particularly social, but there was little choice if she wanted to eat. She was trapped, sandwiched between two of the other guests. One was a peddler who spent most of the meal trying to sell anyone who would listen one of his kettles. Another was a young vicar. At least he claimed to be a vicar. It was difficult to imagine him as a man of the cloth. He spent an inordinate amount of time drawing her into conversation and touching any part of her he could reach. He patted her shoulder, her arm. Once he brushed a hand to her chin claiming she had something there.

Leaning close, he peered at her plate. "My child, you hardly have any meat on your bones. Help yourself to a second bread roll."

Weatherton watched from across the table, glaring back and forth between the two of them. Clearly, he was aware that she had earned the vicar's undivided attention and he didn't like it.

She had the niggling suspicion that the vicar was no vicar at all and he laid claim to the title to gain the trust of females. She, however, wasn't a trusting female. When she felt his hand close over her knee beneath the table, she slid her fork out from beside her plate and stabbed his hand.

He gave a quick yelp before catching himself and pressing his lips in a flat line.

She blinked innocently. "Something amiss, vicar?"

He resumed eating, scowling at her as though seeing her for the first time.

Her gaze lifted to meet Weatherton's amused stare. Gone was his glare. His lips twitched and he looked on the verge of laughter.

The rest of the meal passed tolerably without the vicar's cloying attentions. Weatherton excused them as soon as they finished their desserts, pleading travel-exhaustion. Not an untruth. She was weary.

Mrs. Collins offered to send up hot water so that they might bathe. Alyse had washed her hands and face before dinner, but she gladly accepted the offer of a bath.

"Thank goodness that's over," she declared once in their room.

"What? You didn't care for Mrs. Collins's mutton?"

"I didn't *care* for the vicar!"

He chuckled. "You handled him aptly enough."

She huffed. "Vicar, my foot."

"Well, I would gladly have had the vicar fix his attentions on me rather than endure the peddler. He was relentless. I bought two kettles I didn't want! What am I supposed to do with them?"

She outright laughed. A deep laugh that swelled up from her belly. It felt good. Real. It was nice. She could not recall the last time she had laughed in such a manner.

"Well. You could have conversed more with Gregoria. She had eyes for you."

"Did she? I hadn't noticed."

"You didn't notice how many times she asked you to pass her something?"

He shrugged and she realized female admiration was likely nothing new for him. He probably never even noticed the stir he created in the female population. Even Mrs. Collins was caught under his spell.

He sank down onto a chaise and started tugging off his boots, his face creasing in mirth.

"And what did you think of Mrs. Collins's infamous scones?" she heard herself tease. "As wonderful as promised?"

His eyes widened and he pointed to his mouth. "I think I left a tooth buried in the one I bit into. Truly, they can't be digestible. She could use them as artillery. The army should be notified."

Alyse giggled. "So we won't be staying an additional night in order to indulge in more of them?"

"Another night of enduring those scones and I fear I shall have no teeth left."

They were still chuckling when a knock came at the door. Weatherton admitted Gregoria inside the room. He quickly relieved her of one of her sloshing buckets.

"Ah, much thanks, sir." The young woman

stared up at him with an expression of wonder. She moved slowly, casting him several admiring glances.

Gregoria filled up the hip tub tucked behind a dressing screen. Finished with that, she carried both empty buckets to the door. Casting a final lingering glance Weatherton's way, she promised to return with two more buckets and then departed.

While she was gone, Alyse stared at the dressing screen, satisfied to see that it was not made of any kind of translucent material. It was impossible to see through the thick blue fabric. Even if Weatherton remained in the chamber whilst she bathed she should be afforded her privacy. That was some comfort.

Gregoria soon returned and added water to the half-full tub. As soon as she left the chamber, Weatherton motioned toward the dressing screen. "Your bath awaits."

She nodded, not bothering to even decline the invitation. She was eager for a bath to wash away the rigors of travel.

A few strides carried her across the chamber. Safely ensconced behind the screen, she made quick work of shedding her clothes. Aware that the water was losing its heat and there was little more miserable a thing than a cold bath, she hurriedly sank into the water and went about her washing. Stepping from the tub, she reached for the nearby towel, valiantly trying *not* to listen for Marcus on the other side of the screen.

She rubbed herself dry, first her body and then her hair. Slipping on her nightgown, she smoothed her hands down her length and exhaled. When she emerged from behind the screen, she noticed that he was donning his boots again.

"Er. Are you going somewhere?"

He stood. "I thought I'd check on our mounts. Make sure they're properly stabled and fed for the night."

She nodded a tad too jerkily, wondering why he seemed to have trouble meeting her gaze.

"G'night. You'll likely be asleep when I return."

"Oh. Of course. Good night then." She supposed she should be thankful that he was giving her some time to herself. She'd fall asleep without any anxiety because he wouldn't be there in the bed beside her. When she woke in the morning the worst of it would be over. She would have slept throughout their nerve-racking proximity.

He glanced her up and down as she stood in her nightgown, her bare toes peeping out from beneath the hem. She fidgeted self-consciously. It was just a hasty examination but her face burned from it. She didn't know why his glance should unnerve her. He'd seen her in her nightgown before.

Over the course of this journey there would be all manner of intimate moments between them. She understood that now. Traveling together— just the two of them—modesty would be elusive. Still, knowing that and accepting it were two very different things.

Without another word, Weatherton spun around and exited the room.

She sank down into the chair before the fireplace and began combing out her hair, pausing more than once when she heard footsteps in the hall, wondering if he was returning. And wondering why her pulse leapt at the possibility.

MARCUS TOOK HIS time checking on Bucephalus and the mule. He lowered himself down onto an old wood stool as they munched on fresh hay in their stalls. Stretching out his legs, he watched them distractedly, sticking a stalk of hay in his mouth and rolling it idly between his lips.

He needed a little space. He actually welcomed the bite of cold air. It shocked his body and helped get rid of the infernal warmth he had felt as he heard Alyse getting undressed behind that screen . . . the swish of water and her throaty sigh as she eased into the tub, the scratch and drag of the sponge against her skin.

It was a torment he had not anticipated. He'd

had no choice but to listen to the sounds of her bath and imagine her naked, all that warm and wet flesh . . . sudsy water running down the curves and hollows of her body. It wasn't to be borne.

He fully intended to avoid that room . . . avoid *her* in that room until he'd put such manner of thinking from his head and came to his senses.

He lingered on the stool until the chill started to seep into his bones. Confident she was in bed by now and likely asleep, he left the stables, telling himself he was being cowardly. She was but one small female. He didn't need to run from her. He frowned as he considered that he had been running from a good many things lately. His life, in fact.

Mrs. Collins waylaid him in the foyer and invited him to help himself to some of the whisky she kept in the parlor for her gentlemen guests.

Deciding a drink wouldn't hurt—nor would warming himself back up by the fire in the parlor—he accepted the offer and settled himself in an armchair with a glass of fine whisky and a week-old Edinburgh newspaper. He must have dozed off because he woke with a jolt sometime later. Running his hands through his hair, he groggily rose from his chair and made his way upstairs.

The room was mostly dark, only the dim light

of the fire saved the chamber from complete darkness. He made out the vague shape of her lying in the bed. As still as stone. Although he knew she wasn't stone.

She had a fierceness to her, without a doubt. But there was a softer side to her, too. He'd seen it. Watched her as she interacted with the crofter's wife. There had been something in her eyes . . . compassion that he rarely saw in the drawing rooms of London. She'd been dealt a difficult life, to be sure, but she still possessed a tender heart and cared about others.

He'd never really considered how privileged he was . . . never counted himself particularly fortunate, but she made him think about that. She made him feel like a churlish, ungrateful wretch.

He approached the bed, his eyes acclimating to the near darkness. Peering down at the outline of her body, he identified that she slept with her back to him, her hair a loose and flowing trail winding over the lighter counterpane.

Inhaling, he caught the clean, soapy scent of her. She might be still as stone, but she was no inanimate lump. She was flesh and blood—a living, breathing female for whom he was responsible.

The idea pinched at the center of his chest and he couldn't fathom why. He was accustomed to having servants. Why should the addition of one more give him pause? His lips twisted wryly. He supposed she was different from the rest. He had never shared a bed three nights straight with any of them. That made her a little different, indeed.

He moved away from the bed to stand before the fire. Holding out his hands, he let the warmth penetrate. A small sound from the bed drew his attention. She stirred and he held his breath for some reason, not releasing it until she settled back down, falling to stillness.

He removed his clothing, garment by garment, draping them over the back of a chair. Moving back to the bed, he stopped at the edge. His hands twitched at his sides as he stood there, hesitating. Damn. They really needed to stop sleeping in the same bed.

Their first night together he had simply climbed into bed with her, giving it little thought. Then, she was nothing more than a woman he had bought at auction. Someone he'd taken pity on and helped through a difficult time.

Now she was something more.

No longer a stranger.

In the matter of days, it was no longer so simple to dismiss her from his mind.

Scowling, he pulled back the covers on his side of the bed and slid in beside her, determined to not let this affect him.

When he left London alone it was because he wanted to be *alone*—and yet here he was. With her. Decidedly not alone.

But that wasn't the real problem. The problem was that he *liked* her. He was enjoying her. Enjoying *not* being alone. Bloody hell. He was enjoying being with his new housekeeper.

The sooner they reached Kilmarkie House the better.

Chapter 14

The dove was unaccustomed to being touched.
The cage bars were narrow and made it
difficult to be reached.

*S*he didn't know what woke her, but it wasn't a nightmare. Not this time.

She lifted her head with a tiny gasp. It was still night outside. Dark air peeped around the edges of the curtains and pressed against the narrow strip of visible glass.

The fire in the hearth had burned low but there was enough of a glow to make out the shape of the window and a framed landscape hanging on the wall beside it. A single cow marked the landscape, facing the viewer, wearing an expression that was much too shrewd for a cow.

Despite the waning fire, she was warm and snug beneath the covers. She contemplated rolling over, but she was aware of a weight draped over her, pinning her in place on the bed.

Her heart raced as she grew more and more aware of what that weight was: an arm around her waist and a leg draped over her thigh.

She was wrapped up in a man. A big man.

Even after these last two nights of sharing a bed it was a shocking and alien sensation.

She twisted her neck to risk a peek behind her.

It was indeed Marcus Weatherton, dead to the world. He slept soundly, his lips parted, emitting a slight snore. She hadn't noticed he snored before. It only made him all the more human to her.

Some of her unease faded. Of course, he slept. He wasn't falling on her like a slavering beast. He wouldn't do that. He wasn't even aware of her existence in the bed next to him.

She looked down at the bare arm wrapped around her. She inhaled a ragged breath and willed her composure to remain in place. After a moment, she lowered her fingers to his skin, warm and lightly roped with sinew just beneath the flesh. He might be hugging her like a pillow, but he was unaware that he was doing so. It was quite safe. A harmless snuggle.

Then why were her nerves all tangled? They

were not man and wife. There would be no con-summating of marriage vows. By now she knew that.

Her fingers relaxed on his arm, easing, tracing idly.

She could not help wondering if this was what it would be like every night to sleep with and be held by a man who loved her. Her parents had been a love match. Once upon a time she had assumed she would marry for love just as they had. Before Papa died and life became about what was necessary.

Her eyelids grew heavy again. She trailed her fingers up and down his arm, pretending, believing in the fantasy for a moment that she had that.

He released a sigh. She felt it against the back of her head, ruffling her hair.

Suddenly she was pulled closer, her back dragged up against his hard chest. She swallowed a squeak. Her eyes flared wide and she stilled her touching of his arm.

She shifted slightly, trying to put some space between them, but that didn't work either. He pulled her back against him.

The heat of his chest radiated through the cotton of her gown. How much clothing was he wearing? Or rather . . . how little? Had he reverted to his tradition of sleeping naked?

That great leg of his still draped over her. It bore down on her thigh like a tree trunk, pinning her.

And then she felt it. An increasing hardness against her bottom. It stirred and grew, nudging into her backside until she had a fairly good idea she was feeling the swell of his manhood. She sucked in a breath.

She understood the mechanics of sex. She'd lived too long on a farm not to know such things.

He was asleep. Completely unaware of his body's reaction. She could wake him and he'd withdraw, no doubt with an apology.

Only *she* was awake.

She knew what was happening. She was wholly, achingly aware and the sensations seizing her body were hard to ignore. Heady and enticing. Her skin hummed very much like it had the night before when he touched her palms, his fingertips feather soft. Only this was . . . more. *More* intense. *More* breath-robbing. Her flesh felt tight, as though it didn't fit over her bones.

She wanted to lean into him and explore these new sensations a bit longer. Her limbs felt languid and heavy, her lower stomach tight, pulsing. And between her legs something unfamiliar pulled there. Different and frightening but no less exciting.

She surrendered to it.

Holding herself still, she enjoyed the drape of his body over hers far more than she should. So heavy and male. She inhaled. Oh, he smelled so good. She closed her eyes in the semidarkness in one long agonizing blink. It was wanton, she knew. Guilt flashed through her until a voice rose up inside her in swift defense. Wasn't this the *thing* she had been longing for? A new life? New experiences?

Besides, she wasn't doing anything. She wasn't even moving.

She was just lying here. No harm in that.

His hand shifted. Those fingers that had brushed her palm and arm so intimately the night before covered her breast now. Heat shot through her from her breast to the throbbing at her center.

She whimpered and arched her spine, thrusting upward.

Even though his palm was broad, it didn't fully cover her breast. A rather embarrassing fact. She'd bemoaned the state of her chest all her life, wearing baggier dresses so she did not call attention to her bosom. She'd been a late bloomer and she had continued to develop after she moved in with the Beard family. When the older Beard boys had started to notice, snickering at her and fixing their gaze on her bodice and even being so bold as to toss pebbles at her chest, she'd felt so shamed. She'd done everything to hide them.

Now this man had his hand on her and she wished there was no layer of fabric between them. She wished she felt the texture of his hand, the calluses of his skin, on *her*.

Her nightgown only made it worse. The fabric bunched beneath his palm, a barrier she loathed. Unthinkingly, she arched, pushing herself up into his hand until her nipple brushed the valley of his hand. The slight pressure made her moan. She bit her lip, killing the sound. She waited several moments, making certain she hadn't woken him.

Still. Her pulse didn't slow. The burn didn't abate. The throb didn't lessen.

He was dead-to-the-world asleep. What would it hurt? She shifted, bumping back into his swelling manhood while simultaneously pushing her aching breast up into his cupped palm.

His hand flexed on her and her lips parted on a little mewl.

Suddenly he went rock-still behind her, his entire body going rigid at her back.

He was awake.

She stilled, too. Not a breath escaped her.

She held herself tight and waited. Waited for him to fall back asleep. Waited until she could fall asleep, too, and wake up in the morning and pretend this entire thing was a dream.

Only he didn't do that.

"What game are you playing at?" he growled.

Don't breathe. Don't speak. Don't make a peep. He'll think you're sleeping.

He whispered her name against her hair. "Alyse?"

She was actually proud of how motionless she held herself. Still and silent as the night.

He brought his face closer until his lips were right at her ear, brushing sensitive skin as he spoke. "Asleep, are you?"

She jammed her eyes shut and fought back a shiver.

That liquid-dark voice continued its slow assault on her ears. "Did you think you could push on my cock and I wouldn't wake?"

Sheer determination had her choking back a gasp. He couldn't prove she'd been awake. She simply had to feign sleep . . .

The hand covering her breast started to move then, squeezing and fondling until a cry climbed her throat. He dragged his palm across her already distended nipple.

It was useless. She was lost. A choked sob escaped.

"I warned you this would not be a real marriage. Did you think to trap me? That I would take you in a wild attack of lust? I have more control than that."

"No, I didn't think that at all."

He rolled her onto her back then, staring down at her and that was tragic. Because then she saw his face. All sharp lines and hollows. That too beautiful mouth. The wildly mussed hair that begged for her fingers.

She fidgeted beneath his weight.

What was wrong with her? He'd accused her of seducing him so that he would be her husband in truth. She shouldn't be admiring his looks.

"You woke me," she accused. "With your big body smothering me and your hand on *me*!" A partial truth.

His eyes narrowed. "And instead of extricating yourself you start purring like a cat in heat."

"Oh!" Before she could help herself, she lashed out, slapping him across the face.

"A couple days together, a few conversations and you decided you liked me . . . that I might make a good husband, after all."

Stunned, she stared up at him. Perhaps she had begun to like him a little bit, but he was mad indeed if he thought she had set out to seduce him. "You arrogant bastard. How could I ever want to be married to you?"

He stared back, looking equally astonished. But also furious. It was the fury that made the metallic taste of fear rush into her mouth. She'd just called him a bastard. What if she had pushed him too far?

He gripped her by both arms, his fingers digging. She braced herself, prepared for a reprisal. A hard shake. A slap. She knew it was done. She'd seen other women bearing bruises in Collie-Ben and vowed it would never be her. She'd not be an outlet for any man's fists.

He looked prepared to retaliate. Prepared to commit violence. She braced herself.

But it didn't happen.

His mouth came down over hers. Hard. Punishing. She knew that was what he intended. She'd struck him and this was his way to strike back at her.

She couldn't have pushed him away or slapped him again if she wanted to. Her hands were crushed between them. She struggled to unwedge them, ignoring the way his mouth on hers made her feel alive. As though she had been struck by lightning. Woken from a hundred years' sleep. Plunged from icy depths into the brilliant sun.

His skin, from the waist up, pressed sleek and hot against her, singeing directly through her nightgown. Her breath caught, beating like a madly fluttering bird in her too-tight chest.

She managed to release one hand. Tearing her lips free, she pushed with all her might, shoving him in his smooth-skinned shoulder, forcing space between them. Not a great deal of space but it was something. It was separation. At least his mouth wasn't branding her. That intimacy was gone even if her lips still stung and hummed.

Gasping, she stared at him, her hand burning where it pressed into his skin.

Their breaths crashed together as they stared at each another. His eyes gleamed in the near dark, like water floating over gemstones.

"What was that?"

"I think it seemed rather obvious."

"Not to me."

"Then it's called a kiss. Shall I show you again?"

"Of course not, you brute! I didn't like it."

The air crackled, alive with energy and prickling heat.

"I think you did."

"You're mistaken." Her heart beat so hard and fast in her chest she was sure he could hear it.

"And you're lying."

Her hand was free. She could strike him again as he most certainly deserved. Lying, indeed! The man's temerity was boundless.

Except she didn't want to hit him again. Her gaze dropped to the shadowy outline of his mouth. She wanted . . .

With a whimper of defeat, she dove in and kissed him again.

He growled in approval.

The kiss started hard, as it had earlier, but it didn't stay that way for long.

His lips softened. Turned to nibbling, kissing entreaties where he managed to husk against her lips, "Open your mouth to me."

Bewildered—at her reaction, at him, at *this*—she obeyed. She was helpless to resist him. Helpless to resist herself.

His tongue entered her mouth and stroked her own. She gasped and jerked at the strange act. He pulled back slightly, staring at her with eyes that were as inscrutable as ever but also brighter, as gleaming as polished gems.

This was it. Her turn. The time to pull back before things got any more out of hand.

The opportunity slipped past. He dipped his head, kissing her again, rubbing his tongue against hers until she was moaning and turning boneless beneath him at the shocking friction.

He settled his big body between her thighs, his hands falling to her hips, yanking at her night-gown until it was hiked up to her thighs and no longer barring him.

They kissed and kissed until her lips went numb, until her tongue felt raw from mating with his. He began moving, rocking his hips between her thighs, his manhood thick and prodding in the fabric bunched at the apex of her thighs.

"It would be so easy," he said against her lips. "I could just lift your gown and slip inside."

She nodded senselessly. He could . . .

Want pulsed through her. Right now it sounded like the most perfect thing ever.

"Can I touch you, Alyse?"

She nodded, knowing she would have agreed to anything in that moment. Anything to quench the pulling ache between her thighs.

She didn't even fully understand what she agreed to until she felt his hand forage under her nightgown and slide against her folds.

She jolted at that first brush of his fingers.

"So wet," he declared. "So ready." Sharp little pants escaped her as he stroked his fingers up and down, learning her intimately. "It wouldn't even hurt if I eased . . . inside." His finger tested this theory, pushing in her channel.

"Oh!" She arched beneath the sweet invasion and the shift in position did something. Brought him deeper, brushing against some place that made her shake and moisture rush between her legs.

Shame had her seizing his wrist. "I'm . . ."

"Let yourself go." He pushed deeper, curling his finger and rubbing it in a small circle against some hidden place inside her.

She shattered, a scream wrenching from her throat. Impossibly, she was wetter now, slicking his fingers. She'd never been so mortified in her life.

His forehead dropped against hers. "That was . . ." He couldn't finish the word. His eyes were closed and he looked in physical pain. "You're going to kill me," he whispered.

"W-what did I do?" she whispered back.

"I won't shag you," he choked, opening glazed eyes to stare down at her.

She stiffened. "I don't remember asking—"

"No, you just came apart in the most splendid fashion and left me so aching I can taste my teeth."

"Oh."

He withdrew his hand from between her legs. "How am I going to resist you now?" His voice was strained.

She stared at him in confusion. He'd made her feel magnificent, but now he looked in pain. His face was the perfect expression of torment.

"You're a witch," he muttered, shifting slightly, the motion rubbing the bulge of his manhood directly into her. "From the moment I saw you, I've been doing things entirely out of my character."

"Is it in your character to deny yourself what you want?" The question popped out of her mouth before she could consider it. She was baiting him and she knew it was ill advised, but it stung. It hurt that she was so very objectionable to him that he was not only angry at her but at himself, too.

"I'm not legitimizing this union," he growled even though he didn't pull away from her.

"I didn't ask you to!"

A muscle ticked in his jaw. He remained above her, between her splayed legs, his arousal pressing directly against her core. Clearly, despite his words, his hunger hadn't abated.

She fidgeted, both satisfied and anguished, her arousal twisting sharper as he pushed his hips forward, grinding himself into her softness with an ill-concealed groan.

She clucked her tongue. "If you'll have naught to do with me, then you best go find some other female to satisfy your very *pressing* needs," she flung out.

"The kitten has claws."

"And whilst you do that perhaps I shall find someone who can finish what you've started."

His eyes flared. "The vicar is only a few rooms down," he reminded.

"Oh?" She feigned consideration with an angle of her head. "Convenient, indeed."

"Brat," he snarled and then his mouth claimed hers again.

She gloried in it.

She didn't even know herself, the woman lying in this bed with this man, provoking him into acting, into kissing her when he clearly did not want to . . . but then everything had changed in the span of a day. Why wouldn't she be different, too? Why *couldn't* she be?

She'd brought him to the brink. His hands went to the laces at her scoop-necked nightgown, tugging them open. Then the bodice was down and her breasts were exposed. His mouth followed, sucking and licking until she was writhing under him in joyous torture.

"Marcus," she pleaded, latching on to his name in the throes of passion, saying it when she couldn't even think it before. She ran her fingers into his thick head of hair. "Please . . ."

He groaned and stilled, dropping his head between her breasts. "Temptress . . ."

She? A temptress? It didn't seem possible.

She was no beauty. Her hair was likely her best feature, although people often remarked about the unusualness of her eyes. Still. A gentleman like him . . .

He had to have seen his share of beautiful women.

"I'll not do this," he said, his voice soft but no less firm. He pushed up to look at her. "I'm not that weak." He stopped with a swift shake of his head. "You'll have to appease yourself as my housekeeper. You'll not have me for your husband."

She let out a breath. "I don't seek to trap you."

"Good." He stood from the bed, staring down at her. His gaze raked over her, taking in her exposed breasts and her bared legs. "I confess you offer more enticement than I expected."

She scrambled to set her nightgown to rights, covering her breasts back up and shoving the gown down to her ankles.

The corner of his mouth kicked up as though he found her attempt at modesty amusing. "But your wiles will not work on me."

Her eyes traveled over him, a thousand prickles of heat flashing over her skin. "You're fully naked!" Truly naked. Naked from the waist down. He'd climbed into bed with her without wearing a stitch of clothing—*again*.

"You well know my sleeping habits, by now." He shrugged a shoulder.

"I thought we discussed you discontinuing those habits."

"Did we?" Another shrug. "Perhaps I will adjust and start wearing clothes to bed. I did not expect you to throw yourself at me."

"Me?" she choked. "You have a very high opinion of yourself."

He splayed a hand against his chest, drawing her attention to that lovely chest, firm and well-formed. She'd seen it before but it still unsettled her. She didn't know a man could be fashioned in such a way. Mr. Beard had been pasty pale with a definite paunch. "You were begging for me quite sweetly. I didn't anticipate that."

Nor did she.

She yanked the coverlet back up to her chin. "You are quite safe from me."

The look he gave her was full of skepticism and right then and there she vowed she would not touch him again. Never permit him to so much as stroke her palms. *Never* kiss him even if he should change his mind and attempt to kiss her. She wouldn't even *look* at him with admiration lest he think she was mooning over her.

He reached for his trousers. Once he had those on, he sank down in the chair before the fire and tugged on his boots.

"Where are you going?"

"As you said. I'm sure Gregoria can satisfy my needs. You've left me with quite the raging cock."

She gasped, glaring at him. "You are a foul man."

"You weren't saying that moments ago."

With a huff of outrage, she rolled over, presenting him her back.

Fuming, she stared at the curtained window as she listened to his movements, angry and reminding herself that she had no right to be.

Certainly he had kissed her and it had been magnificent. Yardley's bland fumbling kisses paled beside the sensation of Marcus's lips on hers, his tongue in her mouth, his hand between her—

She pulled her thoughts up hard, killing them with a mental rebuke. No. She was not enamored. True, he was handsome and blessed with a ...g, fine body that made her belly tighten in strange exciting ways. He spoke well and moved with a panther-like grace and at times he demonstrated a kind nature.

But she had not—would *not*—form an attachment.

He was a rude, cold man.

He could dally with all the maids in Scotland and she would not care.

She was his housekeeper and nothing more.

Chapter 15

The wolf feared he might be a hunter of prey, after all.

When Marcus returned to his chair in the parlor, he had no intention of finishing out the night in the arms of Gregoria despite Alyse's scathing suggestion.

Even if he accepted the invitation he read in the maid's eyes, it wouldn't make him feel better. It might alleviate the ache in his groin that had started the moment he woke with Alyse, but it would not get Alyse out of his mind. Or wipe the taste of her from his lips. Or rid his ears of her voice.

No, soon he'd be back to wanting her and he would feel the perfect wretch for slaking his lusts on some hapless maid whose name he would not remember within the week.

He sighed. Wanting Alyse. He feared that was now a perpetual condition. At least until they got to Kilmarkie House. Then they would resume their proper and respective roles. He probably wouldn't even notice her anymore. She'd do what housekeepers did and he would do what he . . . did.

He helped himself to another glass of whisky and brooded. Brooded. There was no other word for it. The fireplace burned, casting the comfortable parlor in a warm red glow that was almost demonic and fitting for his mood.

Gregoria entered the room and sashayed over to him, the invitation he'd read in her eyes from earlier still clear as day in her eyes now. She took his glass and refilled it. There was no mistaking her look or the hand that lingered on his thigh as she poured his whisky. She would be agreeable to a tryst. He considered it. Except, he soon discovered as he searched inside himself, that was not his desire, at all.

Nursing his drink, he stared blindly into the fire.

His father would not have turned down Gregoria's overture. Hellfire, he would not have walked away and left Alyse untouched—well, largely untouched—in that bed. Not before slaking his own needs first. He would have used her and still refused to call her his wife. That was his father's way. Take. Use. Leave.

"Bloody hell." He downed the remainder of his glass, but it did no good. Two whiskys and he could still taste her.

He should not have touched her at all . . . should not have groped her breast the moment he grew aware of her rubbing against him. His father would have done the same thing, of course. He would have touched, grabbed and fondled her without invitation. Not Marcus.

He had stopped himself and he would be more circumspect in the future.

He and Alyse would resume their journey and even if they had to share a bed the entire way north he would not touch her. Even if she invited him, he would not go there. She could strip naked and launch herself at him and he would have all the restraint of a monk.

He wasn't a slave to his base desires. He had more restraint than that.

Even so, he did not wish to test his strength further this night. He'd pushed himself far enough. It was all too fresh. The taste of her. The sensation of her satiny flesh beneath his lips . . . fingers. She felt too good.

He'd never have thought the temptation of her would be so overwhelming. He'd had several alluring women over the years, and they knew the power of their allure. They worked tirelessly at it and wielded it with utter proficiency. Their skin fragrant and soft from lotions and perfume. Their hair styled to silkiness. They were artfully arranged.

Alyse Bell did not require such manipulation. She was no skillfully wrought construction of feminine beauty. She was just as she was, fresh off a farm and sold at auction without any embellishment.

So, contrary to his earlier avowal, he moved to the sofa. He removed his boots and set them on the floor. He was too tall for the piece of furniture. His feet hung over the end, but the discomfort wasn't enough to send him back upstairs.

It was a decidedly better sleeping arrangement than the temptation of returning to that bed with Alyse.

It did not take him long to fall asleep.

Only it wasn't the peaceful rest he'd craved. It was a dizzying collage of faces. Alyse. His stepmother. His sisters. Colin. They all called his name, pulled at him and chased him.

Then, he saw his father's face, angry and contorted, spittle flying from his lips as he shouted.

Marcus woke with a start, his ears still ringing with their voices.

He was gasping, the sounds wet and ragged in his ears. He dragged a hand over his face. He hadn't trembled like this since he was a child. He laughed hoarsely. Last night he admitted to

Alyse that he'd suffered nightmares before, too. Except it hadn't been recently. Perhaps the ailment was contagious.

He glanced around the room. The fire had died overnight. He inhaled and rubbed at his chest, hoping to massage loose the painful tightness.

He glanced to the room's single window. The gray of dawn pressed against the glass panes. It was time to greet the day.

THEY LEFT A little after dawn, taking the road north just as the sun rose to streak the sky in shades of pink and orange. It was cold and grew only a little warmer as they moved north—a condition he expected to continue.

When he had returned to their room to rouse her, she had looked at him as though he were some unwanted vermin sneaking in from the cold.

"Did you sleep well, sir?" she'd asked icily as they packed their things. That stiff *sir* and her cold eyes and the colder tone of her voice said it all. She thought he'd taken her suggestion to heart and spent the night in another female's bed. Let her think that. Better she thought him loose with his favors than harboring a tendre for her.

Noticing she was shivering atop her mule, he stopped and foraged through his pack. Finding an additional jacket and pair of gloves, he tromped back to her.

"Put this over your cloak," he advised, staring at her on the mule. Her lips were ashy.

She opened her mouth and he knew some fool protest was about to emerge. "Come now," he snapped. "It's cold and only going to get colder. I don't need you to freeze to death."

She relented with a nod and slipped the jacket over the cloak. The scarf followed. She wrapped it several times around her face and pulled the fabric up to cover her lips and nose.

She flinched when he seized her hand and guided his too big gloves on over the well-worn wool gloves she already wore.

"In the next village we will see about outfitting you better for this weather."

She nodded stiffly, watching him with those wide topaz eyes as though he might lunge at her. Tension crackled between them.

Last night crackled between them.

He wasn't so stubborn he wouldn't admit that to himself. He'd tasted this woman. Touched her. Felt her shudder and come apart in his arms. Usually when he knew that much about a woman he knew everything about the woman. He knew what it felt like to be inside her, how she fit around him.

He could only imagine what that would be like with Alyse Bell. He didn't know. He would never know.

Swallowing back a curse, he turned away and remounted, determined to cover as much ground as they could today. Every moment with her increased his urgency to reach Kilmarkie House, where she would be firmly implanted as his housekeeper and he would again be the Duke of Autenberry and not some random wanderer who buys brides in irrational flights of pity and then spends way too much of his time lusting after said bride.

As they continued on, he looked behind him several times to make certain her mule didn't lag too far behind.

"Bucephalus," she would call as though his gelding were a cat or hound that she might lure back to her side.

"You needn't call for him," he finally instructed. "I won't leave you behind."

"Only being cautious. You did warn me to trust no one."

Yes. He had uttered those stupid words. Not that it had seemed to help.

Last night she had placed her trust in him. She had responded to him, kissing him back and arching under his touch as though he were the lover she had counted on rescuing her from the auction block. The lover who had abandoned her. The man she had known and loved and trusted.

At the thought of that faceless bastard, his temper sparked along with a deep throb of possession. That man had failed her. He lost her.

She belonged to him now. Him . . . *Marcus*. No one else.

Shaking off the troubling line of thought, he realized she was speaking again.

"Where did you get such a horse?" she was saying. "I've never seen anything like him in Collie-Ben. Bucephalus is quite the mouthful. I can't quite accustom myself to it. I think I shall call him Bucky."

Bucky? He winced. "Please *don't* call him that."

"Bucky, hold up," she called, ignoring his request.

A glance over his shoulder revealed that her bloody mule was lagging behind again. That or Bucky—damn it all, Bucephalus!—had increased his pace. He sighed as he forced his mount to slow his stride. Now she had him thinking of his own horse as Bucky. "Must you be so irritating?"

"I'm only talking. It's called conversation."

He angled his head. "Is it, though?"

"Yes," she responded with a cheerful surety that grated his nerves.

"I think it's called maddening," he returned.

"Girls . . . women like to talk. Surely you know that. You have sisters. A mother, presumably?"

He shrugged. "Yes. Two sisters and a step-mother."

"I always wanted siblings. A big family. You're very fortunate." He shifted in discomfort in his saddle. She thought he was fortunate because he had a big family? He inhaled. A family he happened to be avoiding. "You're close with them, yes? The way you talked about Clara . . . it sounded like you're close."

A simple enough question and yet he took his time in answering because the answer was not so simple. And that summed up his life succinctly lately. *Not* simple.

"I'm close with my sisters, yes," he admitted, wondering why he was telling her more than he told anyone before. "Clara is the baby. Very animated. She's easy to love. Enid is more re-served, but a wit. Full of quips and clever observations. With my stepmother . . . things are complicated."

"Complicated?"

"Strained."

"Strained? That sounds intriguing."

Annoyance flashed through him. "Not at all. It's rather . . . disappointing. I had admired her greatly once."

He knew he'd lectured Alyse not to trust any

man, but trust in general hadn't worked out for him, be it man or woman.

Trust was for fools.

"What happened?" she pressed.

He compressed his lips shut. The last thing he wanted to do was discuss Graciela and Colin. He was doing his best not to think about them.

"Come, come," she coaxed, smiling. "It helps to talk about these things, you know?"

"Does it?" he asked, unconvinced. The only person he'd confided to over the years had been Colin. He was like a brother to him. They'd roomed together at Eton. And considering his best friend had betrayed him by shagging his stepmother, he didn't think all that *talking* had helped much in regards to anything.

"Of course."

He sighed. She wouldn't stop pestering him. He might as well give her an abbreviated version of events. "A little over a month ago I caught her in a compromising position with my best friend."

"Oh." The single word was restrained, but rife with interest. There was no mistaking it.

"That intrigues you, too, does it? The sordidness of my life?"

Nothing about it had felt *intriguing*. Not then. Not now. The fact that Colin had toyed with his stepmother and gotten her with child still made his blood boil. He'd had to leave town before he did something regrettable. Something like challenge his former friend to a duel.

The scandal of the Dowager Duchess of Autenberry taking up with the young Earl of Strickland was going to be salacious enough for the wagging tongues of the ton. He refused to add to the fires by putting a bullet in his friend. That would definitely not help his sisters' marriage prospects and he still had them to worry about.

At the time, it had made sense to leave. Now he wasn't so sure. It had been rash. A reflex to catching Colin and Ela together. Perhaps he'd behaved badly. Like the spoiled privileged sot he knew Alyse Bell thought him to be.

"It was far from intriguing, believe me. I lost a friend and my stepmother."

She shook her head. "I am sorry. I did not mean to make light of it." She paused, but he could have guessed she was not done talking. "But I do not see how you *lost* them simply because . . ."

"Because they're shagging one another?" he finished bitingly, his sense of betrayal surging to the surface.

Heat flared in her cheeks at his language.

He shook his head. "I cannot fathom how you can still blush. Days ago you stood on an auction block whilst all manner of ribald things were shouted at you." Although that did feel a long time ago. It felt as though they had been together for quite some time now. Every moment with her felt full . . . significant.

"That doesn't mean I'm accustomed to such coarseness."

Coarseness? Meaning she thought he was coarse? He . . . a duke, godson to the queen? Not that she knew any of that, of course. He knew her well enough to know that it would not impress her in the slightest.

Her judgment did not sit well with him. His father had been coarse. Unequivocally. He was the definition of that. He did not care to be lumped into the same category.

Marcus stifled a groan and dragged a hand over his face. What did it matter what she thought of him? She was a member of his staff. She should be beneath his notice.

"I'm only saying," she continued, "perhaps they love each other. Perhaps they couldn't help themselves because of that. You couldn't blame them for—"

"Love," he snorted. "Lust more like it. And I do blame them. They could have exhibited self-control. Restraint." Instantly his mind drifted to last night and his decided lack of self-control. There had been no restraint on his part. He'd acted impulsively and let his desire rule him. Could it not have been the same way for Colin and Ela?

The comparison did not sit well.

"Love. Lust. Perhaps it's both. Do the emotions have to be exclusive of each other? Can people feel both things?"

He contemplated that, wondering if he'd ever pondered the subject of love and lust with anyone, much less a female. "More often than not lust is just that. Two people giving in to base desires and forgetting everything else." Propriety and obligations. Friendship. Family loyalty. As the mental list grew, he actually felt a familiar tightening in his gut. Graciela and Colin hadn't considered any of those things as they succumbed to their base desires. They had not considered Clara or Enid or him. Not how Society would react and what the consequences would mean for *all* of them.

"I believe you are a pessimist, Mr. Weatherton."

For a moment, the sound of his family's surname jarred him. He'd never been addressed by anything other than his title.

"It's not pessimism. It's called experience. I've seen . . . things." Hard things. Ugly things.

He knew a great deal about base desires and lust. Less about love. Perhaps nothing. Nothing at all about love.

She made a sound. It was nothing he had ever heard from a woman before. At least never directed at him. It was a kind of like a . . . jeering snort.

He sent another glance over his shoulder. Her expression was scornful, one of her dark eyebrows cocked over those cat eyes of hers. "So life has taught you to doubt love?"

"In a manner . . ." Again, that sound from behind him. He wheeled around to face her. "What?"

"*I* don't doubt love. I was so young when my mother died I can't even remember her. At fifteen my father died and I married a man old enough to be my grandfather. I had to work his farm, raise his children, cook and launder for him. That same man sold me at auction. So I've seen things, too, you know. *I've* seen ugly things and I still believe in love. Your life must have been very hard indeed for you to be such a nonbeliever."

She finished her tirade with flashing eyes and a deep exhale and nudged her mule ahead, for the first time bypassing him and Bucephalus.

Marcus started after her, admiring her and marveling at this female who had just made him feel like a rebuked child. He couldn't even be annoyed with her. Not when she was right.

SHE TOOK A fortifying breath. Little Bit couldn't keep up with Bucky's pace and she soon fell behind again. She rocked on the contrary beast's back, staring hard at Weatherton ahead of her, sitting so stiffly in his saddle. He was a cold man. She was foolish to let such a man rouse emotions in her.

Alyse was never one to despair. It was not her way. Even when life had been the hardest. When everything felt like a rock to break herself against. The last few years with her father, when he was sick and suffering and it became clear she would be left on her own, she had not given in to despair. Not even then.

When Papa died and she had moved into Mr. Beard's small gable room she still clung to hope. She'd grown up reading fairy tales. Papa had filled her head with them. His romantic nature had been infectious. He'd gifted her with the ability to dream. Perhaps that's why she so readily believed in Yardley.

In Papa's stories, the peasant girl always found love. Good always prevailed. The witch always died and princes never failed. Never abandoned you when you most needed them.

She had always believed in these ideas.

Except riding in this dark wood, following a dark figure, she knew her story was not written yet. She couldn't see into the darkness ahead. She couldn't know for certain if her happily ever after would come.

But she had a plan.

She would make the best of her time at Kilmarkie House, even if she hadn't counted on these confusing feelings for the man who held a deed declaring her his property.

She wouldn't get too comfortable. She wouldn't grow to like him. That would be foolish. Her future was elsewhere.

The wind blew and her teeth chattered in response. The hills above the tree line were growing more craggy—turning into steep, snow-blanketed shapes against the graying sky.

It was getting darker. They'd have to stop soon. Maybe then she'd feel warm again.

Chapter 16

*He was a wolf without a pack, but that
didn't mean he needed anyone.*

The next few days passed without incident.
Thankfully, there were no more problems with
overcrowded inns. Marcus was able to acquire
separate rooms every night they stopped. The
relief reflected in her eyes wounded his ego
more than he cared to admit. She really didn't
like him.

For three nights, they stabled their mounts.

For three nights, he walked her to her door,
seeing her safely to her chamber.

He ordered their meals to be delivered each to
their separate rooms. They did not have to endure
one another's company once the sun went down

and that seemed for the best. He needed the respite . . . and to avoid further temptation.

She chattered unflaggingly during the day, her words flowing in an endless stream as they rode along.

And yet when he was alone in his room every night he actually found himself fidgeting. Tapping fingers. Pausing every time he heard footsteps near his door. He could still hear her voice in his head and he actually longed for it in the humming silence of his room. He came to resent that silence.

He would idly pace until his dinner tray arrived, always grateful when it did so he could eat and fall into bed and sleep. In sleep, he could forget her. Escape.

For three nights this was their pattern.

The fourth morning continued as the others had. Even her mule seemed to know the routine and trotted along at a more obliging pace. They were nearing Glasgow now. He tried not to think about that . . . or the man he knew who lived there. He planned to bypass the city.

Except every time he managed to put thoughts of Glasgow and Struan Mackenzie from his mind, a sign would appear alongside the road in a cruel twist of humor, announcing the distance to the city. The signs seemed to taunt him to confront his half brother. He wasn't certain what he would say or do in such an instance. Past confrontations between them had never gone well. After all, this feud between them had nearly killed him.

As the noon hour approached, he noticed that Alyse was not as garrulous as usual. In fact, she was quiet.

He glanced over his shoulder. She was lagging behind again. The mule, contrary beast, had reverted to his old crawling pace. She sat on his back rather listlessly, not even bothering to prod him forward as she usually did.

Marcus wheeled his horse around and galloped back to where she plodded along, determined to nudge the mule ahead for her. Her head drooped. It almost appeared as though she were dozing.

"Alyse?" Concern pricked at him as he reached for her reins, dipping his head to better view her face.

At the sound of her name she gave a small start and lifted her gaze. Whatever else he was going to say died a swift death in his throat.

Her eyes were bloodshot and glazed like she wasn't in full comprehension.

"Alyse?"

She swayed in her saddle.

With a sharp oath, he leaned between their two animals and caught her the moment she toppled. He swept her atop his lap, cursing a fury.

Her head lolled limply as though too heavy for

her neck to support. He tapped her cheek with his fingers, hoping to rouse her. Her eyes remained closed. Her skin felt hot. She was raging with fever. He expected cold in this freezing air, but she was hot to the touch.

"Bloody hell. Alyse!" He glanced around as though he would see salvation somewhere near, perhaps lurking in the trees crowding the road. Except there was no help to be had. Wind blew through creaking and brittle limbs stripped bare of leaves. Never had the world felt so desolate. Never had he felt so helpless.

There was no one and nothing about. It was just the two of them on this wild stretch of road separating one village from the next. He glanced down at her face again. Eyes closed, a soft rattling rasp escaped her parted lips. She was dead to the world.

"Ah, sweetheart. Why didn't you tell me you were ailing?" he muttered as he adjusted her in his arms. He didn't expect her to answer, but he couldn't stop talking to her. As long as he talked to her it was as if she were still here. Still with him. Not gone. Not lost.

"You're going to be fine." He was responsible for her. No one else. It fell to him. Shaking his head, he whispered close to her ear, feeling the heat radiate from her like a burning grate. "Everything will be fine." *She* would be fine.

He looked away from her and sent one last desperate look around.

He knew what he had to do. There was only one hope for her.

She needed the very best of care and she had one chance of that.

SHE FLOATED LIKE a bird, her wings sailing with nary a flap on the air. There was no cage. No locked door barring her escape, but she didn't quite feel free yet. She felt every bit as trapped, as penned, as she always did.

She wandered through the fog blindly, unable to see anything save rolling gray.

It was hot. Then cold. Then hot again.

Time suspended as she drifted, floated. Aimless wandering.

She whimpered and called out. For anyone. For someone. For *him*. Marcus.

At one point she felt him there. Knew it was him before she felt his hand on her. Gentle as wind on her skin. Soothing her ruffled feathers, touching her almost tenderly as though careful not to crush her feathers.

His voice eased over her. Deep, dark, luxurious satin closing over her, promising her that everything was going to be fine.

She knew that voice. She felt it deep in her soul. And she believed it. She believed him.

Everything was going to be fine. *She* was going to be fine.

Somehow these words had the power to make her muscles soften and relax. His voice made the fog seem less dense, less suffocating . . . and it pushed her to keep going, keep searching for a way out.

A way back to him.

ONE LOOK AT the mammoth structure and he felt confident it belonged to Struan Mackenzie. The man wouldn't live in a home any less grand than this. He'd clawed his way out of the gutters of Glasgow and was now rich as Croesus. Such a man wouldn't have anything short of a palace for himself and his wife—a wife with whom he was profoundly besotted.

If Marcus was wrong and at the incorrect house, he didn't give a bloody damn either. He had reached their final destination. He couldn't continue dragging her through the city in her condition.

He would not lose her. She needed care and this place would be it. If he had to reveal himself as the Duke of Autenberry to gain entrance then so be it. Experience had taught him that people generally gave way once they knew that.

He lowered himself from his mount, careful to not lose his hold on her. He didn't bother to wait for a groom to approach and tend to their mounts.

Standing, he adjusted the weight of her in his arms and rushed toward the front door, his boots biting into the frozen ground. He left their mounts behind, letting them wander aimlessly in the courtyard, expecting a footman would see to them.

He pounded on the great double doors with his boot. No response. Cursing, he kicked at the door again, glancing down at her ashen face as he did so. His chest squeezed tighter at the glimpse of her face. She was still so pale.

After what felt like an eternity, the door swung open. A ginger-haired man in full livery stared back at him, his expression already fixed in annoyance—no doubt from Marcus's demanding boot knocking.

He looked Marcus up and down before pinning his gaze on Alyse and asking drolly, "Is she dead?"

"No, and she's not going to be." He swept past the servant. "Send for a physician and direct me to a bedchamber. Do you have a maid that can help undress her? She's damp from the snow. She needs something warm—"

"Who are ye?" the man blustered with a shake of his head, his composure slipping.

"We haven't time for introductions," Marcus snapped.

"Sir, I insist on—"

"Is this the residence of Struan Mackenzie?"

"Aye."

"Then let him know the Duke of Autenberry is availing himself of his hospitality."

The butler stared at him with his mouth agape, unmoving, scarcely even blinking.

With a muttered curse, Marcus bit out, "Tell him Autenberry is here . . . his brother." That proclamation delivered, Marcus strode past the man and up the winding marble stairs leading to the second floor, not about to wait for the butler to direct him.

Once on the second floor, he bypassed the double doors of a drawing room. The doors to that room were cracked and voices floated out into corridor, but he didn't care. At the moment, Alyse needed a bed. That was his foremost concern.

He turned a corridor, dimly aware of the squawking servant trailing behind him.

Holding Alyse in his arms, he managed to push the door latch down on one room, only to discover it was a music room full of instruments. With a grunt of dissatisfaction, he continued searching until he arrived at a vacant bedroom at last.

He strode inside and lowered her on one side of the bed. Moving around the monstrosity, he pulled the covers down and then picked her up and tucked her inside beneath the heavy coverlet.

"Stoke the fire," he barked at the hovering servant. "And call for a maid to help undress her." He paused to glare at the unmoving man. "Has the physician been sent for yet? Why must you stand there and gawk?"

The man sputtered and looked ready to object when a feminine voice spoke his name, "Marcus?"

At the sound of his name, he looked toward the door where Poppy Mackenzie stood, formerly Poppy Fairchurch. "What are you doing here?"

"I need your help," he answered, almost not recognizing the thick, stark quality to his voice.

Her wide gaze swept over him before drifting to Alyse in the bed. Color heightened her cheeks. "Oh!" She hurried forward in a rush of elegant skirts. "What's amiss with her?"

He followed her gaze to Alyse where she lay as still as death. "I don't know. She sickened on our journey north . . . she's feverish."

Poppy looked to her servant. "Have you sent for the physician?"

"Mrs. Mackenzie," he said in a strangled voice. "What—who—"

"At once, Givens," she said, her voice commanding for all its gentleness. "Make haste now. Can you not see our guest is ill? There's no time for explanations. Do as you're bade."

With a final frustrated glance at Marcus, the man hurried from the room.

"Thank you," he murmured, watching as she pressed the back of her hand to Alyse's forehead.

"Of course." She tsked, glancing up at him over Alyse's alarming inert form. "We're family, after all."

The proclamation startled him for a moment. He certainly hadn't embraced her or her husband as family.

He stifled a wince, an odd tightness wrapping around his chest. He should be grateful that she had such an attitude, he supposed. Without his connection to Struan Mackenzie, he would not have access to this place or access to what would unquestionably be an excellent physician. Mackenzie would settle for no less.

"What are *you* doing here?"

This time the voice to arrive in their midst was decidedly unfriendly.

Marcus straightened from where he hunkered over Alyse. "Mackenzie," he greeted, eyeing the giant of a man eating up all the space in the threshold.

"Autenberry," he returned, stepping into the room, his steps thudding over the thick rug. The man stopped beside his wife and looked over Alyse where she slept in the bed. "Who is she?"

"Alyse," he returned. "Alyse Bell."

Mackenzie flicked him a cold stare. "One of your . . . intimates?" Marcus was immediately aware that he had to search for that word and would have likely said something far more ugly if not for the presence of his wife.

"My housekeeper," he snapped.

"Housekeeper?" Poppy looked bewildered. "You're traveling with your housekeeper?"

"I'm taking her to my property in the north. She's going to manage the house there." Even to his own ears it sounded ridiculous. The only thing more ridiculous was the *other* version of events. That other truth.

She was the wife he had bought at auction in the market square.

"Housekeeper?" Mackenzie echoed with a curl of his lip, clearly in disbelief. He thought she was his bedmate. A consort. Marcus would greatly like to take a swing at his half brother, but he stopped himself. He needed the bastard. For Alyse's sake, he had to play nice.

"She's ill. She needs help. *I* need your help."
He held Mackenzie's gaze as he said the words—
words he never thought he would utter to
this man.

Mackenzie said nothing, merely continued to
glare at him.

"Struan," Poppy hissed, her gaze meaningful
as she looked between him and her husband.

Mackenzie finally nodded, relenting. "Very
well. I'm not a heartless man. Of course, they
can stay here until she is well. We will see to her
care." He turned to look down at his wife and his
expression turned soft and besotted and Marcus
felt like retching.

A knock sounded on the partially open door.
A maid peered in the room holding towels and
what appeared to be fresh clothes in her arms.
"Mrs. Mackenzie?" she queried. "You've need
of me?"

"Yes, yes, come in and help me with our guest."
Poppy gestured for them to go. "Out with you
two. Struan, get him a drink. We will change her
and tend her until the physician arrives."

Marcus nodded, but still he hesitated, reluctant
to leave her side. He looked down at her. She was
still so pale. Ashy. Lips tinged blue. Those fine
arched eyebrows of hers looked even darker than
usual against her pasty skin.

"Come," Mackenzie advised. "Poppy has spoken.

There will be no changing her mind, believe you me."

He nodded but still did not yet move away. He couldn't. He couldn't get his feet to work. It was like he was rooted to the spot. "She's very cold. Don't have her out from the covers for very long." He glanced to the fire. "That needs stoking."

"Marcus. We know what to do. Now go." Poppy shook her head at him. Behind her the maid pulled down the covers from Alyse and started on her shoes, unlacing the ugly boots. The toes were almost worn through, he noticed. Why hadn't he noticed that before? They were more than ugly. They were inadequate. Hardly ideal for this weather. He cursed himself, not liking himself very much right then for his thoughtlessness.

"We have this under control, Marcus." Poppy touched his sleeve, her tone softer, her eyes gentle as she scanned his face. "Now go. We will send for you."

Mackenzie was waiting at the door.

Poppy made shooing gestures with her hands for him to go. "Go with Struan."

With a sigh, Marcus obeyed. Reluctantly. He strode out of the room backward.

"Come now," Mackenzie said as they stepped out into the corridor. "I'll get you some whisky." They walked in silence for a moment, their steps a scratching hush over the carpet. "Housekeeper, huh?" His voice was rife with amusement.

Marcus bristled. "That's correct."

"I never once looked at a housekeeper the way you're looking at that lass in there."

"That so?" he asked tightly.

"Aye. I've only ever looked at Poppy that way."

Marcus stopped in his tracks.

The fair-haired giant lumbered away. Marcus glared after him, certain he didn't know what the hell he was talking about. His hands opened and shut at his sides, curling and uncurling. He'd only been in the company of Struan Mackenzie a handful of times. But every time did this to him. Made him so mad he could taste it like copper in his mouth. It didn't make sense. He knew that. It was an irrational anger.

"I'm not you," he tossed out. Indeed not. They were nothing alike. Not even in appearance. Well, not *too* much alike in appearance.

Mackenzie chuckled lightly. "That much is clear. You were the golden one, our father's pride and joy . . . I was the dirty secret."

"Only not so secret," he reminded.

Mackenzie shrugged. "Well, not anymore."

True. Not anymore.

Mackenzie had surfaced a little over a year ago, making himself known to the family and rattling Marcus. He had never imagined he had

another sibling . . . much less an *older* brother.
Struan should have been his father's heir. Had he
been born on the right side of the family blanket,
he would have been.

It was also a strange bit of irony that Mackenzie
looked *more* like the late duke than Marcus did.
Same fair coloring. Same eyes. Similar features.
Stranger still that Marcus was the heir. The
legitimate one. The one that counted among
the ton. The one that had mattered to the old duke
himself.

Only a twist of fate determined that Mackenzie was the by-blow. The bastard.

Shaking his head, Marcus followed the man
down the hall. None of it mattered now. His
father was dead. He was the duke. Struan was
not. And the two of them were strangers to each
other, blood related or not.

They entered a rich, mahogany paneled study.
Mackenzie poured them a whisky.

"So." His half brother offered him a glass. He
accepted it with a nod of thanks. "Who is the girl
really? And don't say housekeeper. I won't believe it. You care about her and *not* like one cares
for a housekeeper."

He opened his mouth to deny it, but then
closed it with a snap. Mackenzie had already
made his mind up about the two of them. Why
protest?

He couldn't bring himself to deny Mackenzie's allegation. The girl was sick. Clearly, he cared. He'd ridden Bucky hard to get her here. He cared, damn it.

He glanced to the open door of the study. Alyse was several rooms down being well cared for. She was in Poppy's hands, so he had no doubt of that. She would be well. She would recover and they would resume their journey.

He lifted his glass to his lips and took a heavy sip, wondering how soon he could return to her chamber and check on her without looking fool- ishly anxious. Swallowing, he peered down into the amber liquid and was reminded of her topaz eyes. Hopefully they would open soon and he would once again see her usual fire there.

With a muttered curse, he downed the re- maining whisky and set his glass down with a clink. "I'm going to see how Alyse is doing. The physician should be here by now." And if he wasn't here Marcus would do something about it. Even if it meant going out and scouring the city himself. He would not fail her.

"I wouldn't. Poppy said she will send for you and I wouldn't disobey my wife."

"Disobey?" He looked his giant of a half brother over coolly. "I'm not afraid of your wife."

"You should be. She's tenacious and fearful when thwarted."

He lifted up from his chair. "I don't think it's unreasonable that I'm concerned for my employee. Poppy will understand."

Mackenzie chuckled. "Employee. Right."

Ignoring that gibe, Marcus exited the room and proceeded down the hall, determined to claim his place in that bedchamber and oversee Alyse's care, making certain everything was done for her. Everything within his power.

He'd taken responsibility for her the moment he opened his mouth in that village square. He wouldn't shirk his duty now. They'd come this far together. She fell ill on his watch. He felt to blame.

He saw a flash of those shoddy shoes. The pale face. The feverish skin and glazed eyes. He should have done better for her.

He'd do better in the future.

Chapter 17

The dove had never fallen ill before.
She always told herself the bars of her cage kept sickness out.
She told herself this because she needed to believe there was
something good about being in a cage. She'd been wrong.

Searing pain lanced her skull as she first opened her eyes. Immediately she closed them again and took several shallow breaths. After a moment she tried again, opening her eyes to a shadowy room and, thankfully, less pain.

Without moving her head, she swung her gaze left and right. A big room. No. This wasn't a room. It was a chamber. A chamber fit for a king. Not for the likes of Alyse Bell.

She swallowed and cringed at the dryness of

her mouth. She must have made a sound because suddenly someone was there.

"Here." A hand slipped under her neck, lifting her. A cup pressed to her mouth and water met her lips. She gasped and then drank, greedily, sloppily. Water dribbled down her chin. "Whoa. Easy there."

"Oh," she murmured, feeling a little embarrassed.

Her gaze followed up the arm to the person being so very kind to her . . . so very—

"Mr. Weatherton?" she managed to get out. She didn't know who she expected it to be, but she didn't expect him. Not that she had been traveling in the company of anyone else, but he was her employer. He shouldn't be caring for her as though she were a child.

His lips twitched. "I think we are beyond surnames now, don't you, Alyse?"

She swallowed and this time it didn't hurt quite so much. "That wouldn't be appropriate. We should cling to some manner of propriety."

"We've been traveling together. *Alone* together. I think we've left *appropriate* far behind." His smile slipped and his eyes took on a somber gleam. "I was worried about you."

Her chest tightened at the look in his eyes . . . at his words. She did another quick glance around. He seemed sincere and she didn't know what to do with that. She didn't know what to do with his sincerity or her reaction to it. Pleasure suffused her. Contentment to know he had been worried. He cared that much.

Clearing her dry throat, she asked, "Where are we? This chamber is . . . impressive."

He seemed to search her face before arriving at words. "People I know live here."

People he knew? Well that sounded mysteriously vague. "Well, that's good to know. At least we've not made ourselves comfortable in a stranger's home."

He didn't even crack a smile at her joke. "How are you feeling?" His gaze crawled over her face as though he would find evidence of her health status in the lines of her features.

"My head aches a bit. And I'm thirsty." She paused, assessing herself. Arriving at a new conclusion, she added, "Hungry. I'm hungry, too."

"I'll ring for some broth."

Broth. "Hm. Sounds . . . appetizing."

He hopped from the chair beside the bed, behaving as anxiously as a child released to play. "Just start with that and then we will see."

Her gaze followed him as he made his way across the room and pulled a bell. In a blink, he was back. He reclaimed his seat and picked up her hand and chafed it between his. And that was strange. And confusing.

She told herself the action wasn't affection-based. He was trying to warm her hands. That was all. There was nothing intimate about it. Her heart shouldn't beat a little faster at the act.

She sat up a little higher in the bed. "How long have I . . . how long was I sick?" She brushed back a lock of hair and then winced at how grimy the strands felt between her fingers. She must look a mess. Not that she was ever any great beauty, but she had a feeling this was a personal low even for her.

"We arrived here three days ago."

Three days! She shook her head in wonder. Three days in this bed. She didn't just look a mess. She probably looked frightening. She wouldn't even consider how she must smell.

"Three days? I never get sick. For years it has been me taking care of everyone in the Beard household." She was the strong one. The one everyone could rely upon. "I thought I was immune." She choked out a laugh. "First time I manage to leave Collie-Ben and *I* fall sick. You must think me terribly weak."

He shook his head, his expression somber. "No. I should have taken better care of you."

"No," she was quick to say, bristling. She didn't want to think she required anyone to take care of her. She wanted to think she was stronger than that. Even broken in this bed, she wanted to believe she was dependent on no one. She didn't want to be a constant duty for him.

"Alyse," he said her name quietly. "Everyone needs help now and then. There is nothing wrong that."

Could he read her thoughts? A lump formed in her throat that she fought to swallow down. "You've done a great deal for me. I have been nothing but a burden on you." She looked him over, taking in his handsome face and the shadowy growth of his beard coming in. It appeared he had neglected to shave again.

"Do I look burdened?"

She choked out a laugh. "Actually, yes. You look tired and haggard." He simply held her gaze, his thumb stroking a small circle on the back of her hand.

A knock sounded at the door and a servant poked her head in.

"A tray please," Weatherton instructed. "She is awake."

With a quick glance to Alyse, the girl nodded and ducked back outside of the room.

But they weren't alone for much longer. Apparently that bell had roused more than a servant to the room. The door burst open and a woman strolled into the room in an elegant gown of blue. In fact, all of her was elegant. Her wheat-colored hair was swept up into an elegant chignon. The smooth skin of her face creased in a delighted smile. "It's true then! Our patient is awake. How wonderful."

He rose and offered her his chair beside the bed. "Our Marcus here was quite beside himself over you," she said with a clucking tongue.

"Was he?" Alyse looked over at him curiously. His smile from earlier was gone. In fact, he stood rather stiffly beside the chair.

"Indeed. He could scarcely be lured from your side. We gave him the room adjoining yours. Not that he ever made much use of it."

Alyse glanced toward the door on the opposite side of the room. That was his room? But he had not been using it. He'd been *here*. Presumably in this chair beside the bed—next to her—for the past three days. For her.

"Oh!" the woman exclaimed, throwing her hands up in the air with a puff of breath. "How remiss of me. I have not even introduced myself to you. Let's not stand on formalities. My name is Poppy. I am married to Marcus's brother, Struan." She leaned forward to squeeze Alyse's shoulder.

"Brother?" Had he mentioned a brother? There had only been talk of his sisters and stepmother. Why had he not mentioned this Struan? For some reason, she felt unaccountably stung. They'd shared things. Talked of family.

PROMISED, A bath was delivered to her cham-
r. She felt like a new person afterward. Clean
d less achy; her head less throbbing. She ate
nner alone at a small table before the fire, a
id standing close in case she had need of her.
e wore naught but a silken dressing robe with
e ermine trim, her hair plaited in a neat coil
ut her head.

She tried to pretend the situation wasn't awk-
ird. Any time she glanced at the maid, her gaze
s fixed somewhere on the wall above Alyse's
ad. Apparently she was trained in stoicism.

Alyse tried not to think about how that girl
s likely more cultured and sophisticated than
e could ever hope to be and a reversal of their
es would probably make much more sense.

She dipped her spoon into the bowl and lifted
soup to her lips. It was rather tasty, heartier
n the thin broth delivered to her when she
woke. It warmed her from the inside and
greedily ate it to the last drop.

espite having slept for three days, she went
d again and slept another twelve hours—a
dreamless slumber. When the morning
ed, she woke up refreshed and ready to
he world again. Only she couldn't.

haid stood sentry at the door, stopping her
eaving her room.

el fine," Alyse protested.

How was it he didn't mention he had a brother
who lived in Scotland?

He didn't remark on any of this. He simply
stood, an uncomfortable air surrounding him as
he shifted on his feet.

She stared up at him, marveling at Poppy's
words. As confounding as it was to believe, he
really had been worried for her.

She was simply his housekeeper. He had made
that abundantly clear. Surely he had not forgotten
that fact? Why would he have been so worried?

"I'm sure you would like to get cleaned up."
Poppy stood and moved toward the bell. "I'll
ring you a bath."

"Thank you."

Her gaze moved to Marcus as he inched away
from the bed.

"I'll leave you then." He turned his back on
them rather hastily. Almost as though he couldn't
wait to depart the room. Strange considering all
she had been told about his level of concern. Now
he looked like he couldn't get away fast enough.

He passed through the adjoining door and
shut it behind him. She stared at the wood panel-
ing for a moment as though it would open again
and he would emerge.

"He was very frightened for you."

She looked at Poppy again. The young woman
wore a soft knowing smile on her lips. "Some-

times men don't know what it is they feel when they're feeling it because they've never felt it before."

Alyse rubbed her forehead with the base of her palm. It was aching again. Perhaps even more than when she first woke.

"Confusing, I know," Poppy added, her smile deepening.

Alyse shook her head. "I beg your pardon?" She was not even certain what the woman was talking about.

Poppy blinked and leaned down to gently squeeze her hand. "I'm talking about how confusing love is, of course."

Alyse just stared at her for a long moment and then she did the unexpected. Unexpected even for her. She laughed. Even though it made her head throb, she laughed heartily. She couldn't help herself. "Love? Oh, no no no no no. We are *not* in love. Most assuredly not."

Poppy nodded with annoying conviction. "That is what everybody thinks, m'dear. It's even what I thought with my Struan. Love? Absolutely not. It had to smack me in the face several times before I accepted it." She laughed lightly. "I was so blind . . . so foolish."

"Isn't that what Mr. Thackeray says? That 'love makes fools of us all, big and little'?"

Poppy's eyes shone in approval. "My, bright well-read girl."

"My father was an admirer of his Alyse replied self-consciously.

Poppy continued nodding with app proval. "No wonder Marcus is taken You have a fine mind . . . to say nothin pretty face."

Heat bloomed in her face. "He is my Nothing more." She would be a fool anything else. Anything more.

Poppy's smile turned knowing. "Ver you say so. But I shan't be surprised whe differently later on."

Alyse nodded, her fingers curlin around the bed linens, drawing them to her neck.

Poppy's words were a dangerous were the kind of words that fed h heart and filled one's head with use

She already had dreams.

She didn't need any new ones, fetched ones of this variety.

Gentlemen did not fall in love bought on an auction block. Not she ever read.

* * *

"I'm sorry, miss. The gent said ye must—"

"Who?" she demanded, determined to know who was controlling her actions.

The maid swung her wide eyes to the adjoining room.

She followed her stare to the adjoining chamber. "Him?" *Marcus?*

He said she couldn't leave her chamber? She squared her shoulders. "Very well. I will address it with him." And then she would leave this room. She hadn't stepped from it in four days. It was starting to feel too much like a prison for her taste. Even if she had been unconscious most of the time, she felt a little itchy. Trapped.

Turning away, she strode across the room and knocked briskly on the adjoining room door. No answer. She attempted several times over the next hour, all to no avail. She considered storming past her guard, but it was hardly dignified. She was a guest in this home. She didn't want to tussle with one of their servants. Certainly Marcus would stop by to see her. If he had stuck to her side for three days, then she couldn't imagine he wouldn't want to check in on her.

Except he did not visit her. Not all day. Servants popped in and out. Her meals were brought to her.

Desperate, she decided to risk appearing undignified. She attempted to emerge from her chamber, but a new maid stopped her—a much taller and broader maid than before. The very formidable female ushered her back inside with a stern look.

Alone in her room again, she glared at the adjoining door. Perhaps he was in there and ignoring her.

She crept across the room and pressed her ear to his door. She listened for several minutes. Nothing. Even after everything he had done for her, never leaving her side as Poppy claimed, she began to wonder if he had gone. If he left her here? Perhaps he had decided she was more trouble than she was worth, after all.

She supposed being abandoned here was better than being left stranded in the countryside. Or up on an auction block before a jeering crowd. Perhaps Poppy would give her a position as a maid. Of course in that event she would have to move into the servants' quarters. She glanced around the well-appointed bedchamber. Understandably, she would not be treated to such luxury as this.

The lady of the house visited her in the afternoon, thankfully breaking up the monotony of her day. She even brought an assortment of books for her to read. When Alyse explained to Poppy that she was more than ready to be up and about, Poppy replied, "You feel strong enough then? I will put the matter to Marcus."

Well, that answered her question. He was still here. He had not left her. He was simply avoiding her. That stung more than it should have. She bit back the impulse to demand why *he* was in charge of her. He was her employer. Technically he was in charge, and she might look like an ungrateful shrew for objecting. He'd brought her here—an action that likely saved her life. If he wanted her to recuperate in an unhurried fashion, who was she to object?

She availed herself of the books Poppy brought her. It helped pass the time until dinner. Dinner was a lonely affair yet again. The food was delicious, of course, but she ate alone at the small table before the crackling fire, a maid nearby staring at a fixed spot on the wall as before.

After dinner, she took another fragrant bath.

This life was not hers. It was beyond extravagant, but she could not resist reveling in it. She did not know when she would ever receive such pampering again. She was determined to enjoy it and not feel guilty about it.

Curled up in a great oversized armchair, she brushed her hair out before the fire and sighed in contentment. As the mass dried, she read again from a book Poppy had been kind enough to bring her from the library. She tucked her feet under her and snuggled deeper into the fine lawn of her nightgown. A tartan was draped over her lap. The only thing missing to make it truly idyllic was a dog. A furry little mongrel to nestle in her lap or at her slippered feet.

Perhaps as the housekeeper at Kilmarkie House she could have a pet of her own and then take it with her when she left. It would be a lovely companion in whatever humble dwelling she occupied. A constant in her life.

The hour was late. She should go to bed, especially if they were leaving on the morrow. She would need her rest. And yet she could not drag herself away. The chair, the fire, the lovely nightgown that smelled freshly laundered . . . it was all so nice. So cozy and indulgent.

She turned a page and then paused, lifting her head. She thought she heard a sound. Turning, she fixed her stare on the adjoining door. It remained closed, but she watched it as though it might open or perform some miraculous feat. Moments ticked by and nothing happened. She sighed and turned her attention to the book in her lap.

A muffled cry passed through the door. There was no mistaking it. It sounded as though someone was in trouble. Or hurt. Whatever the case she needed to help whoever was on the other side of that door. The door to the room that belonged to her Not Husband.

Setting the book down, she rose to her feet. She had to do something. She had to check on him. It was the least she could do. He would do the same for her. She rubbed her palms at her sides.

Taking a breath, she knocked lightly. Nothing. No response. She knocked a little bit harder, stinging her knuckles a bit. This time, almost as though in response, she heard it again. Him. Marcus. Was that his muffled voice? Was he bidding her enter?

Closing her hand around the latch, she pushed the door open and stepped inside the dark room.

Chapter 18

The dove pecked at the twine holding her
cage door closed, ready to fly.
She was growing impatient and tired of watching
the wolf prowling on the other side.

Marcus lurched upright in bed, his chest heaving, sheets pooled around his waist. Something clattered to the floor beside the bed.

"What the . . ." He sat up, peering into the gloom, trying to place his location.

He wasn't at his home in London. The room dimensions were all wrong to be his bedchamber. The dimly lit fireplace was on the wrong wall, as was the large balcony window.

The back of his hand mildly stung as though it had collided into something. Rubbing at his knuckles, he glanced down to the floor. Darkness swam there. He could see nothing.

He stretched out his arm and gingerly felt around the rug until his fingers brushed against something hard. His hand closed around it, assessing, measuring. It was a vase. Several sharp-edged porcelain flowers decorated the outside of it. That must be why the back of his hand stung. He'd scraped his knuckles when he knocked it off the nightstand in his sleep.

He recalled it had held actual flowers, too. His hand continued its search over the rug until he met dampness and flowers and stems.

"Marcus?" The side door to his room eased open with a slight creak.

He tensed at the sound of the soft voice and peered into the shadowy dark, almost expecting to see Nancy there, coming into his room to sneak him a biscuit as she often did when he was a child. The young maid had been so kind to him, checking in on him at night. Always ready with a story of her childhood in Kent.

But it wasn't Nancy from his childhood. He wasn't a boy at his town house in London. This was now. This was reality and that soft voice belonged to Alyse.

Her voice came again. "Marcus."

"Alyse," he whispered, dread filling him. He'd been avoiding her since she woke up for a reason.

He really didn't want her here in his room in the middle of the night. It wasn't advisable.

"I heard you. Is everything all right?"

He evened his breathing. "It's nothing. I warned you. I talk in my sleep."

She approached, her bare feet whispering over the carpet.

"Is the rug wet?" She was near the bed now.

"Er. Yes. I knocked over a vase of flowers. My apologies for waking you." He sat up, resting his back against the headboard. Bending a knee, he propped his elbow on it, rubbing his face with a hand.

"I don't mind. I've slept enough lately. You're the one that needs some sleep. Poppy said you spent a lot of time in the chair by my bed. It doesn't look to be a very comfortable chair."

Poppy and her big mouth. "I'll be fine."

She stood there, unmoving, a shadow looking down at him. Her hair flowed in a nimbus around her. The dim firelight set the brown strands aflame. A few feet separated them, but he could smell the clean scent of her. And something else. Something that was inherently woman . . . and *her*.

He needed to tell her to go, but his body pulsed with different words. Words he dared not utter.

She took a step forward, sliding closer hesitantly.

Thoughts warred within him. Silent commands, pleas.

Come closer . . .

Go away . . .

He held his breath, watching as she lifted an arm, stretching it toward him. Her hand brushed his face, palm down. Cool fingers curled against his forehead, her thumb grazing the bridge of his nose. "You're warm."

"Don't touch me," he said under his breath.

"You may be feverish." Her hand shifted against him as though assessing. He heard the concern in her voice. He knew what she was thinking, what worried her.

"I'm not sick." He might very well have a fever at this moment . . . but it wasn't because he was ailing. It would be because of her. It would be because her hand was on him. Because her body was so close. Because the aroma of her filled his nose—her feminine, soapy, floral fragrance intoxicating him. "Go, Alyse. Leave me."

"How can you be certain you're not sickening? Perhaps I was contagious and you picked up what afflicted me?" She shifted even closer and it was misery. He closed his eyes in a tight, pained blink. "Perhaps we should send for the physician, to be certain?"

He was definitely in need. But not for a bloody physician. He needed *her*. Somehow, some way, he had developed a yearning for Alyse.

Her hands on him were like a balm to his soul,

and she wasn't even trying to entice or arouse. That made her all the more dangerous. A woman who didn't know her power over him. Who had no clue how very attractive she was—to him or any man, for that matter. She was modest and guileless.

He snatched hold of her wrist, circling it with his fingers, stalling her exploration of his face.

She hissed sharply. He wasn't certain if the sound was from surprise or pain, but he quickly loosened his grip. "I asked you to go."

Now it was too late. Now he couldn't let her leave.

Still gripping her by the wrist, he tugged and rocked her off balance. The move brought her sprawling down on top of him. He was awash in the scent of her. A cloud of soft sweet-smelling hair fell over him, curtaining them. He let go of her wrist and took her face in both hands, spearing his fingers through the wild fall of her hair and pulling her face to his.

She released a gaspy breath the moment before he covered her mouth with his own. Her lips melted against him. All of her did. The delicious weight of her sank over him . . . into him.

He settled her over him more snugly, fitting her against him like a warm, well-loved blanket. Her thighs parted and slipped over either side of his hips, straddling him. Her body was pliable and warm but her hands felt so cool, almost chilled against his skin.

Only the sheet pooling around his waist served as any barrier to his nudity. She wore her nightgown of sheer lawn. It slid against his flesh like the most sinuous of material. The two fabrics were insubstantial. A tug to the side. A yank. A rip. He could be directly against that silken core of her. Against her slick heat. A thrust and he'd be inside.

He gripped the curve of her hips in both hands, fingers digging through her nightgown as he rubbed his cock into the cleft between her legs. She moaned and lowered both her hands on either side of his head for leverage.

His hands curled into fists, strangling handfuls of nightgown. She moaned and tossed back her head. Slapping one hand on the headboard, she ground down on his cock until they both groaned. Moisture rushed between her legs as she started rocking against him, working her hips and sliding up and down the hard length of his erection.

One thing was certain. There was too much damn fabric between them.

He dove his hand into her hair, fingers sinking and tangling in the mass, the strands soft as silk against his palm. "You should go," he growled, fingers delving deeper, cupping her skull.

She released a soft whimper. "I . . . I don't think I can."

Just like that, something snapped in him. The last invisible thread that had been holding him together.

"Your choice," he growled, thrusting his hips, letting her feel him, rock hard against her, letting her know exactly what was going to happen if she didn't leave.

He tugged lightly on her hair and another one of those little sounds escaped her as she arched her throat. He pressed his open mouth to the flushed skin at the side of her neck, directly beneath her ear.

She moaned in response, rocking into his hardness.

She might come to regret it, but she was still here. Still here and his restraint was gone.

She started to shake. "It's happening . . . like before . . ."

The material between them was damp with both their desire, slicking all their movements. They slid and rocked desperately together. His balls swelled tight. He slid his hands up her back to grip her shoulders and bring her harder down on him.

"What are you doing to me?" he growled, loving how she quivered, how she was so responsive, so close . . .

She shook her head. "I—I don't know. This isn't . . . I don't know . . . what is . . ."

He felt her trembling against him as she moved on him like an animal, desperate for her own pleasure, seeking her release.

He spoke into her ear as his own release twisted up and rose in him. "I said I wouldn't do this . . ." But here he was, lost in her, drowning.

A shudder racked her and vibrated into the length of him.

Her hair fell into her face and he swiped it back, so he could see her in the shadows, her contorting expression as she shattered over him. It was enough. The sight of her undone. Knowing she did this because of him. Because of what he did for her.

He kissed her, swallowing her shriek even as he moved under her, grinding into her yielding heat until he joined her in release, shattering as completely as she did.

She lowered her face until their foreheads were pressed together. Their ragged breaths merged, mingling. He relaxed his grip, his hands smoothing over the nightgown covering her hips.

She pulled back slightly, blinking wide, glittering eyes at him. He stared back, his chest tightening. Her breath fell hard on his lips and he had to resist another taste.

He'd thought her artless. Unworldly. Now he wasn't so certain.

She'd had a lover. The man who abandoned her. Perhaps she knew precisely what she was doing—snaring herself a husband.

He tightened his hands and moved her off him, seating her at the edge of the bed. Her gaze turned wary as she hastily tugged her nightgown down over her legs.

"You're looking at me that way again," she murmured.

"What way is that?"

"Like I might pounce on you . . . but then I suppose I've already done that, no?" Her voice broke a little, shook between them like a wobbly, drifting feather.

He flung back the covers and rose from the bed, walking naked across the room to the washstand. He heard her suck in a breath, but didn't bother to cover himself. It seemed a little late to adopt an air of modesty.

He used a linen and washed himself off, his back to her. He felt her stare boring into him, thorough, scouring as a heated blade. He looked over his shoulder at her. "We've done nothing irreparable here."

"Irreparable?" The eyes that gazed at him looked rather haunted. "What does that even mean?"

He turned to face her. Again, she sucked in a breath.

"You're a clever girl." He braced a hand on the table behind him. "I'm not saying you manipulated this into happening." He waved between them.

She made a choking sound. "Oh, that's generous of you to allow . . . seeing as I only came in here because I heard you cry out. Because I thought you might have fallen ill and be in need."

He lifted a shoulder in a shrug. "Perhaps . . . but put a bed near us and this is where we always end up."

"Is it so wrong? If we both want each other, if we both—"

"I warned you not to want more from me. Don't expect more than an offer of employment."

She laughed bitterly. "Don't flatter yourself. This was only a tryst. It happens between people from time to time. I'm not so naïve I don't know that. I did not mistake it for more."

He studied her profile. The clean line of her nose. The slightly pouty push of her bottom lip. They really were luscious lips. Her mouth brought forth all manner of carnal ideas. Staring at it, at her sitting on the edge of his bed, he wanted to cross the distance and claim that mouth again. He wanted to spend hours on it, tasting and exploring and committing it to memory.

"You should return to your room and get some rest. We resume our journey in the morning. This won't happen again, Miss Bell."

She stood from the bed, brushing at her night-gown as though smoothing out wrinkles in the fine lawn. She took several steps toward her door, appearing unsteady on her feet. Her voice came out jagged as broken glass, sharp enough to cut. "You really are a coldhearted bastard."

Then she fled into her room.

He blew out a breath and dragged a hand through his hair. Better that. He could live with being cold.

It would get easier. Once he had her at Kilmarkie House and she was set up properly as the housekeeper it would be easier. He might not even stay very long, after all. He might just leave her there and keep going. Keep riding.

Chapter 19

*When the dove looked out from her cage it
wasn't just her wolf out there anymore.
There were wolves everywhere.*

*H*e wanted to get rid of her mule. She glared at Marcus. He stared back steadily, looking quite unperturbed by the announcement or her obvious distress over it.

Alyse wasn't quite certain when she began to think of the animal as *hers*, but she did, and the thought of giving him up was intolerable.

"We're not leaving Little Bit," she announced, staring at the lovely doe-eyed mare that stood placidly beside Bucky, ready to take the place of her mule. Rare sunshine peeped out from the clouds, highlighting the red in the beast's mahogany coat.

She crossed her arms over her chest and tapped her foot, much in the manner she had done when being firm with any one of the Beard children.

Marcus stopped and stared at her, his expression full of exasperation. "Alyse, he's much too slow. I would like to reach Kilmarkie House this decade if possible."

She resisted reminding him that they were back to formalities. He had called her Miss Bell last night. "We cannot leave him behind. He has tried his best—"

"He simply is what he is. An old mule."

Just as she was what she was. Unwanted. Without family. Homeless. Constantly reminded by him that she wasn't worthy to be his wife. What if he deemed her worthless as a housekeeper, too? Would he cast her aside?

"He. Is. Coming." She propped both hands on her waist, determined to stand her ground. Which was odd. She hadn't particularly enjoyed riding the mule. She didn't know why she was so stubborn on this point.

He stared at her for several moments before releasing a frustrated growl. "Very well. We don't have time to stand here and argue." Turning, he barked at one of the servants, "Fetch the mule please. Take this one back."

She couldn't help herself. The mule was going with them. She smiled widely. When he turned back to face her, she was still smiling. He paused as if the sight took him aback.

"What?" Her hand lightly drifted toward her face.

He shook his head. "Nothing." But he continued to gaze at her as though he had never seen her before.

"Is there something on my face?"

"You look happy. You're smiling."

Her smile slipped. She shrugged awkwardly. "Sorry?"

"Don't be sorry." Now it seemed it was his turn to look awkward. "You're happy. No apology necessary for that." He winced and watched as a groom led out the mule. The beast looked resentful and took several nips at the lad as he tugged it forward. "Even if it is because of a stupid mule."

She forced down a laugh. He looked aggrieved as he stared at the sulky animal.

They mounted without another word on the matter of the mule and her state of happiness (or lack thereof). She sent a look over her shoulder where Poppy Mackenzie stood before the threshold of her massive home, waving them off from the courtyard. They had already exchanged very proper and polite farewells.

Alyse waved back, deciding that Poppy Mackenzie might be one of the nicest women she had ever met. She couldn't help hoping that she would someday see her again although that seemed unlikely. "Your sister-in-law is very lovely. Very kind."

"She is that," he agreed as they trotted out of the courtyard.

"You seem to know Poppy well. I'd almost say better than your brother." When they departed the two men had behaved rather stiffly toward each other. Gruffly. Almost not like brothers. At least not brothers who were close. She had noticed. Poppy had watched, too, frowning at the pair of them and bidding them to say farewell to each other like two ill-mannered boys.

He shrugged atop his mount. "I don't know if I'd say I know her *well*."

She stared at him thoughtfully, prompting him to continue.

"But yes, I suppose I know her better than Mackenzie."

He called his brother by his surname?

"How is it possible you know your sister-in-law *better* than your own brother?"

"It's a long and complicated story."

She snorted. "Considering I am bound to this mule for the better part of the day . . . I have all the time in the world."

"We were engaged for a brief time."

All of her froze, went cold inside. He had been affianced to that paragon of womanhood. That lovely and kind lady . . . but somehow she had married his half brother instead.

The information didn't settle well with Alyse. In fact, the information sank like rocks in her stomach. The awful sensation was unfamiliar . . . but suddenly she didn't feel so kindly disposed toward the other female. It was uncharitable of her. Inexplicable. She owed the woman a debt for taking such good care of her during her illness.

"As I said, it's a long and complicated story," he began. "Struan is my father's illegitimate son." He cleared his throat as though it were difficult to admit that. She could imagine how such a thing might be complicated . . . how that might bring a whole host of issues. "It took me some time to accept that. To even recognize it as truth." He grunted. "I believe I was the last one in my family to accept it. I suppose that makes me a stubborn ass."

"You think?" she managed to tease.

He cast her an uncomfortable glance. "Yes, we have a history of . . . tension. I suppose I proposed to Poppy because I knew he wanted her. It was spiteful. I did it to nettle him."

"Oh," she replied, rather surprised he would resort to such a low thing. "You would have married her out of . . . vindictiveness?"

"Yes. I suppose I would have. I was led by different emotions then. And once I offered for her, I was bound to honor the proposal. Thankfully, she broke it off with me."

"For Mackenzie?"

"Of course. Her heart was as bound to him as his was to her. It was inevitable. *They* were inevitable."

Inevitable. She marveled at that and felt a twinge of jealousy. What must it be like? *Feel* like? To be *inevitable* with another person? For your love to be that unavoidable?

"She is a good soul," he added. "Poppy, like the rest of my family, hopes we can put aside our differences."

"Do you want to do that?"

He was quiet for some time before answering, "Yes. I do. I'm not the same person I was when I first learned of his existence."

"Well. You should make peace. Family is important." She knew that better than anyone since she lost hers. Since she didn't have anyone to call kin. Since she knew the ache of loneliness. "And your brother seems . . . nice." It was all she could offer on the subject of Struan Mackenzie. She'd met him only briefly. He was handsome and fair-haired. Even bigger than Marcus. They hardly spoke beyond the obligatory greeting. The brief exchange was hardly enough to pass any kind of judgment, but she felt compelled to say something positive about Marcus's brother to encourage the solidifying of their relationship.

"Struan Mackenzie is *many* things, but *nice* is not a descriptor that pops to mind." He didn't say anything more beyond that as they left the Mackenzies' lavish neighborhood behind and clattered down the cobbled streets between shops and buildings. It was quite the largest city she had ever been in. Considering she had been insentient the first time she passed through it, she took it all in with avid interest.

She thought about Struan and his brother as they rode through the streets of Glasgow. She always wished for siblings and here he had a brother . . . along with the sisters back in London. A brother he didn't like and yet he brought her to his home for tending. Struan Mackenzie had been there for Marcus. For her. As a brother ought to be.

She was still thinking about that as they left the city behind and continued north. "I suppose it is lucky your brother lived in Glasgow so that you could prevail upon him during my illness."

He was ahead of her on the road as usual thanks to Little Bit's plodding pace. He stopped and turned sideways, staring at her. "Aye. Lucky indeed. His home was near and despite the shakiness of our relationship it seemed the obvious thing to do at the time. The only recourse, really."

"Perhaps not that obvious." He had characterized the relationship with his brother as complicated, but he had put that aside and ignored their differences. For her sake. For *her*. "You could have taken me somewhere else. Found lodgings and sent for a physician."

"First, I don't hate Struan. Perhaps once I did. But this was good for us . . ." His voice faded. "Regardless of what I felt for him before I carried you into his house, you needed—"

"Saving," she finished. "It seems you are always saving me."

Yes. It was a good thing. Of course. She was glad to have him. Of all the men who could have bought her in that market, she was fortunate to have ended up with him.

And yet she just wanted to be somewhere in life where she didn't need rescuing. Or at least in a place where she could save herself. Or even better yet . . . be with someone she didn't feel so beholden to for every gesture, every act of kindness.

He stared at her across the distance, so strong and solemn atop his gelding. Because he was that. Noble and strong atop a beautiful fairy tale horse whilst she was a peasant girl on a mule.

She willed him to say something. To say he cared about her even a little. That helping her wasn't about pity or simply because he was a good man and it was the honorable thing to do.

Honorable. Like both times now that he had stopped himself from consummating their sham of a union. Stopping himself just as he compelled her into wanting him with a desperate fervor.

Again and again he had proved himself honorable. And she was sick of it. She wanted him to be a little bad. *With her.*

Staring at her, he didn't say anything. He simply turned his horse around and continued on.

THEY CONTINUED NORTH and managed to avoid any proximity to beds. Although she felt the strain of it. Not avoiding beds, but avoiding his touch, avoiding his gaze for any significant length of time. His rejection stung and she vowed not to endure it again.

The villages became smaller. The lodgings less like inns and more like boardinghouses with only a few rooms, but fortunately there was no risk of not securing two rooms. Travelers this far north this time of year were not in abundance.

For the next few days, she stared at the back of him, wondering at the unfeelingness of him.

How could he have touched her, done those

things with her, and now he scarcely looked or talked to her? Was that the way of all men? Was it so easy to go from hot to cold?

Admittedly, her experience was limited. The one man she thought she could rely upon, the man that had said all the right things, had let her down when she needed him the most. Whereas Marcus Weatherton had been there for her every single time. So what if she longed for his touch, his kiss, his body to take her over that precipice they toyed upon . . . he was not obligated to give her those things.

On their fourth day out of Glasgow, they stopped midday to eat and stretch their legs. They moved off the road into a small copse. A stream burbled nearby as he removed food out of a pack. Poppy had sent some fresh bread, cheese and apple pasties. They'd finished the cheese days ago, but the bread was still tasty as were the apple pasties.

Their fingers brushed as he handed her a portion of crusty bread and some dried meat. She tried not to notice. They were both wearing gloves. It shouldn't have produced a spark, but heat traveled up her arm and spread throughout her chest contrary to that.

Locating a rock, she brushed the snow off it with a gloved hand and sank down, trying to pretend the ice-cold was not a shock to her derriere. The warmth triggered by his hand brushing hers quickly dissipated.

What she wouldn't do for that comfortable bedchamber in the Mackenzie household. Warm beds. Warm baths. Warm sofa chairs before the fireplace.

She lifted her face to the sunlight as she ate, imagining it helped warm her up a little. Her gaze drifted to where he sat. He took a swig from a bottle.

"What are you drinking?"

He pulled back the flask and squinted at it. "My dear brother was good enough to pack this as a parting gift. Care for a draw? It might warm you until we stop for the night."

She thought about it for a moment and then said, "All right then."

He stood and brought her the flask. She accepted it, careful not to touch him this time. The container felt lighter than expected. She gave it a slight shake. "Had more than a few nips, have you?"

He shrugged. "It's cold out in case you did not notice."

She took a small sip and hissed out a breath at the potent drink. Goodness. It tasted awful. She held it out for him to reclaim. "So you thought you'd pickle yourself, is that it?"

He chuckled as he took it and leaned back

against a nearby tree, crossing his boots at the ankles. "Not much of a drinker, I take it."

"My father never drank and Mr. Beard only imbibed at the tavern, once a week or so." He always returned home intoxicated on those nights, stumbling about through the house until he found his bed. The following morning she would have to rise extra early and do his chores before her own. The cows couldn't wait to be milked until he managed to drag himself from bed.

"And what of your lover? Did he imbibe at the tavern, too? Or was that when he visited you? On the nights your husband was away?"

"I don't understand."

"Yes. You do. The bastard that promised to show up and buy you in that auction . . . is that when he visited you?"

Why did he sound so angry? She was the one who was wronged.

Heat flushed her face. Suddenly the food she'd just ate felt like rocks in her stomach. "I never dishonored my vows."

True, she'd kissed Yardley, but when he'd pressed for more, promising they'd soon be man and wife, she had resisted. Not because she doubted his promise but because it had not felt right.

Even though she and Mr. Beard were not husband and wife in the truest sense, she'd taken vows of fidelity. Vows that had been transferred to this man before her now. Not that he wanted her fidelity. Because he didn't want her.

He took another swig of whisky. "Such loyalty. It's a shame you're such a poor judge of character and didn't settle your sights on a more reliable man."

She hissed out a breath, stung. It was almost as though he was trying to hurt her feelings.

He continued, "Then you wouldn't be stuck here with me freezing off your arse."

"Are you trying to be cruel?"

"No. It comes rather easily. No effort required." He took another drink. "Especially after a whisky or two. Perhaps you've come to expect too much of me?"

"Perhaps you are right," she charged, her voice rising an octave. "I *am* a poor judge of character. And I do expect too much of you. You're a drunk. And a boor . . ." She sniffed and glanced around, wondering how much longer until they reached Kilmarkie House. Certainly they could not be too far from it. She looked at him again, her anger welling up inside her.

He chuckled and took another drink. "Lady, it's worse than that . . . I'm a duke. That essentially guarantees I'm an insensitive sod."

She stilled. "What?"

"An insensitive—"

"No, no. Not that! The other thing you said."

"Oh. I'm a duke?"

"But your name . . . you said you were Marcus Weatherton."

"That's not untrue." He shrugged. "I'm both. By title, however, I'm the Duke of Autenberry."

She shook her head, believing his outrageous words for it all now made sense. Everything about him proclaimed this to be truth. His airs. His absolute refusal to consider her his wife. A duke did not marry the likes of her. If she'd thought him far removed from her before, he might as well live on the moon now. He was gone from her. Not that she had ever had him.

And yet an inconsolable sadness swept over her, hollowing out her insides and leaving a stinging ache in her chest.

She suspected he wanted that. He wanted her to know the truth so that the divide between them was out there in the open. Fully visible. Not simply in his awareness, but hers, too. A great mountain that she would never climb. A commoner could not dare ascend such heights.

"Why didn't you tell me sooner?" Before she started developing feelings for him . . . before she began hoping that they could be something. Yes. It was true. She had hoped despite his rejections. She had felt . . . *feelings.* Emotions. Desire. She'd hoped because when he kissed her and touched her she thought he must feel something that went beyond obligation.

Now she knew. Now that their journey was coming to a close, he'd admitted who he was. What he was. The gulf that yawned between them was inaccessible.

A horse neighed softly somewhere just beyond the copse and it wasn't Bucky or her mule. No, they stared blandly, not making a sound.

"Marcus?"

He cut a hand swiftly through the air, silencing her, his gaze suddenly hard and intent.

She held her tongue and waited, angling her head, hoping it was nothing. Merely a rider passing through the woods. Nothing to fear.

Except she was wrong.

Several horsemen emerged from the trees, moving like wraiths, silent as the wind itself. Surrounding them. Flanking them.

"Wot 'ave we 'ere?" one of the riders asked, looking between Alyse and Marcus. "A bit of domestic strife?"

She eyed the newcomers. Highlanders. Unquestionably. They wore full tartan. It was almost as though they stepped out of the pages of a book. Vestiges of an era before Culloden.

Marcus was beside her, his hand tight around her arm. "We don't want any trouble. We're simply travelers passing through."

"Travelers," a dark-eyed Highlander at the center of them proclaimed. He was maybe the youngest of the pack, no older than herself, but he held himself with an air of authority. "Nice bit of horseflesh ye have there, Englishman." He nodded to where Bucky munched on grass.

Alyse glanced at Marcus's gelding worriedly. Fearing they were about to lose Bucky, she blurted, "He's not for sale."

The Highlander turned his attention on her. "Oh, I'm no' interested in *buying* the beast. I'd love nothing more than relieving so fine a creature from an Englishman. Actually it's my duty as a Scotsman tae do so."

Marcus's arm tensed under her fingers. She tightened her grip. "It's not worth it." Not worth his life. Marcus looked down at her with glittering eyes.

"Listen tae your wife," the Highlander advised.

"I'm not his wife," she automatically replied.

"Are ye no'?" The man looked back and forth between them, his gaze bright with interest.

"She is not," Marcus said slowly, for the first time appearing almost reluctant to agree to that fact. His gaze prowled her features, almost as though memorizing, as though loath to look away for any reason at all.

"Nay? Then what is she tae ye?"

Alyse held her breath and forced herself not to look at Marcus even as she wondered what the answer to that question would be. She told herself it shouldn't matter. His answer didn't amount to anything. Not when they were nothing to each other. He could say anything, however marginalizing of their relationship, and it shouldn't matter.

Marcus didn't answer immediately and as the silence stretched she felt compelled to fill it, to answer for him, "I'm his housekeeper."

"Housekeeper? Och . . . is that what they're calling it these days?" All the men laughed at the younger man's quip.

Her face caught fire.

Marcus cursed and surged against her grip, ready to lunge at the other man.

She clung tighter to him and snapped at the Scotsman, "Mind your tongue."

The group of Scotsmen *ooohed* at her harsh reprimand.

The dark-eyed Scot stared at her as though she were suddenly something fascinating. A trickle of unease ran down her spine. "You're right. My apologies. I was verra rude." The leader grinned then, appearing as mischievous as a lad—a handsome one at that. "The fact that ye are no' married to this Sassenach is something tae recommend ye, lass."

Marcus growled and attempted to step forward again. She struggled to pull him back before he clashed with the Highlander. That couldn't end well. They were outnumbered and the group of Scots was armed to the teeth.

"Lass," the Highlander tsked. "Ye keep verra poor company. I heard ye two squabbling through the trees. In fact, that's what caught our notice and we decided to investigate. You see these are my woods, and I canna have any lass being mistreated in my domain."

She fidgeted.

"She is fine," Marcus said tightly and took her hand, his fingers lacing through hers. "We are both fine. You need not be concerned."

"Allow me tae disagree. She sounded verra unhappy and as laird of these lands I'm honor bound to assist any lass in need." He snapped his fingers then and a man dismounted, moving forward to fetch Marcus's gelding. Alyse pressed a hand against Marcus's chest and felt his growl rumble against the flat of her palm through their garments. "I'm a great admirer of fine horseflesh. We'll leave ye with the nag."

"You cannot do that," she protested, looking uneasily between Marcus and the men surrounding them. Tension crackled in the air. Her nerves pulled tight, waiting. Something was coming.

She knew it as much as she feared it. Something that made her stomach knot and clench.

The black-eyed Highlander assessed her a moment longer before snapping his fingers yet again. "Ye ken I'm going tae do my good deed for the day and relieve ye of the lass, too."

"What? No!" she cried as men descended on her.

Marcus shouted but she couldn't make sense of the words. She only saw the men . . . the hands coming at her, seizing her and pulling her away.

"That's right," the leader continued. "Ye won't have tae suffer this lofty bastard anymore, lass."

Marcus surged for her, fighting like a wild animal, but men descended on him as well, pulling him back.

He turned on them, fighting, swinging his fists. It was hopeless. Three-to-one odds. They pummeled him. Awful bone-smacking blows. His body jerked beneath the impact. It was a terrible sight. She felt each blow as though it were inflicted upon herself.

"Please! Stop! You're hurting him. Marcus, stop fighting!" *Stop fighting.*

Let me go. Let them have me.

He went down and suddenly the group of men stepped back.

She pushed forward. "You killed him!" She lunged to where Marcus had fallen. His eyes were still open, his gaze wild and unfocused. "Marcus!" She reached out to touch him, but was pulled away.

One of the Highlanders moved to crouch beside him. "'E's no' dead. Just grazed 'is 'ead on a rock when 'e fell. 'Ead wounds always bleed like the devil. 'E'll be fine."

Not dead. Not dead.

The words rushed through her and she grabbed at them like marbles rolling past, curling them in her palm and holding them tightly, letting them fill her with hope. She expelled a sobbing breath.

"Fetch her bag," the leader gestured to her floral valise on the back of the mule. The man crouching beside Marcus stood and claimed her bag.

His devil-dark eyes landed on her then.

She shook her head. "No, no . . ."

She attempted to back away, but she didn't get very far before her arm was seized in a vise. She was tossed up on the horse in front of the leader.

She had one last glimpse of Marcus and he didn't look well despite their assurances. He was flat on his back on the ground. Only this time, his eyes were closed. He didn't move a muscle. Not a flicker.

Not even when she called his name.

Chapter 20

Finally. The wolf unleashed the predator within him.

*T*heir tracks were easy to follow.

He scarcely felt his injuries. He was aware of them distantly, as one might be aware of the weather outside. Remotely and indifferently. He pushed Little Bit hard. The beast had likely never moved with such haste in all his life.

Fortunately it did not snow during the time he was unconscious and he was able to follow the deep ruts left by their horses in the snow.

Even more fortunate, he did not have far to travel. The great stone castle he'd arrived at looked like something out of a medieval fairy tale.

No one had to tell him this was the local laird's castle.

Certainly the gray stone itself looked medieval. It was crumbling in several places and one of the towers actually looked hazardous, as though it might topple over at any moment.

The main gates were open and he rode right through them, earning more than a few stares. He was a big man riding a mule after all, with the soles of his boots skimming the ground. He read the mirth in their eyes. He hardly posed a threat to them.

He dismounted and let the mule idle in the crowded courtyard.

He didn't bother to think about how he was going to get out of here once he had reclaimed Alyse. He couldn't worry about that now. He could only worry about locating her and making certain she was safe. Making certain they hadn't harmed or molested her in any fashion. He continued to ignore the throbbing in his skull and the crusted blood matted in his hair where he'd struck his head.

His mind worked feverishly with one goal as he walked inside the castle. Find Alyse.

The hall was full. They were in the midst of dinner. A long dining table was positioned at the far side of the room resembling something from the feudal age. It felt like a forgotten era. There were men and women all about garbed in the tartan colors he'd seen on the men from earlier. The men who'd taken Alyse.

At the head table sat the man who took her. The young leader. Marcus walked down the open space between the tables, stopping once he was a few feet from the table's edge.

"I've come for the girl," he addressed the lad.

He was cold and wet and furious.

And worst of all, he was terrified. Terrified for *her* . . . wherever she was in this castle. His mind conjured all manner of horrific things. Alyse chained in a dungeon somewhere . . .

His stomach knotted as he thought of all the things that could happen to her. That could have *already* have happened to her.

This was worse than the day he'd seen her standing on that auction block in the middle of the square, men haggling over her like she was some bit of horseflesh. It was worse because he knew her now. She was no longer a stranger. She was more than some hapless nameless female.

As annoying as she could be with her prying and chatter, she meant something to him. She had come to be . . . something to him. She mattered. He couldn't imagine a day without her in it. Alarming as the thought was, he couldn't take the time to examine it right now. He had more pressing concerns. Like getting her back. Getting her back and keeping her.

His gaze skimmed the hall, searching for a glimpse of her among the revelers. There was no sight of her, but his presence before the head table was finally noticed. His declaration had seen to that.

The smug bastard at the head table stood up, still holding a goblet. "And who might ye be looking for, ye fine sir? A girl, ye say?" He took a long, leisurely sip, behaving as though he didn't remember Marcus.

The hall fell silent, everyone looking back and forth between the young laird and Marcus.

"You know damn well who I'm here for."

Marcus's hand went inside his coat to pull out his pistol. Earlier the weapon had been out of reach, but not this time.

A growl rippled through the great hall. Several men moved toward him, but Marcus kept the barrel trained on the man responsible for taking Alyse. The laird in command and, apparently, his neighbor. The man he would kill if he didn't set her free.

It didn't matter to him that *he* might die. True, he was standing in the veritable lion's den, but he didn't care. There were things a man had to do. He understood that now.

His father had never understood that. He lacked the instinct to do right by others. His rank and wealth had bred in him a callous indifference to others—especially others who were of lesser rank. Considering his father had been a duke, that was essentially everyone.

Even though he had raised Marcus to be just like him, somehow Marcus wasn't. He would not let them take Alyse and forget all about her.

The laird motioned his men back, an amused lift to his lips as he addressed Marcus. "You're either verra stupid or verra brave tae stroll in here and point that at me. In my own home, no less." He nodded at Marcus's weapon.

He was neither stupid nor brave. He was desperate, but he didn't bother pointing that out.

The cocky bastard continued, "This is a great deal of fuss over a housekeeper, is it no'?"

"Where is she?" Marcus repeated, not bothering to respond to that allegation.

"Readying for bed," the laird said with decided satisfaction, seeming to relish the word *bed*. He gestured upstairs with a flippant wave of the hand and Marcus wanted to shoot him right then. He might as well as said she was readying herself for *his* bed. An amused light glinted in the man's eyes. He was enjoying himself.

"She doesn't belong here with you," Marcus insisted.

"Nay, she doesn't belong wi' ye."

"Hunt, wot is 'appening 'ere?" An older woman appeared, her hair white as snow and plaited in several ropes elaborately around the crown of her head.

"'Tis nothing, Nana. The Sassenach here thinks he has claim on the wee lass I brought home." His lip curled as thought the notion was distasteful.

"I do." Marcus stepped forward.

The old woman looked Marcus up and down. "Och. So yer the Englishmon. She was fretting over ye. Feared ye might be dead. She will be verra relieved."

She had spoken of him and she was worried about him. It lightened his chest to hear that. She couldn't be too unwell if she was fearful for him, could she?

The old woman added, "Me grandson 'ere said ye dinna want 'er." She shot the young man an accusing look.

Rather than address the untruth of that, Marcus flung out, "He abducted her!"

The laird shrugged. "They were bickering. Seemed like they would be happy to part ways."

"Your men beat me."

"Lower that weapon, would ye," the old woman asked, waving at his pistol. "Before ye 'urt someone. Ye stand in the hall of Clan MacLarin. Show some respect and put that thing away."

Sighing, he lowered his pistol.

She looked with fond reproach to her grandson. "The lad 'ere always 'ad a soft spot for damsels in distress and she is a bonny lass." She shrugged one bony shoulder. "For a Lowlander."

Marcus gnashed his teeth. Alyse was no damsel in distress. Not since he freed her from that auction block. She was more. So much more. An infuriating magpie, to be sure . . . but somewhere along the way he had begun to think of her as *his* infuriating magpie.

"And," the old woman added, "this could have something to do with Hunt having a hatred for all things English. No doubt he relished tweaking your nose."

"I don't give a damn how he feels about me. He needs to free Alyse—"

"Free 'er? Ye think we're holding 'er against 'er will? We're no kidnappers." Nana laughed. Cackled really. "The lass is no' hostage 'ere."

He snorted. "Your grandson carted her off against her will."

The old dame shrugged again and snapped at a nearby serving girl. "Fetch the lass." As the girl scurried off to do her bidding, she looked back at Marcus again. "Perhaps she was a reluctant guest in the beginning but—"

"Abducted," he insisted. "She was *abducted*!"

"Och, well, she's quite comfortable now," the woman finished. "Ye needn't fash yerself."

"Aye, quite comfortable," the smug laird echoed with a waggle of his eyebrows, enjoying himself immensely.

His grandmother cackled again. "That one." She waved a hand at him. "Such a way wi' the lassies. But in truth, ye can rest easy. She is in good 'ands 'ere. Nae need tae feel obligated further."

Obligated?

It was as though she could see into the past and all the times he'd flung that word at Alyse. Had Alyse said anything to the woman to lead her to believe he would so easily let her go?

"Marcus?" At the sound of his name, his gaze jerked from the old woman.

Alyse emerged through a large arched threshold, one hand lifting her skirts so they didn't catch on her feet as she hastened forward. She pressed a hand to her stomach and all of her body seemed to sag with relief as her gaze swept over him. "You are alive! They said you were not dead, but I was not certain."

He inhaled. "Indeed, I am not dead." He had perhaps never felt so alive. So furiously alive.

She grinned rather widely then. Her happiness to see him was heartening at least.

She wore a fresh gown of red velvet and her hair shimmered from a recent wash, a set of jeweled combs held the strands back from her face. Gone was her worn and ragged clothing. She looked elegant and noble. Immediately, he felt like a wretch for not supplying such nice things for her. Instead he'd dragged her through the cold on the back of a mule, prompting her to sicken.

He shot a scathing look to the blackguard for giving her the things he had not.

"See," Laird MacLarin declared effusively. "We've no' put 'er in chains."

Alyse's smile slipped. An air of restraint came over her. "Aye. They've treated me quite well."

"There now," the laird's grandmother chimed in. "All is well."

All was decidedly *not* well.

"I appreciate you coming after me," Alyse started. "But you needn't put yourself to such trouble."

"Trouble?" he echoed dumbly.

"Aye. I am well cared for here. They've invited me to stay—"

"Like bloody hell!" Did she think he would leave her to a bunch of brigands? Is that what she thought of him? That he would gladly abandon her at the first opportunity? *Wouldn't you have done so? That first day of your meeting?* Perhaps but that was then. This was now and he wasn't letting her go.

"Marcus!" she exclaimed at his outburst with a small shake of her head, looking truly bewildered. "What is so objectionable about leaving me here?" She stepped forward to whisper for his ears alone. "You can't have really wanted me as a housekeeper. You made the offer out of pity. We both know that." The look she gave him then was fairly indulgent and it set his teeth on edge. He didn't want her condescension. He wasn't so naïve that he didn't pick up on it.

She continued, "I don't need your generosity anymore. I will be quite safe here. You can go. Continue on your journey without me as a yoke about your neck."

A yoke about his neck. He looked her up and down. She hardly resembled that. Her gown of rich red that brought out the amber in her eyes, making them appear all the more afire. They gleamed like topaz in the firelit hall. The bodice was snug, as though it had belonged to a smaller woman before her. The fabric pulled tight across her chest, emphasizing the curve of her breasts.

She looked at home here. As though she fit in this castle. As though she were a lady that belonged in this hall. A lady that could stand at the helm of any fine household . . . a lady of the manor. *Not* a housekeeper.

"I've come for *you*," he bit out. "I'll not leave you here."

Her gaze traveled over him. She cleared her throat and said slowly, "But . . . why?" She shook her head as though truly puzzled. "Why should I go with you?"

"Because . . ." He motioned to the clan laird who was watching them as though they were quite the diverting spectacle. "He abducted you."

Her chin went up. "We've put that aside."

"Have we?"

"Of course. Now," she began in a rather dismissing tone. "You've saved me enough. Fret no more on the matter. You will not be required to rescue me further. You are free of me."

"Alyse," he said tightly, stepping closer. "We had an arrangement. What happened in Collie-Ben—"

"Speak not of it." She waved a hand. "You needn't concern yourself with that anymore."

He stared at her, unblinking, wondering what he needed to do or say to get through to her. "I cannot do that. You are my obligation."

Something flickered in her eyes, but then the emotion was gone before he had a proper read on it.

Her expression returned to mild amiableness.

She smiled tightly and nodded as though reaching a decision. "I release you from our arrangement. There. I've said it."

"You release me?" He shook his head. "You cannot do that."

She propped a hand on her hip, indignation coloring her cheeks. "Well, that doesn't feel very fair. I say you are free to go." She motioned to the laird. "Hunt has been kind enough to promise me a place here for as long as I wish to stay."

Hunt. She addressed the laird as Hunt. As though they were intimate friends now. It was unendurable.

"I need not travel any farther with you." She angled her head as she went on, "I thought you would be relieved. Why do you look so cross?"

"Alyse, you cannot expect me to feel comfortable leaving you here among these strangers." He motioned to his head. "Strangers, need I remind you, who beat me and left me for dead."

She winced. "I am certain Hunt is sorry."

He inhaled sharply against his rise of temper.

"There is only one way to settle this," the old lady chimed in.

"Nana?" The laird looked slightly bewildered at her interjection.

"Ye both want her . . . clan law dictates ye fight for her."

"Fight for me?" Alyse looked perplexed. "I'm

not property! Haven't I any say? And Laird Mac-Larin doesn't *want* me—"

Nana waved her to silence. "Hush, lass."

Marcus nodded. "Very well." Given his present mood, he would be happy to resolve this with his fists.

Alyse's slight nostrils flared and she once again leaned in to whisper for his ears alone, "Why don't you just leave, *Your Grace*?" His title dripped like poison from her lips. Ah. She was still angry about that, was she? Was that the root of this then? Her contention with him? She shook her head at him. "You don't belong here, *Lord Autenberry*. And I don't belong with you. Rip up that bill of sale and forget all about me."

He stiffened. "I can't do that."

He didn't know why. She wanted him gone. She was giving him every opportunity to be rid of her without feeling obligated. She'd said the bill of sale meant nothing—*he* had said the same thing—so why not destroy it? Why not do precisely what she suggested?

And why was he still standing here? Staring at her and fighting the impulse to fling her over his shoulder like a caveman?

"Well, then. Let's have a go at it. A duke, eh?" The laird clapped his hands and moved around the table to the open space where Marcus stood. "I appreciate a good fight and I've nae fought wi' a blue-blooded Sassenach before. A duke no less! This should be verra diverting."

"You don't have to do this," Alyse hissed, looking at him with beseeching eyes. Her voice dropped to a whisper again. "You're a duke. You shouldn't lower yourself to fisticuffs. You shouldn't lower yourself to even associate with me."

"Och, let them fight," Nana called with a shrug. "Men need a proper release fer their aggression. And the one who wins? 'E'll be the one that wants ye most. 'Tis the natural order of things."

Alyse sent the old woman an exasperated look before looking back to Marcus. "No. He's never wanted me." She was speaking directly to him then, her eyes willing him to understand . . . to walk away. "You know it's true, Marcus. Let. Go." Her voice quivered with weariness. "Leave me here." She donned a wobbly smile then. "Really. It's all right."

"I'll not leave you, Alyse." A great ball of emotion welled up from his chest and released itself, erupting from him in a hot flow of words that could be heard across the hall. "You're my wife," he exploded, his voice echoing over the great hall, reverberating up to the high beams of the ceiling.

Silence fell. Deafening as the loudest drum.

He glanced around, the sudden quiet strange and unnerving. It was as though he had said or done something profound. He supposed he had. He'd just laid claim to Alyse as his wife.

Oddly enough he didn't regret the words.

Alyse shook her head. Her eyes went wide at his declaration. "Marcus," she whispered. "What have you . . ." Her voice faded away.

"Yer wife?" Nana proclaimed. "Well now. That changes everything."

Chapter 21

Even a wolf sometimes has to face what he is . . .

It was a mistake. His words reverberated through her head so she knew they had come out of his mouth. But he didn't mean it. She knew he didn't mean it. He couldn't have. He had made it clear they were not man and wife and now she knew how impossible it truly was because he was a duke. She understood his earlier resistance. She didn't even blame him. She couldn't be a duke's wife. She was a commoner. Less than that. A peasant who happened to be in possession of a first-rate education, but peasant no less. Marriage between them was impossible.

She swallowed and moistened her lips. "I fail to see . . ." She paused, searching for words, for a resounding denial to his outrageous announcement. "This changes nothing." Now her head was spinning in confusion. Before she had had a plan . . . a future that did not include him. Now she didn't know what to think. That's not true. She knew one thing. One thing for certain. More than ever they needed to go their separate ways.

Marcus's hard eyes fixed on her, but he said nothing. She waited, hoping he would retract his words, but he uttered not a sound.

She looked around rather helplessly at all the faces staring back at her, lingering on Nana, who had made the dramatic pronouncement that everything had *changed*. Whatever that meant.

Her gaze collided with Laird MacLarin and he shrugged as if he didn't know what his grandmother meant either.

"Is it true?" Nana asked evenly. "Are ye 'is wife?" She pointed at Marcus.

Alyse fidgeted. Marcus cocked that infernal eyebrow at her, daring her, challenging her to lie. "Well . . . in a manner. I suppose I am."

Nana didn't let her finish. She clapped her hands. "Fetch 'im a plate. Are ye 'ungry, sir? Forgive our lack of 'ospitality . . . and the abduction of yer wife." She shot a glare at her grandson.

He held his hands up in the air. "How was I tae ken? The Sassenach said she was 'is housekeeper," he blustered in defense even though his dark eyes glinted in humor.

"Scamp," Nana chastised without any heat. "Yer lucky ye be m' favorite grandson."

"I'm your only," he returned.

"Thank you for the offer, but I think I should just like to retire for the night," Marcus spoke up, gesturing to his disheveled person. "It's been a long day."

"'Course." Nana swerved her gaze pointedly on Alyse. "P'raps ye can show 'im tae yer chamber and treat 'is wounds?"

She felt herself scowl. *Her* chamber? She knew this monstrously large castle boasted more than enough bedchambers. "I am certain it would be more appropriate to show him to another room."

"Come now, lass." Nana clucked her tongue. "Dinna be an ill-tempered wife. No man wants that."

Releasing a gust of frustrated breath, Alyse lifted her skirts and turned, walking back the way she had come. It would do no good to argue. He'd announced them husband and wife and that was that as far as everyone here was concerned.

She heard him behind her but she didn't look back. Her blood simmered. Soon they'd be alone. Then she could unleash everything that was burning inside her. Her hands opened and closed at her sides as she fought for composure.

She located her chamber in the shadowy halls of the castle. The large fire still crackled in the hearth. It wasn't as big or as lavish as the room she'd slept in when they stayed with his brother, but it was still far finer than anything she had before. The four-post bed was a monstrosity and looked like something out of the Middle Ages with its ornate wood posts and headboard. A four-step stool was required to gain access to the bed.

She heard him close the door behind her.

Crossing her arms, she whirled around to face him.

He moved across the chamber and dropped in a wingback chair before the fireplace with a heavy groan. As though nothing untoward had happened.

He lifted a hand to his face, lightly probing his swollen jaw. She felt a twinge of pity that she quickly squashed. He would not have her sympathy. Not now when she was angry with him.

She stalked toward him, arms still crossed tightly over her chest. He dragged a hand through his hair, wincing.

That softened her somewhat. Slightly. Evidence of him in pain deflated some of her ire.

She was glad he wasn't dead, after all. Sighing, she dropped her arms and inched closer. Closer to him. "Why are you doing this?" she asked, her voice so low it was practically a whisper.

"Did you think I'd leave you here?"

"Why not? They wouldn't harm me."

"You don't know that."

"That's right." She snorted. "Trust no one."

He pointed at himself. "Have you seen me? They left me for dead."

"Aye, *you* for dead. Not me," she retorted.

"Oh, that's splendid. As long as they didn't wound you they are trustworthy." He glared at her and pushed to his feet. "And you *know* you would be safe here? With absolute certainty?"

"Nothing is certain in life. I don't know my fate with you . . . as your . . . whatever I am . . ." She stared at him, waiting, hoping he would fill in that silence so she could at least know what he was thinking and then she would have some indication as to what was happening here. This was when he would explain that he did not really consider them married—that he had just said that to appease the crowd downstairs.

Except he didn't do that.

"There's no point arguing about this. You're my wife. You heard me say it. They know that now." He shrugged. "And apparently they respect it."

"Stop saying that," she hissed.

"What?"

"That I'm your wife!" she exploded. "You know I am not."

He pushed to his feet. "You *are* my wife!"

His claim sparked something inside her. Fear. Hope. And that hope only made the fear twist tighter because she had no business feeling such a way. There was nothing to hope for with this man. They had no future.

"I've got the bill of sale to prove it." His words dropped like heavy rocks inside her, settling in the pit of her stomach.

Fury spiked through her. Fury at this world that deemed her property. Fury at he who would remind her of that and make her feel suddenly lower than she did when the auctioneer was shouting her attributes to a frothing crowd.

"No!" She slapped both hands against his chest and shoved. Hard. Hard enough to sting the palms of her hands. Hard enough to force him back a step. "Stop saying that. From the very beginning you've insisted we are *not* that. I've never been that to you! I'm simply your burden!" Her chest lifted with savage sobbing breaths. "I never will be your wife."

The words tore from her like a bandage being ripped free. She couldn't blink, couldn't look away from his face. A muscle pulsed to life in his jaw. He looked fierce—like some warrior walking into battle . . . or emerging from it. All that was missing was his sword.

Too late she realized her mistake. She was still

touching him. Her hands were still on his chest. His heart beat hard and fierce under her fingers.

She'd forgotten herself and laid hands on him.

She forgot who she was. A simple commoner without a penny to her name. And, more importantly, she forgot who he was. A duke moons above her.

There was no sound save the crash of their breaths filling the space between them. She slid back a step, but his hand shot out, looping around the back of her neck, hauling her close until all of her pushed up against the longer length of him.

It was like being pressed up against a living, breathing wall. A wall radiating its own heat. Their breaths collided, mingled. Their gazes devoured each other.

Then he broke. He moved. His head swooped down, his mouth claiming her own.

She couldn't move. Her hands were trapped between their bodies. His other arm stole around her, pulling her in tight, wrapping her up in him. It was impossible to break loose. Not that she wanted to. The moment his lips touched hers, she was lost.

His kiss was demanding, punishing and yet seductive. Her head swam as his mouth softened against her lips, coaxing. His fingers delved into her hair, fisting in the heavy mass and pulling her head back, better angling her mouth.

Her lips parted on a gasp, and his tongue slid along her bottom lip. Her blood sang, everything in her going soft. She opened her mouth wider, inviting him in. Their tongues touched and it felt like a bolt of lightning shot through her.

All hesitation fled. She leaned forward, diving into the kiss, into *him* like he was the air she so needed for survival.

He growled, deepening the kiss, his grip tightening in her hair. He took. He claimed, and that only made need pulse more swiftly inside her. Made *her* need *him* more.

She struggled to free her hands from between them, so that she could wrap her arms around his neck and climb inside him. There was no such thing as too close. No such thing as too much or too far. No such thing as impossible.

It was the longest kiss of her life. Not that she'd had many. Only chaste ones with Yardley and her recent ones with him . . . Marcus. She didn't know that a kiss could make her lips all tingly and numb. Her entire being ended and began where his mouth melded with hers. Sensation flooded every nerve in her body

Minutes ago there had been fury and now there was this. Desire. Want. Fury of another manner.

A twisting ache started at her core and spread like wildfire.

He broke away, one hand in her hair, an arm locked around her waist.

He looked down at her with blazing eyes.

She moistened her tingling lips. Her fingers flew there, touching the tender flesh. His eyes tracked the movement of her tongue. The dark blue of his eyes went darker, almost black.

She waited expectantly. She knew what would come next. He would pull away and put a stop to this. That's what he did the previous times.

Only that didn't happen.

His dark head swooped in and kissed her again. He picked her up in a sudden move and brought her body flush against his. He carried her . . . somewhere. She couldn't see and she didn't care. Her head spun, eyes closed as his mouth moved on hers. She opened her mouth wider and increased the fervency of their kiss, her tongue stroking and tasting his.

A growl rumbled up from his chest, vibrating into her. The sound made her feel desired. *Wanted* by this man with his too beautiful face and piercing dark eyes. A duke! She shoved that thought away. She didn't want to think about that right now.

He lowered her on the bed, following her down. He came over her, pushing the red material of her dress up to her hips so that her legs were bared and freed. He sat back and eyed her as he peeled her stockings off her legs, slow inch by slow inch, tossing each one aside. Finished, he paused to stare down at her with his relentless gaze. She fidgeted, her dress rustling around her.

"I should have been the one to put you in a fine dress."

She glanced down at the ruby fabric. He touched the edge of her bodice, pinching the fabric between his fingers as though testing the texture. "This makes your eyes glow."

She wanted to tell him the dress had nothing to do with making her eyes glow—that it was *him*. It was what he did to her. Instead, her hands went to the laces at the front of the dress. Loosening the ribbons with shaky fingers, she watched him under heavy lids.

He stilled, watching her fingers work. She loosened them enough so that her bodice gaped open, exposing her shift—along with the top swells of her breasts.

With a curse, he yanked off his jacket and vest, casting them aside with anxious movements. His hand went behind his neck and he pulled off his shirt in one move, sending it flying like a bird on the air. His hands gripped her thighs and she hissed at big hands on her flesh as he leaned over her, his big body fully wedged between her welcoming thighs.

Her hand drifted between them. She curled

her fingers around the edge of his trousers, letting her fingers slip inside, nails lightly scoring the tight skin of his abdomen. She watched him, transfixed by the intensity of his stare. He made her feel like she was at the center of his universe, this moment—*she*—was everything. This castle could crumble down around them and he would still be looking at her like this.

And she would still be wanting him.

She tugged him toward her. He fell forward, his hand falling beside her head on the bed, bracing himself. She didn't even care that she was acting the wanton.

He sucked in a breath as she slid her hand deeper inside his trousers, led by some impulse, some instinct that lived inside her. He was easy to locate. She wrapped her fingers around him. He filled her hand, overflowing. She gave his member a slight squeeze, and he pulsed, grew in her hand. A throb answered between her legs.

"Alyse," he panted, his own hand delving between her thighs, finding the slit in her drawers to touch her, stroke her, slide along her opening. He touched that little nub nestled at her center and she cried out, arching under him. His hand set to work, fingers rubbing in fierce circles, bringing her to a frenzy. Moaning, she ran her fingers into his hair, learning the shape of his skull beneath her palm. His head lowered, his breath moist and warm on her neck and it was all too much. Overwhelming. Her release welled back up inside her again. She couldn't stop it. She didn't want to. She rode the wave, arching under him.

He pushed, touched, stroked.

"God. You're so bloody responsive," he grunted against her mouth before claiming her lips in another scorching kiss full of their mingled pants and moans.

And then, suddenly, he pushed one finger deep inside her, curling up and touching her so deeply that she shattered, crying out loudly. Wildly. Unashamed.

His hand stayed between her legs. It was like he wasn't going to give up until he wrung out every last drop of joyful release from her.

Her hands dropped to her side to twist tightly in the bedding. She tossed her head from side to side, fighting the overwhelming sensations.

"Let go, Alyse," he commanded. "You can do it again."

With a choked cry, she did, breaking apart as his fingers toiled over her, not even slowing down as another wave overtook her. Her hands rolled over his shoulders, palms skating down the smoothness of his muscled back, ripples of feeling eddying throughout her.

This couldn't be her. A creature of passion.

Without shame. And yet it was. It was and she didn't regret it.

His member bulged in his trousers, prodding rock hard against the inside of her thigh. She was acutely, achingly aware that there was much left to explore between them. The hunger was still there, pulsing and throbbing in her . . . unanswered in him.

He made a deep sound in his throat and claimed her mouth in a kiss again, his fingers cupping her face. They kissed and kissed and kissed, stoking the fire hotter between them again. She didn't know kissing could be like this. So mind-addling. So consuming. Endless and yet not enough.

She gasped and his tongue entered her mouth, slicked over hers in total possession. She leaned in, moaning, giving as much as she took.

He muttered against her lips, pulling back to seize her gaping bodice and chemise. He yanked the material down to her waist, leaving her naked from the waist up.

Cool air wafted over her. Her hands covered her breasts self-consciously in an attempt to hide her chest from him. His fingers circled her wrists, exerting only slight pressure, but she was fully aware of his power, the strength in his big hands as he tugged her hands down.

"I want to see you," he whispered, his night-blue eyes dark and intense, moving down her throat to her breasts. Her nipples tightened under his stare.

He eased his hands off her wrists, and this time she didn't try to cover herself. She held still, stopping herself from covering her body up again.

She blocked out her embarrassment and focused on him, reveling in his breath-stealing beauty, the intensity of those deep-set eyes on her, the lush mouth.

She gasped at the first touch on her breast.

Her head dropped back and she moaned senselessly as he rolled both fingers over her rigid nipple. Back and forth, back and forth, he toyed with the peak, making the point harder with every swipe of his fingers.

"So beautiful," he growled. He turned to her other breast, rolling the quickly hardening nipple.

She squeaked as he pinched her pebble-smooth nipple. She felt a rush of wetness between her legs and she squirmed under him, desperate for relief, for the ache to be filled.

He looked at her from beneath heavy lids and then ducked his head. His hot mouth closed over the tip of her breast like he was starving and she the long-denied food.

She cried out as his warm tongue laved and

sucked her nipple. She grabbed the back of his head, pulling him closer, likely smothering him at her chest.

Everything in her tightened and squeezed, pleasure centering where his mouth fed on her, his tongue swirling wildly. Her core pulsed, clenching in agony.

She cried out again as he turned on her other breast, sucking hungrily, licking and nipping. Her noises were wild. Embarrassing. Especially when his teeth scraped one stiff nipple while his fingers simultaneously pinched down on the other one.

She rolled her head side to side on the bed. She felt out of control. Too wild, too removed from her own body. She inhaled a thick breath, fighting for control.

Then he was at her mouth again, kissing her. Savage kisses that she met with equal fervor. The possibility entered her mind that there would be no stopping this time.

He tunneled his hands into her hair, dragging the loosened mass.

"Please," she whimpered, writhing against him.

He hopped off the bed. She watched as he shed his trousers until he was naked beside the bed. "Oh, my," she breathed, allowing herself to have a good look at him. All of him. *All* of him.

All *all* of him. Her face caught fire and a trickle of unease ran through her. How was that going to fit inside her? As nervous as the sight of him made her, her core throbbed, almost hurting in her need to be filled.

He was big and looming and jutting straight out and it made her intimate parts clench in anticipation.

His lips curved in a cocky smile as he returned to the bed, doubtlessly reading her mind.

He slid back in between her thighs, his own solid thighs rubbing against hers. It was shocking for a moment, the sensation of a man against her, the hair on his skin tickling hers.

His hands touched her everywhere. Touching, stroking. She was bombarded with sensation, another climax rising up inside her again from all his ministrations.

His hands slid under her, cupping her derriere, lifting her up so that his manhood prodded at her entrance. She gasped. It was really happening. This . . . him . . . *them* . . .

"Please," she choked, reaching down between them, closing a trembling hand around him. Keeping a careful eye on his face, she wrapped him in her palm and pumped several times, enjoying the way the lines and firelit shadows of his face seemed to grow more stark, more torment-ridden.

His breathing grew ragged. "Enough." He grabbed her hand and peeled it off him.

His big hands gripped her thighs, holding her, splaying her wide as he settled between her, his manhood rubbing against her where she was wet and throbbing. She moaned slightly, tilting her hips up to him.

He looked down at her, all of him tense—one hard, lean line curved over her, ready to snap.

His thumb worked small circles inside her thighs as his gravel-deep voice stroked over her. "I feel as though this were inevitable . . . I was a fool to think otherwise."

Her eyes widened at that declaration. She must not let such words wheedle into her heart. This was not a matter of the heart. This was lust. Desire.

She looked down between them. Holding himself up with one hand, he fisted his manhood and guided himself to her.

She gasped as he started to slide inside her, all thoughts fleeing. Her hands flew to his arms, fingers clenching around his taut biceps as he filled her, easing in slowly, stretching her until he was buried to the hilt.

She felt her eyes widen, shocked at the unfamiliar sensation. She felt so full . . . so invaded . . . bursting with him.

"You feel perfect," he whispered against her mouth.

"And I feel you . . . *everywhere*," she returned, talking against his lips. He was all around her, over her . . . in her. She didn't know it could be this consuming.

Then the ability to speak was lost.

He started moving, holding her hips, positioning her in a way that built the friction and made her arch and cry out. Tears burned her eyes as everything tightened inside her. Snapped. Some invisible, coiling band broke and she came undone, her muscles going limp.

Marcus didn't stop. He didn't slow down as shudders overtook her. His hands slid under her and gripped her bottom, pushing her to that precipice again. "It's too . . . much."

"Run toward it," he panted. "Embrace it."

She relented with a moan.

He dropped over her, his mouth on her ear as he thrust in and out of her. Fast and hard. "That's it, sweetheart. Come again for me."

His deep voice served as its own aphrodisiac. She flew apart again. His arms wrapped around her, holding her tightly. With a few more strokes he joined her, crying out.

Their ragged breaths fogged the air between them. For a brief moment, she worried awkwardness would instantly follow. Regret. He would look at her with cold eyes.

Except that didn't happen.

Marcus rolled off her and left the bed, moving to the washstand. There was the splash of water and moments later he returned, sliding in the bed and pulling her against his side. He curled her leg around him, one hand splaying over her hip—and began to clean her with a damp cloth.

She made a strangling sound at the first stroke of the cloth against her and shrank away. "What are you—"

"Let me take care of you." His eyes fastened on her face in the dark.

They were quiet for a long time. She splayed a hand over his chest, fingers fanned over his warm skin, enjoying the feel of his heart against her palm.

She nodded and relaxed. He washed her in careful swipes. His ministrations were thorough, but detached, efficient. She shouldn't have felt anything . . . shouldn't have made an aroused little whimper. His hand stilled and his eyes locked on her.

Embarrassment sliced through her. She really was the wanton. She wanted to bury her face.

The washcloth disappeared between them and then it was his fingers again, toying with her oversensitive folds. She grabbed on to his wrist, "Marcus, we can't . . . not again."

"Oh, I'll give you some time. I won't ill-use you," he promised, his eyes glittering in the fire-cast room, but his fingers continued to stroke and play over her swollen mound.

Her head rolled on the pillow. "Then . . . what are you—"

He slid down between them, between her thighs. He wedged himself down there . . . his head down *there*.

"Marcus!" she shrieked at the first swipe of his tongue, her hands flying to his hair and gripping fistfuls. What he was doing . . . she didn't know it was done . . . it had to be *wrong*. Wicked.

"I've dreamed of tasting you." His voice rumbled against her most intimate flesh.

Her shriek faded into a moan as his tongue loved her thoroughly, latching on to that tiny nub that made her quake and weep. He sucked and she bucked under him, instantly flying, bursting, shattering. His lips continued to pull and his tongue rolled over the little button of pleasure. He worked her as her climax rode out, until tears streamed from her eyes and a fine sheen of perspiration coated her heaving chest.

Sated and thoroughly ruined, she went limp.

Vaguely, she felt him move and drop beside her. Felt him pull her against him, his warm arm wrapping around her waist. She opened her mouth to say something. She felt like she should. After something as profound as that, she certainly should say *something*.

But her eyelids drifted shut, heavy as twin stones. No words passed between them.

Chapter 22

*Occasionally, in a sudden change of light, the dove
imagined her cage door was opening. And then
she realized it was just a play of the light.
She was still trapped.*

Marcus left her asleep, curled up, spent
and luscious in a bed that could sleep an army.
He didn't imagine he could sleep, so he went in
search of a drink and found one in a room set off
from the great hall. He poured a glass and sank
down in a chair, grateful for the warmth of the
fire in the hearth.

"Stealing my whisky, are ye?"

The voice startled him. Marcus's hand jerked
and whisky sloshed over his fingers and dribbled down onto the floor.

"Mind what ye do there . . . that's fine whisky."

He glanced over to where the young laird sat, shrouded in shadows on a corner sofa. He shrugged. "You steal my wife. I steal your whisky. Seems ye are on the winning side of this." Tilting his head, he took a deep drink from his glass.

The laird chuckled. "It seems you reclaimed your fair bride. I'll never reclaim that whisky sliding down your throat so I'm no' thinking I'm the winner here, ye ken?"

Marcus shook his head in amusement. "Well, we're to be neighbors. I'm sure over time we shall impose on each other too many times to keep count."

The Scot propped both elbows on his knees and leaned forward, putting his face into better view. The scant firelight threw the angles of his face into stark, hard lines—all angles and hollows. He couldn't be much over twenty years of age, and yet he looked fierce and hardened. A man already . . . a man for some years. Nothing like the young men Marcus saw about Town. Dandies with soft hands and softer middles more concerned about their diversions.

"Interesting, Lord Autenberry." He nodded rather smugly. "Aye, I put it together after yer wife addressed ye by title. Yer family has always been in possession of Kilmarkie House and its attached lands, but never in my lifetime has anyone

occupied it. Are ye saying ye plan tae stay then?"
His dark eyes fixed on him with intensity.

"I might well stay awhile, yes," Marcus replied
with a slow nod.

He hadn't yet arrived at Kilmarkie and seen
it for himself, but London seemed a world away.
For all the rigors of traveling, he was enjoying
these lands. The Highlands agreed with him and
he was eager to explore his property. The Highlands weren't all he was enjoying. *You're enjoying
Alyse, too.*

He meant what he had said. She was his wife.
He wouldn't go back on his word. Perhaps they
could begin forging their lives together at Kilmarkie House where they would be on more
equal footing . . . both a pair of newcomers. The
place would neither be his nor hers but *theirs.*
Eventually he'd bring her to London, of course,
and introduce her to his family, but for now he
would take this time. For her. For *them.*

"This is verra unexpected—Kilmarkie House
tae be alive wi' yer noble presence. Well, that is
something. I dinna ken how I feel about that."

"I was not aware that you had any say in the
matter."

"Oh . . . ye will soon learn that I 'ave a great
deal of say in what goes on in these parts. Nothing 'appens about here that is no' my concern."

"Perhaps," Marcus allowed. "But that was

before I got here." Kilmarkie House sat on a large portion of land north of here. It belonged to Marcus. What occurred there was *his* concern. *His* responsibility. The land and the livelihood of the people who lived there fell to him.

The laird chuckled. "Ye're a right arrogant bastard. But I would expect no less from an English lord."

"You're no English lord," Marcus retorted. "What is your excuse then?"

The younger man hooted. "I 'spect I am an arrogant bastard . . . but no one in these parts save my Nana is so bold tae say so."

Marcus shook his head. "Glad to introduce you to new experiences."

Why did it feel as though he was conversing with a man still stuck in the Dark Ages? A Highland laird, ready to wield his battle-ax with anyone who dared cross his land.

The man rather reminded him of Mackenzie. Perhaps it was just the brogue . . . or the size of the lad. He certainly was big for one of tender years. "How old are you?" he asked abruptly.

"I will be one and twenty in a fortnight."

As he had guessed. Still. Marcus scoffed.

"Aye, young tae one as ancient as ye." Mac-Larin flashed a grin.

Chuckling, Marcus shook his head, thinking of himself at the age of twenty. He certainly wasn't as intense as this young man. He was all about staying out all night and bedding actresses and lonely widows. He realized with a start that he wouldn't have liked himself were he to meet the young man he had been today.

Hell. He didn't even like the version of himself he had been a few weeks ago. He'd been a spoiled privileged snot, nursing wounds that he now realized were flimsy grievances. He stared into the fire's licking flames, wondering what had prompted this change in attitude.

And then he knew the answer.

Alyse, of course.

Alyse was the reason. A humble farm girl was the reason he went from a shallow individual to someone who wanted a life of meaning.

She had humbled him . . . and he was desperate for her.

"And wot does yer wife think of yer plans? Is she content tae be a duchess stuck in the wilds of Scotland?"

The question gave him pause, of course, because he didn't know. He didn't know what Alyse felt at all about staying at Kilmarkie House.

He didn't know what she felt about him.

HE RETURNED TO their chamber after finishing a second drink with MacLarin. He stood at the side of the big bed and studied her by the light of the fire.

Her eyelids flickered and he wondered at her dreams. Hopefully, they were peaceful. Stripping off his clothes, he pulled back the covers and slid in beside her.

Sleep, however, remained elusive. He dozed in and out through the waning night, staying close to her, loath to peel himself from her side. One of his hands lingered on her body at all times. As though he needed that contact . . . that assurance that she was still near him.

Watching her curled up on her side, the bedding wrapped enticingly around her naked body, his mind skirted around tricky thoughts. Such as were they really married? He'd convinced himself that their transaction in the village square did not constitute a binding marriage. That being the case, they would need to rectify that.

She murmured incoherently and fidgeted. He rubbed her arm soothingly and she relaxed as though his touch calmed her.

She was the sweetest thing he had ever touched. She was good and pure and deserved better than him, but she was his. Their lives had collided and tangled together that day in Collie-Ben and it was too late for anything else. There would be no untangling of them.

He brought his hand up in the small space

between them, trailing his fingers up and down the exposed ladder of her spine, relishing the feel of her skin, the bump of every vertebra.

She shivered and stirred and he slid down deeper into the bed against her, burrowing under the covers. He curled alongside her body, her back to his chest, spooning her with his longer length. He wanted to learn everything about her . . . know her shape and scent as well as he knew himself.

"How are you awake?" she whispered into the thick space around them, letting him know she was awake without turning around to face him.

Her breath fanned against the pillow, rasping the cotton. He was so attuned to her. Every little sound and movement. He'd never felt this connected with another person. It was rather alarming. His fingers brushed the silk of her hair off her nape. He couldn't stop touching her.

"Hard to sleep next to you."

She turned her head to look back at him, a ghost of a smile tracing her lips. "You're going to be exhausted tomorrow."

"I won't complain. It will be a good kind of exhaustion."

He slid farther down on the bed, until they were face-to-face, nose to nose. Her lids were still heavy. She sighed sleepily. She was tired. He'd worn her out.

She rolled over and brought her smooth palm to his face. She held his cheek. "You're starting to bruise," she tsked. "Does your face hurt?"

"No." He slipped his arm around her waist and pulled her lush curves more firmly against him. She was deliciously warm wrapped around him. His hand slid down her back and cupped the swell of one cheek, using his grip to haul her even more firmly against him. He gave it a firm squeeze and her breath caught on a whimper. She was so soft with her sweet-smelling hair and rounded ass.

His body knew her now. Wanted her. His desire for her hadn't even been whetted. It wasn't close to being quenched.

Without calculation, he rolled her so that her back was flush against his chest. He curled a hand around her hip and dipped down her navel to her beckoning quim. Her thighs parted sweetly at the first foray of his fingers. He eased inside her clenching heat. She was wet. Soaking for him. He thrust his fingers, pumping into her contracting channel.

She cried out and moaned his name, rubbing her backside against his cock. With a growl, he removed his hand from inside her and seized hold of her hips, lifting her to her knees on the bed so that she was on all fours before him.

He admired the swells of her ass, smoothing

both hands over the firm cheeks. She trembled and sent him a heavy-lidded glance over her shoulder. Hot want gleamed in her eyes . . . along with a fair amount of uncertainty. She wasn't sure about this position.

His lips curved in a knowing smile. "You're going to like this," he promised. He parted her thighs for him and touched her again, stroking the entrance to her core. He eased a finger inside her again, reveling at her low, keening moan. He couldn't wait. He removed his hand and slid inside her, pushing his cock deep.

Tight heat surrounded him and he ground down against her, pumping faster, sliding through her slick wetness. Nothing had ever felt this good. So perfect.

"Marcus!" she cried, her hands fisting the bedding, her knuckles whitening.

"I told you," he panted. "You would like it."

"I love it!" she gasped and he felt a flood of wetness come over his cock. Her core tightened and pulsed all around him. "You're . . . Oh. My! What's happening?"

Her sharp cries filled his ears and his hands slid around her rib cage, found her breasts, molding the plump mounds as he rolled her over, pinning her under him and working in and out of her body in a fast frenzy.

"Lord, help me! Marcus! Yes, yes, yes . . ."

The sound of his name drove him into a frenzy. As her quim grew ever tighter around him, closing and squeezing him like a fist, he pumped in and out of her, crashing into her. He pushed and pulled and erupted with a groan, spilling himself deep inside her sweet, milking heat.

He collapsed on the pliant body under him, feeling as warm and satiated as he had ever felt. It had never before been like this with a woman and the sudden thought shook him. Left him desperate and as vulnerable as a newborn. That was how he felt then. Newly born in this moment.

She cleared her throat from under him. "Uh, you're a little heavy."

"My apologies." He lifted himself up into a sitting position.

He fixed his eyes on her as she lifted into a sitting position beside him. She pushed her long tangle of hair from her face and looked at him rather reticently.

"That was . . ." she began and then a blush stole over her face. After all that, she was still capable of blushing. She was still his innocent bride. He rather suspected a part of her always would be.

He reached out and brushed a finger against her cheek. "I enjoy your blushes." She ducked her head with a timorous smile. "I look forward to doing many more things that prompt the color to rise in your face."

She lifted her gaze back up, arching an eyebrow in interest. "Indeed?"

"I promise you that."

SHE WOKE TO an empty bed. Dawn tinged the room a purpling blue. Somehow he had roused himself before her despite how little they had slept. She'd think that after the night they had—in addition to the fact that he had been trounced by a band of Highlanders—he would have slept like the dead.

Her arm stretched out beside her, searching and finding nothing. Sitting up, she clutched the bedcovers to her chest and rubbed at her eyes. She couldn't have slept very long. A few hours maybe. She had fallen back to sleep after their second bout of lovemaking and their talk of blushes.

Her hand drifted over her stomach, sliding up to her sensitive breasts. It had been faster. Frenzied. Needier if possible than the first time. That position had been wild. Primitive. She came apart in a way that she could never have dreamed.

She stretched her body, wincing at her aching muscles. She was an early riser but she was convinced she could sleep until afternoon.

It wasn't even light out yet. The purpling blue was turning into the barest gray of dawn now, pressing against the mullioned pane of the chamber's single arched window.

A rustling sound captured her attention and she turned, tracking the source. Marcus sat before the fire, already dressed, sliding on his boots.

"Marcus?" she queried in a tremulous voice before she could think better of it.

He turned and for a moment they simply stared at one another across the room. Everything hovered between them, the intimacy of the night before, the memory of his body sliding against her, into her over and over . . .

Heat singed her face and that felt silly. Despite his seeming approval of her blushes, it felt silly.

After everything, her face shouldn't be so quick to catch fire. She should be more composed than this. He was undoubtedly accustomed to taking much more sophisticated women to his bed. And then she flinched at the thought of him with other women. Why did she have to think of that?

"I wanted us to get an early start," he said. "We're close and I'm becoming anxious to finally see Kilmarkie."

She nodded jerkily. "Oh. Yes. Of course."

Coward. It wasn't what she was thinking. She couldn't find the nerve to say any of the things she was thinking. All the many things she was thinking.

So many questions whirled around her mind.

What were they to each other?

Had things in fact changed like Nana proclaimed?

Did he mean what he said last night now in the light of day?

Did he consider her his wife?

And yet despite all those questions running through her mind, something else blurted from her lips. Something she had not anticipated even asking.

"What are you running from?"

He stopped. Stared. "I'm not running from anything."

"It's just you have never been to Kilmarkie House before . . . and yet you've been so very determined to reach there."

"I'm not running from anything, Alyse," he repeated. The warmth had bled from his eyes. He looked stern. Distant. Cold even. It was a hard thing to reconcile after the inferno that had raged between them last night.

"I'll leave you to get dressed and go ready our mounts," he added, clearly finished with the subject. "I'll ask a servant to fetch us a breakfast, too."

She nodded, still clutching the covers over her nudity. He snatched up his coat and left the chamber. The door clicked shut behind him.

She dropped her head back down on the bed with a sigh. She needed to get up and get dressed so they could resume their journey.

She supposed there was no question of her staying here. Not after last night. She would be leaving with him.

And yet she still had other nagging questions. She didn't know what she was to him. She no longer felt like his employee. They were much too familiar now. She had never been a house-keeper before, but she was certain a soon-to-be-housekeeper didn't interact with the master of the house the way they did. Not a proper house-keeper, at least.

Nor did she feel like his wife, though. That would make her a duchess and that could never be. Awkward or not, she would still be his employee. That would be less awkward than becoming his wife.

With a groan, she flung back the covers and stood, determined to get dressed before he returned.

She knew about persevering. About squaring her shoulders and moving ahead despite everything. Despite all disappointments and pain. This was just more of the same. It should feel quite customary by now.

When he returned, she'd be ready to depart.

MARCUS LEFT THEIR bedchamber shaken. He paused outside the room and leaned his back against the cold stone wall of the corridor, letting the chill seep through his garments and into his skin. Her voice echoed through his head. *What are you running from?*

Her eyes told him she did not believe his denial. Hell, even he didn't believe himself.

How did she see into him so clearly? It was hard enough to cope with the fact that he felt such a deep and growing attachment to Alyse. Must the girl now peer with such ease into his very soul?

The truth of the matter . . . the thing he had *not* admitted to her was that he had been running from himself when he left London. At least in the beginning it had been that way.

Now, strangely, he felt as though he were running *to* himself on this journey.

Somewhere along the road north, he had reached a level of peace with life that he had never known.

With her at his side, he had found himself. He had found the man he wanted to be.

They were words he was not ready to admit to her, but they were there nonetheless. A truth he was only now seeing and accepting. A truth he would reveal to her in good time.

THEY REACHED KILMARKIE House the following afternoon, which only hammered home the fact that the laird who abducted her was Marcus's closest neighbor. That might make for awkward relations if the laird seemed inclined to harbor any ill will toward him. Somehow, she thought his bark greater than his bite, though.

He may have thrashed Marcus and abducted her, but MacLarin behaved as though that was all water under the bridge.

They moved along a narrow path and crested a great hill. She could taste the sea wind. It was funny how you knew what something was without having to be told—or without having ever experienced it before.

The briny air sat thick on her skin. As they cleared the hill, they both stopped and looked down the grassy slope.

It dawned on her that she wasn't the only one seeing Kilmarkie for the first time. He was, too. This place was all his to do with as he wished. Whether it prospered or fell to great disrepair was all on him. She slid a look at him.

The wind ruffled his dark hair as he stared out at the view.

"It's beautiful," she remarked of the sprawling stone structure. The broad manor house was constructed of varying shades of gray stone and dark wood beams. The dark sea glinted a distance behind it. The shore was riddled with rocks of pale pink. She'd never seen anything like it.

"It is beautiful," he agreed.

Squinting, she noticed rippling pockets out on the bay. "Are those . . ." Her voice faded breathlessly as a sleek dark body arced out of the water.

"Dolphins," he finished.

"Incredible." Excitement bubbled in her chest. She might just love this place. That would certainly help her endure her time here, however long that may be. She'd have that view . . . that shoreline to walk whenever the fancy struck.

Gazing out at the water, she felt lighter. Buoyed. That sentiment only grew and solidified once she passed through the threshold and stood in the high-beamed foyer of the house. She oohed over the well-worn stone floor, rotating in a small circle as Marcus chatted with the caretaker, Mr. Shepard, listening with half an ear.

"Sorry my missus is feeling poorly. She would 'ave liked tae greet ye both," Mr. Shepard was saying.

"No need. I assume the nearby village boasts able-bodied men and women."

"Yes, Your Grace." The older gentleman looked between the two of them curiously. "Yer staying fer a spell then?"

Marcus nodded. "Yes." He glanced around their surroundings as though firmly deciding he did indeed like the place. He shot her a glance. "As is my wife."

My wife.

There it was then. He was claiming her as his wife again. This time not to a room full of strangers well into their cups. No. He was proclaiming it to the head of his household staff. According to him, she was the Duchess of Autenberry. And this grand home was hers as much as it was his.

She never felt more of a fraud.

She glanced around the foyer again, but this time her excitement had ebbed. In its place was a hollow sensation. She was his wife. He'd claimed her as such. Not out of love or affection but because of obligation. She brought nothing to this union and yet she was his wife.

If only it were that simple.

His saying it didn't make it so. Marriage was more than that.

And she wanted more. No half measures. She wanted all of it or nothing at all.

* * *

THE MASTER AND mistress of the house had their own adjoining rooms. Mr. Shepard showed them to their chambers together. Both rooms shared a balcony, which faced the sea. She lingered on the balcony, marveling that she would wake each day to a view of dolphins.

"I can rouse the kitchen girl, Helen, tae prepare ye both dinner," Mr. Shepard called to her. "She's a right fine 'and in the kitchen. Ken 'er way around a soup pot, she does," Mr. Shepard offered as he hovered in the threshold, worrying his hands together before him. "It may no' be tae yer normal quality—"

"We've been journeying for many days." Alyse emerged from the balcony, cutting him off, hating that he thought she was some fine lady accustomed to fine quality. It made her feel a liar and a fraud. "We aren't particular."

He started as though to leave and then stopped himself. "Well, if ye will permit me tae say so, Yer Grace—"

She could not stop herself from flinching at the designation.

"—we are ever so 'appy tae 'ave ye 'ere. The duke and yerself. This place 'as been vacant far far too long. It will be good tae see life bloom 'ere once again."

She stifled her wince at his kind and supportive words. In her he did not see someone unacceptable, someone unfit to preside as lady of the house. He did not see the truth. Or at least he wouldn't dare let it be known if he did. But she knew.

She would always know. That is the only thing that mattered.

Others would know, too, she reminded herself.

"My thanks to you, Mr. Shepard. You are very kind."

He nodded his head obligingly and backed out from the room. "I will see tae yer dinner tray and send one of the lasses up to 'elp ye unpack."

Unpack. That was almost humorous. She only had a single valise to her name. Only a few belongings within it and yet a maid would come to assist her. That girl would know it at once. She would know the fraud Alyse perpetrated and tell others. The rest of the staff of Kilmarkie House would know.

She took a deep breath and chided herself not to be so anxious. It mattered naught. She wouldn't be here for long.

Mr. Shepard inclined his head and then ducked out of the room to see about their dinner.

She returned to the balcony and that stunning view that beckoned her. Her husband stood there, admiring the sight as well. They stood in restful silence for a few moments. It was easy to forget all one's worries. All tensions just melted away when she stared out at the sea.

"Well," he said after some moments staring out at the sea. "We made it here."

She nodded before releasing a slow breath. "Why did you tell him I was your wife?" It would only make things more difficult for him . . . later. When she was gone.

"Because you are my wife." He arched his eyebrow at her and gave her a sardonic look that seemed to say: *naturally*.

"That's what you said to get me back . . . I didn't think you truly meant it."

"There are certain things men never say unless true. The claim to be married is one of them."

The wind picked up off the sea, fluttering the loose hair fringing her face. "But it's not true."

"We made it true last night. Our marriage is consummated. It's official now. No going back now."

She studied his face, trying to read him. He sounded resigned. Not happy. Of course. But there was something in his eyes, in his flat voice.

Disappointment.

Understandably. She couldn't be the wife he'd imagined for himself.

She swallowed and looked away, out at the sea again. It was hard seeing that in his face, knowing it to be true. She couldn't imagine seeing it for a lifetime.

She didn't intend to.

SHE WENT TO bed alone in another great four-post monstrosity (clearly the rich and noble never slept in anything of normal proportion), listening to the sound of the sea outside her chamber. Distant, steady waves washed along the shoreline, the sound rhythmic and mesmerizing. She wondered if it was ever warm enough to sleep with the balcony doors open—and then she reminded herself that it wouldn't matter. She would not be here in the summer months to find out.

She went to bed alone, but she didn't stay alone for very long.

She had not yet fallen asleep when she heard the adjoining door open.

She felt him stop and stand over the bed, near enough to touch her. His presence radiated energy . . . fire. "You're awake." It was not a question. A statement.

"Yes."

Pause.

"Do you want me to go?"

He was giving her a choice. Her life had been one of few choices.

She thought about how he was the kind of man who did the right thing. When he saved her on that auction block. When he'd taken her to Glasgow and imposed on the brother whom he had no relationship with in order to save her life. When he saved her from brigands.

This—coming to her in the night—was the only thing he did out of selfish want. Need. Desire.

She pulled back the covers and he slid in beside her and took her in his arms. He kissed her and she melted into him.

It would be so easy, so tempting, to fall into this night after night. Again and again. To forget why she couldn't stay. To let it happen.

To pretend she was some kind of wife in reality to him. Except she knew.

She knew the truth.

She was not the wife of his choosing. She would always know that. She would have that knowledge for all her days. Deep down he would know it.

She couldn't do it. She couldn't live like that.

This wasn't enough. Desire wasn't enough either.

Coming together in the dark of night like two people trysting in secret. Like what they did was shameful, to be saved for the cover of darkness.

Still, she was helpless to resist him. To resist

herself. Just the sensation of him over her, his big body wedged between her thighs, set her afire. He pulled back slightly, pushing the tangle of covers aside in an attempt to free them. "Damn bedding," he muttered.

As his hands reached for the hem of her nightgown and pulled it up and over herself, she lifted her hips to help him. To help herself. Because she couldn't deny herself this one last time. She couldn't deny her own selfish need.

Free of her nightgown, his hands skimmed up the outside of her calves and then roamed over her thighs. "I dreamt of these," he growled. "They're strong and sleek." He slid down between her knees, pushing her thighs wider to make room for his head and shoulders.

"Marcus," she breathed, her hands reaching for his head.

"Let me taste you," he murmured, seduction dripping in every word. Heavens. He was wicked—and she reveled in it. His fingers grazed the outside of her knees in teasing circles that made her limbs shake. He turned his face to trail kisses along the inside of her thighs, his tongue darting out to lick. His teeth occasionally biting and nipping and making her jerk in delight.

Her hands lifted above her head and grabbed fistfuls of pillow. She arched, loud, undignified pants escaping her, broken by the occasional yelp.

With a groan, he crawled above her and latched on to her nipple. She felt the perfect prod of his cock against her barrierless sex. He teased her there, tormenting her. Not yet penetrated. His eyes looked up at her, devilish and taunting.

"Marcus, please," she begged.

"Please, what?" he murmured, his mouth talking around the aching nipple he was working with his tongue, lips and teeth.

"Oh, you're a wicked man."

He flicked her nipple with his tongue. "Please, what?"

"Take me."

"You're going to have to be clearer with your words, Your Grace."

She didn't even care at the designation. Not then. Not with her body tightened like a bow beneath him.

"Marcus," she complained again, writhing . . . at a loss.

He moved to her other breast, sucking the nipple deep into his mouth as his hand came up to squeeze the other one, his finger and thumb clamping down on the distended peak. She screamed, coming up off the bed as she flew apart. "What. Are. You. Doing. To. Me?" A hot breath punctuated every word as her entire body convulsed.

He moved then, sliding down her body and dropping between her splayed legs. His mouth covered her, drinking her climax deep. She jerked, startled at the sensation of his mouth on her.

"Say it," he prodded, bucking harder against her aching core, grinding his manhood against her sex. "Oh, you're soaking, sweetheart."

Heat flamed her face at his words.

His mouth continued its assault between her legs, sucking at the little nub of pleasure hidden there, taking it deep into his mouth until she forgot everything. Her name, her title—real or false.

She cried out, her fingers clawing through his hair as his hands slid under her, gripping her backside and pulling her closer to his face. He pulled her to his mouth, sucking her between his lips, savoring her with hard licks.

He continued to taste her, drowning in her, it seemed. It would be mortifying . . . if it didn't feel so amazingly good. The tension began again, throbbing in her core and twisting throughout her. She started to shake and rock against his questing tongue. He settled deeper between her thighs, adjusting his hands under her bottom and lifting her higher for him. The torment was endless and yet not nearly enough.

The wicked man feasted on her. She screamed and cried out . . . aware that the entire household could likely hear her. They would know what the duke was doing to her. Still, it did not stop the sounds from tearing from her throat. That was a physical impossibility as long as he continued his sensual assault.

Her fingers clenched in his hair as he increased his mouth's pressure, his tongue playing with her sensitive flesh until she was senseless, tears leaking from her eyes as he hurled her back into the heavens again.

She cried out, pushing into his mouth wantonly and without shame.

Then he added his hand to the mix. As he thrummed his tongue over that tiny pleasure bud nestled in her sex, he slid a finger inside her, pushing deep and hard, curling inward in a way that made her come out of her skin and scream his name.

"That's it, Alyse. Say it. Tell me what you need."

He established a rhythm, pushing and pulling in and out of her body, playing her like an instrument.

She released a muffled screech, convulsing all around him, coming apart yet again, her channel tightening around his finger.

He lifted his body up. She still shook from the impact, clinging to his shoulders. His devilishly satisfied eyes locked on to hers in the darkness. "I'm still waiting to hear it from you, Alyse."

She stared back at him, her heart pound like a drum in her chest. "W-waiting for what?"

"For you to say what you want." His eyes locked on her, encouraging, willing her to let go and embrace this *thing* between them.

"I," she started and moistened her lips. Lifting her chin, she finally said the words he was waiting to hear. "I want you to make love to me, Marcus."

A slow smile spread across his features.

As he came over her, she welcomed him into her body, gasping as he sank deep inside her ready heat. She reveled in the moment, wrapping her thighs around his hips and scraping her nails down his back and telling herself it would be enough for the lonely years to come. The glorious memory of this would be enough.

It had to be.

Chapter 23

*Her cage was gone. But she felt unchanged
just the same. Trapped as always.*

He wasn't in bed with her when she woke.
He was gone. Again. She shoved aside the hurt.
It made things easier after all.

She dressed herself quickly and repacked her
valise. On her way downstairs she bumped into
Helen, the kitchen maid who made their dinner
last night. She carried a tray laden with food in
her hands. She blinked and looked Alyse up and
down, not missing the fact that she was dressed
for the outdoors in her cloak and boots and carrying her valise in her hand.

"Good morning, Your Grace. Your husband

said I should bring breakfast up to you this morning."

Alyse stopped one step above her and perused the tray, ignoring how odd it felt to be addressed in such a manner. She selected a delicious-looking iced bun the size of her head off the tray. "Thank you. This looks scrumptious."

"You're welcome, Your Grace." The maid glanced inquiringly at her bag clutched in her hand. "Could I help you with something . . ." Her voice faded away suggestively. Clearly she was curious as to what Alyse was about.

She forced a bright smile. "No, thank you. I am quite well." She wiggled her bun in the air. "This is all I need. Thank you for this. I'm sure I will quite enjoy it." Bestowing another smile on the bewildered-looking girl, she stepped around her and descended the stairs.

Once outside she made haste for the stables, hurriedly devouring her bun and eyeing the grounds for a glimpse of Marcus. This would be easier to do if she didn't have to see him. Easier on her aching heart.

In the stables, she set her bag aside and went in search of her mule.

There were other horses, of course. Bucky was missing and she assumed that Marcus had taken him to do whatever errand he was about. She knew any of the other horses would be faster than her mule. But that didn't feel right. It almost felt like a trial to pick another horse at this point. The mule was hers. She didn't feel like a thief taking it. Taking another horse would make her feel like she was sneaking off with something that didn't belong to her.

She saddled the mule and secured her valise. Fortunately he was small enough she didn't even need the mounting block.

The mule felt like an old friend. After his customary greeting nip of her flesh, they settled into a familiar routine. He plodded along at a snail's pace. Only without Marcus to lead, the mule would occasionally slow to a complete stop and stare off into the tree line. She would have to do everything just to get him moving again.

At this rate it would take a year to reach London. She sighed, wondering if she should have taken one of the horses in Marcus's stables, after all, whether it felt like stealing or not.

She had hoped to reach the village by noon but it was nearing dusk when she rode into town.

She'd have to stay the night. She had a small purse she hoped to make stretch until she reached London and found work. If she had to, she'd stop at a town along the way and work to build up some funds. If necessary she could sell the mule in Glasgow and take the train south.

That seemed the wisest course of action. But then she had to reach Glasgow first.

And sell her mule. The prospect produced a pang near her heart. Strange as it seemed, this mule was tangled up in Marcus. It was all she had of him. All she had left.

After stabling her mule, she entered the inn from the night before. The innkeeper recognized her and rounded at the counter with a warm greeting. "Welcome! Welcome! I didn't expect tae see ye two back so soon." He looked beyond her shoulder as though expecting Marcus to appear. He probably assumed he was outside yet handling their horses.

She smiled wanly. "Thank you," she murmured. "It is only I tonight seeking accommodations."

"Ah." He frowned as though understanding, but it was clear he did not. Doubtlessly the questions whirled around his mind. Ever the proper businessman, he pasted a smile back on his face and gestured her toward the taproom. "Would you like to warm yourself by the fire with some tea while we ready your room?"

She blew out a breath and rubbed her gloved hands together. "That would be lovely. I confess I am quite chilled."

He waved her ahead to the room she had briefly occupied the night before. She entered the room and walked a straight line toward the fire, not noticing until she arrived at its crackling warmth that another person already sat in a chair before it.

"Oh. Good evening," she greeted the other patron distractedly, shooting him a quick glance—and then yelped. She slapped her hand over her mouth in shock and jumped back a small step. "What are *you* doing here?"

The man in the chair rose to his feet. "Alyse . . . I've come for ye." He brushed his hands over his trousers as though shaking loose crumbs. She glanced at the table to indeed find a plate of food there. She'd caught him in the midst of a meal.

She looked around the room in bewilderment. "You came for me here? At the inn?"

"Well, I stopped 'ere tae change clothes and freshen up. I didn't want tae look a complete waster when I came tae ye. I've come tae apologize. Tae make everything right. Tae make good on my vow tae ye." His thin chest puffed up. "Tae do what I should have done the first time."

She shook her suddenly spinning head. "How did you even find me? How did you know—"

"Nellie told me."

Of course Nellie would have told him. She would have been worried about Alyse. She would have thought that Yardley was her only salvation and she was doing Alyse a favor telling him of her whereabouts.

Emotion thickened her throat. "You abandoned me, Yardley. You were my friend. You promised . . ." Too choked up, her voice faded. And yet even as she said the words she was heartily *glad*. Relieved. For if he hadn't she would never have met Marcus. She would have never known what it was like to love him.

She pulled back with a startling hiss. She loved him. She did. And yet she was leaving him. Sudden doubts assailed her. Should she not stay? Stay and fight for him? Win his love?

Yardley reached for her and she sidestepped him. He looked crestfallen as he dropped his hand back to his side. "I ken. I made a mistake . . . a colossal mistake. I was foolish. I panicked at the notion of marriage." He nodded somberly, both his eyes as wide as the moon. "I mean it is verra permanent. It's forever."

She nodded back, wondering if he had always been this dim. Or had she been the dim one, seeing so much more in him than there really was? "Yes. I'm aware."

"Please say ye will forgive me. Please say ye will come wi' me. We can go tae London. We can go anywhere. We can have that life we wanted together. The one we talked about."

He was saying all the right things. She should be happy. She should leap on what he was offering her and yet his words felt hollow. There was no temptation in them.

Suddenly another voice spoke. A deep familiar voice. "You should go."

She spun around, her heart hammering like a wild drum in her chest. "Marcus?" Marcus stood there, tall and beautiful, snow dusting his great shoulders.

He was here. He had come after her.

He had come after her and found her like this. With Yardley. He had heard Yardley's declaration and he was letting her go. He was giving his blessing to this. And why wouldn't he? It was giving him a way out. An escape from her. It was freeing him of his responsibility to her at last.

She nodded, fighting back tears. "Of course. Yes. I will."

His expression was stony as he stared at her. He didn't even spare a glance for Yardley. He held her gaze as he reached inside his vest pocket and pulled out a folded piece of parchment. She frowned for a moment, not comprehending . . .

Until she did.

Understanding dawned on her.

He held the parchment up in the air before her and tore it asunder. "You are free. Free to go. Free to be with whoever you want to be with." The scraps of parchment fluttered between them, the bill of sale for *her* landing with a whisper on the taproom floor.

That was it then. All it took. He was freeing her to do as she wished. To go with Yardley. To live out that dream of a life with this boy that she had spent so many years fostering. She could do what she had set out to do from the very start.

So why did she hurt so much?

"Only there is one other thing I must do before I let you both go," Marcus added.

"Oh?" She watched him, baffled at what he could possibly have left to do after that very dramatic destruction of her bill of sale.

"Yes." He turned to face Yardley and with no worry, punched him squarely in the face.

Her childhood friend went down hard. His hand immediately covered his spurting nose. Blood seeped out between his fingers. "Wot was that fer?" his nasally voice cried out.

Alyse gawked.

Marcus stabbed a finger in her direction. "For abandoning her. Do you know what could have happened to her had I not been there? The abuse and misery . . ." Marcus's face twisted with rage. "You're lucky I don't haul you outside and give you the true thrashing you deserve. If you ever hurt or disappoint her again, I'll come for you. And the next time, there will only be pieces

of you left. Understand me, lad? Make her happy
or I will end you."

Her stomach fluttered with a thousand butterflies at his words.

Marcus turned back to face her. "If you ever
need . . ." His voice faded as his eyes bored into her.

She nodded, a hot lump forming in her throat
that made speech impossible. She understood
what he was saying—and what he was leaving
unsaid.

He was there for her. He would always be there
for her. He was the person she could trust even
though he had claimed she should trust no one.

With one curt final nod, he turned and left her
standing in the taproom beside Yardley.

And she was free. Free at last.

MARCUS CHARGED A hard line through the taproom refusing to look back.

He couldn't look at her again. He couldn't see
that scene. He couldn't see her with him—that
bastard who had abandoned her and thought he
could now return and everything would be fine.
No, Marcus couldn't look, knowing he had lost
her. She was gone from him forever. And yes,
that hurt more than he could ever have imagined.

He was almost free of the taproom. But on the
threshold the innkeeper watched him with wide

and blinking eyes, clearly aware that something out of the ordinary was afoot.

"Ye really are one verra stupid bastard."

Marcus stopped abruptly and looked around. There, in the corner with two other tartan-clad men, sat the laird who had whisked Alyse from him. He wore a big grin on his boyishly handsome face. It would be his luck that this man was his neighbor and frequented this establishment.

"I'm really not in the mood." Or perhaps he was. Perhaps a tussle with this cheeky bastard would be a proper and suitable release for his current ire. Especially since he could not turn around and lay hands on the man who stood claiming *his* woman. The thought jarred him a little. His woman. Alyse was his. And he was hers. Not that she appeared to want him right now.

"Aye," the Scotsman said, studying his face as though reading Marcus's mind. "You just did that. You just left her with some other man." He chuckled. "After everything you did to get her back from me."

Marcus looked behind him. He couldn't help himself. The Scotsman's words rolled through him in a bitter tide. He watched as the younger man reached for Alyse's hand. He spoke to her earnestly, his face full of emotion.

"She wants him," Marcus murmured, even as those words cut through him like a knife.

"That pimple-faced lad? I think I could snap him wi' a sneeze." He snorted. "Perhaps she wants ye but doesna think ye want her." He shook his head. "Gah . . . fools the both of ye. She be yer wife. 'Ave ye forgotten that?"

Marcus shook his head. He had ripped up the bill of sale. Had severed his responsibility to her. He had no obligation to her and she had none to him.

"She's not my wife." The words were painful to utter. Strange how that had happened. Before he had latched on to them, now they were abhorrent.

She was free of him. He had done that for her.

This time the entire table laughed. He looked down at the three men. "What is so funny?" His hands tensed into fists at his side.

"Ye are," the laird replied. "Ye canna declare yourselves married publicly in Scotland as ye both did and it no' be true. That is all it takes, my friend. Ye are a married man in the eyes of the law." His gaze swung to Alyse. "Married to that lass."

Marcus stared. He couldn't speak.

Could that be true? Granted he was not familiar with Scottish law, but as he had already discovered, things were a little different here.

Elation swelled inside his chest only to be quickly followed with doubt. No. Not doubt.

Fear. Fear that she would not want this. Fear that she would be unhappy. Fear that she still wanted another man rather than him.

So much of his life, he realized, had been caught up in fear. Fear of his father. Fear that his father was everything wrong and evil in this world. Fear that he was cut from the same cloth and would be just like him.

He was done with fear.

Striding across the room he called her name.

She turned quickly, those wide topaz eyes locking on him. He wanted those eyes on him every day for the rest of his life. Stopping before her, he devoured the sight of her. He could look nowhere else. Not at the man beside her. Not at the men stomping their feet and shouting encouragement several tables away.

He dropped down on one knee and took her chilled hand in his. "Alyse . . . Don't leave me. Please be my wife. Because *you* want to be my wife. Because I want you to be my wife. Because I want us together and this life." The cheering stopped. All sound disappeared. "Because I love you. And I want to spend the rest of my life loving you. I may have bought you on that auction block that day, but it is you who owns me, body and soul."

She sucked in a ragged breath as though she had been struck. She didn't say anything for several moments. Finally her flushed face crumpled, and a sob broke loose. "But you're a duke. I can't be a duchess. I'm *not* a duchess—"

"You're you. Be you. That's all I want. I don't want a duchess. I want a woman to love. I want you to love. We already have a home here. You love it. I know you do. I saw it in your eyes. I love it, too. We can make a good home here, a happy home here."

"Yes." She nodded, tears streaming down her face. A laugh burbled from her lips. "Yes yes yes yes."

He hopped to his feet and hauled her into his arms. He hugged her close, tightly, as though he figured she might change her mind. As though he feared she might slip away and disappear like a wisp of smoke.

He released a gust of breath. Perhaps the first breath he'd ever taken. Free of fear. Full of love.

Epilogue

Five years later . . .

*S*he's coming!" Alyse declared as she burst open the doors to Marcus's study and waddled her way toward his desk.

She was fast increasing with their first child and their joy couldn't be any greater.

They had begun to accept that a child may not be in their future, no matter how very much they wanted one, when Alyse suddenly discovered she was with child.

For five years they had focused all their love and attention on each other and Kilmarkie House, building it into a home they were both proud of.

They'd added staff and outbuildings. Made repairs on the house and redecorated its interior. They'd planted more crops and improved commerce in the local village. When Alyse learned they had no blacksmith, she sent for her friend, Nellie, and her husband, a young blacksmith.

Although they did have to contend with the occasional reivers who had a penchant for stealing their cattle and sheep. Inviting Laird Mac-Larin and his grandmother to dinner usually won them the return of their lost flock for they suspected he was the one who liked to abscond with their livestock in the first place. He might be gentry, but he was little better than a criminal and he enjoyed vexing Marcus to no end.

With the impending birth of their child, their blessings only continued. They were finally having a child of their own to love. Someone who could grow and carry on the legacy they were creating at Kilmarkie. A little one who would walk the shoreline with them in the evenings and admire the dolphins. Marcus smiled wistfully. Hopefully a little girl who was the spitting image of her mother.

It was the life he never knew he wanted. A life he doubted he deserved, but nonetheless it was his and he would never give it up.

Looking up from the ledgers spread across

his desk, he lifted his spectacles off his nose to better view his lovely wife. He had succumbed to the need for spectacles last year, much to his chagrin—and much to his darling wife's delight.

Alyse insisted he looked dashing in his spectacles. He would be inclined to think she was jesting—or at the very least, humoring his vanity—if not for the fact that she had ravished him moments after she had first seen him wearing the infernal things. As absurd as it seemed, his wife found him all the more irresistible wearing them.

He didn't question it. He simply counted himself a very lucky man . . . and wore them at every opportunity as it served to incite his wife's desires.

"Who is coming?" he asked, nodding to the missive she clutched in her hand.

"Your sister! Clara! She is coming. She's finally coming. She always said she would like to visit and now it seems she is. Oh!" Alyse glanced down at the letter again, her bright eyes dancing with delight. "We haven't seen her in years. She is a woman grown now, can you imagine it?"

They had not seen Clara and the rest of his family since their one trip to London a few years ago. He'd wanted his family to meet Alyse. He himself had wanted to see them, too. Of course, he missed his sisters and wanted to set things right and make peace with Ela and Colin who now had their hands full with their children. Marcus was too contented with his life to hold any grudges.

Following that trip, he had been happy to return to Kilmarkie House with Alyse permanently. His life was here now away from the noise and bustle of Town and he would not have it any other way.

He frowned as he digested the news his wife happily imparted. "I must confess some confusion. The last letter from Ela said they were busy planning Clara's wedding."

Alyse looked back down to the missive in her hands, her eyes scanning its words. "Apparently not. Apparently . . . the wedding is off." Now it seemed it was her turn to frown. He watched her face as she continued reading from the parchment in her hands.

"What is it?" he prompted.

"Oh dear . . . oh, dear, dear . . ."

The tiny hairs on the back of his nape prickled in foreboding. "Yes?" he pressed.

She met his gaze. "It appears there's, um . . . a bit of a scandal."

Don't miss the rest of
Sophie Jordan's Rogue Files romances!
Available now from Avon Books!

The Scandal of It All

It takes two to make a scandal . . .

What kind of woman ventures into London's most notorious pleasure club? An outsider like Graciela, the Duchess of Autenberry, snubbed time and time again by society because of her Spanish roots. Ela longs to take a lover for a single, wild night, and within the walls of Sodom there are gentlemen to suit every forbidden taste. If only she were not so drawn to the smoldering Lord Strickland . . . a dangerous man who sees beyond her mask, and could ruin her reputation with a mere whisper.

Lord Strickland never permitted himself to fantasize about the sultry, off-limits lady, but then he never expected to find Ela in a place so wicked, looking for what he's more than too happy to give. She may not be to the ton's taste, but she suits him perfectly. First, however, he must convince her to trust in this dangerous desire—and in the promise of forever unleashed by one wild, scandalous night.

While the Duke
Was Sleeping

Sometimes the man of your dreams . . .

Shop girl Poppy Fairchurch knows it's pointless fantasizing about the Duke of Autenberry.
Still, dreams can't hurt anyone . . . unlike the
carriage Poppy spies bearing down upon the
unsuspecting duke. After she pulls him to
safety, the duke lapses into a coma and Poppy
is mistaken for his fiancée. But one person isn't
fooled: his arrogant and much too handsome
half-brother, Struan Mackenzie. Soon Poppy
isn't sure what she wants more . . . the fantasy
of her duke or the reality of one smoldering Scot
who challenges her at every turn.

. . . is not who you think.

An illegitimate second son, Struan may have
built an empire and established himself as one
of the wealthiest men in Britain, but he knows
he will always be an outsider among the ton.
Just like he knows the infuriating Poppy is
a liar. There's no way the haughty Duke of
Autenberry would deign to wed a working-
class girl. It doesn't matter how charming she
is. Or tempting. Or how much Struan wants
her for himself.